QUEEN OF BABBLE
IN THE BIG CITY

Meg Cabot has lived in Indiana and California, USA, and in France. In addition to her adult novels she is the author of the bestselling young adult fiction series *The Princess Diaries*. Meg and her husband live in Key West, Florida.

Visit her at www.megcabot.com

QUEEN OF BABBLE
IN THE BIG CITY

MEG CABOT

PAN BOOKS

First published 2007 by William Morrow
an imprint of HarperCollins Publishers, New York

This edition published 2015 by pan books
an imprint of Pan Macmillan, a division of Macmillan Publishers Limited
Pan Macmillan, 20 New Wharf Road, London N1 9RR
Basingstoke and Oxford
Associated companies throughout the world
www.panmacmillan.com

ISBN 978-1-5098-1139-7

Illustration and design by Kara Strubel

A CIP catalogue record for this book is available from
the British Library.

Printed and bound by CPI Group (UK) Ltd, Croydon, CR0 4YY

Visit **www.panmacmillan.com** to read more about all our books
and to buy them. You will also find features, author interviews and
news of any author events, and you can sign up for e-newsletters
so that you're always first to hear about our new releases.

For Benjamin

Acknowledgments

Many thanks to Beth Ader, Jennifer Brown, Babara Cabot, Carrie Feron, Michele Jaffe, Laura Langlie, Sophia Travis and especially Benjamin Egnatz

QUEEN of BABBLE
IN THE BIG CITY

Lizzie Nichols's Wedding Gown Guide

Finding the right wedding gown for your special day isn't easy, but it shouldn't drive you to tears, either!

Even if you are planning a formal ceremony with a traditional long dress, there are many different styles of gowns to choose from.

The trick is to match the right gown to the right bride before she becomes a Bridezilla . . . and that's where a wedding-gown specialist like myself comes in!

LIZZIE NICHOLS DESIGNS™

• Chapter 1 •

It is still not enough for language to have clarity and content . . . it must also have a goal and an imperative. Otherwise from language we descend to chatter, from chatter to babble, and from babble to confusion.

—René Daumal (1908–1944), French poet and critic

I open my eyes to see the morning sunlight slanting across the Renoir hanging above my bed, and for a few seconds, I don't know where I am.

Then I remember.

And my heart swells with giddy excitement. No, really. *Giddy.* Like, first-day-of-school-and-I've-got-a-brand-new-designer-outfit-from-TJ Maxx giddy.

And not just because that Renoir hanging over my head? It's real. Although it *is,* and not a print, like I had in my dorm room. An actual original work, by the Impressionist master himself.

Which I couldn't actually believe at first. I mean, how often do you walk into someone's bedroom and see an original Renoir hanging over the bed? Um, never. At least if you're me.

When Luke left the room, I stayed behind, pretending like I had to use the bathroom. But really I slipped off my espadrilles, climbed onto the bed, and gave that canvas a closer look.

And I was right. I could see the globs of paint Renoir used to build up the lace he so carefully detailed on the cuff of the little girl's sleeve. And the stripes on the fur of the cat the little girl is holding? Raised blobby bits. It's a REAL Renoir, all right.

And it's hanging over the bed I'm waking up in . . . the same bed that's currently bathed in sunlight from the tall windows to my left . . . sunlight that's bouncing off the building across the street . . . that building being the METROPOLITAN MUSEUM OF ART. The one in front of Central Park. On Fifth Avenue. In NEW YORK CITY.

Yes! I am waking up in NEW YORK CITY!!!! The Big Apple! The city that never sleeps (although I try to get at least eight hours a night, or my eyelids will get puffy, and Shari says I get cranky)!

But none of that is what's making me so giddy. The sunlight, the Renoir, the Met, Fifth Avenue, New York. *None* of that can compare to what's really got me excited . . . something better than all of those things, and a new back-to-school outfit from TJ Maxx put together.

And it's in the bed right next to me.

Just look how cute he is when he's sleeping! Manly cute, not kitten cute. Luke doesn't lie there with his mouth gaping wide with spit leaking out the side, like I do (I know I do this because my sisters told me. Also because I always wake up to a wet spot on my pillow). He manages to keep his lips together very nicely.

And his eyelashes look so long and curly. Why can't my eyelashes look like that? It's not fair. I'm the girl, after all. *I'm* the one who is supposed to have long curly eyelashes, not stubby short ones I have to use an eyelash curler I've heated with a hair dryer and about seven layers of mascara on if I want to look like I have any eyelashes at all.

Okay, I've got to stop. Stop obsessing over my boyfriend's eyelashes. I need to get up. I can't lounge around in bed all day. I'm in NEW YORK CITY!

And okay, I don't have a job. Or a place to live.

Because that Renoir? Yeah, it belongs to Luke's mother. As does the bed. Oh, and the apartment.

But she only bought it when she thought she and Luke's dad

were splitting up. Which they're not now. Thanks to me. So she said Luke could use it as long as necessary.

Lucky Luke. I wish MY mom had been planning on divorcing MY dad and bought a totally gorgeous apartment in New York City, right across the street from the Metropolitan Museum of Art, that she now only planned on using a few times a year for shopping trips in the city, or to attend the occasional ballet.

Okay, seriously. I have to get up now. How can I stay in bed—a king-sized bed, by the way, totally comfortable, with a big white fluffy goose-down-stuffed duvet over it—when I have all of NEW YORK CITY right outside the door (well, down the elevator and outside the ornate marble lobby), just waiting to be explored by me?

And my boyfriend, of course.

It seems so weird to say that . . . to even think it. Me and my boyfriend. My *boyfriend*.

Because for the first time in my life, it's real! I have an honest-to-God boyfriend. One who actually considers me his girlfriend. He isn't gay and just using me as a cover so his Christian parents don't find out he's really going out with a guy named Antonio. He isn't just trying to get me to fall so deeply in love with him that when he springs the idea of doing a threesome with his ex, I'll say yes because I'm so afraid he'll break up with me otherwise. He isn't a compulsive gambler who knows I have a lot of money saved up and can bail him out if he gets too deeply in debt.

Not that any of those things have happened to me. More than once.

And I'm not just imagining it, either. Luke and I are *together*. I can't say I wasn't a little scared—you know, when I left France to go back to Ann Arbor—that I might never hear from him again. If he hadn't really been that into me, and wanted to get rid of me, he had the perfect opportunity.

But he kept calling. First from France, and then from Houston, where he went to pack up all his stuff and get rid of his apartment and his car, and then from New York, when he arrived. He kept saying he couldn't wait to see me again. He kept telling me all the stuff he was planning on doing to me when he *did* see me again.

And then when I finally got here last week, he *did* them—all those things he'd said he'd been going to.

I can barely believe it. I mean, that a guy I like as much as I like Luke actually likes me *back*, for a change. That what we have isn't just a summer fling. Because summer's over, and it's fall now (well, okay, almost), and we're still together. Together in New York City, where he'll be going to medical school, and I'm going to get a job in the fashion industry, doing something—well, fashion-related—and together, we're going to make a go of it in the city that never sleeps!

Just as soon as I find a job. Oh, and an apartment.

But I'm sure Shari and I will find a charming pied-à-terre to call home soon. And until we do, I have Luke's place to crash, and Shari can stay in the walk-up her boyfriend Chaz found last week in the East Village (he rightfully refused his parents' invitation to move back into the house in which he grew up—when he wasn't being shipped off to boarding school—in Westchester, from which his father continues to commute to the city to work every morning).

And even though it's not on the best block exactly, it's not the worst place in the world, having the advantage of being close to NYU, where Chaz is getting his Ph.D., and cheap (a rent-controlled two-bedroom for only two grand a month. And okay, one of the bedrooms is an alcove. But still).

And okay, Shari's already witnessed a triple stabbing through the living room window. But whatever. It was a domestic dispute. The guy in the building across the courtyard stabbed his pregnant wife and mother-in-law. It's not like people in Manhattan go around getting stabbed by strangers every day.

And everyone turned out to be fine. Even the baby, who was delivered by the cops on the building's front stoop when the wife went into early labor. Eight pounds, six ounces! And okay, his dad is locked up in a prison cell on Rikers Island. But still. Welcome to New York, little Julio!

In fact, if you ask me, Chaz is sort of secretly hoping we won't find a place, and Shari will *have* to move in with him. Because Chaz is romantic that way.

And seriously, how fun would that be? Then Luke and I could come over, and the four of us could hang out just like we did back at Luke's place in France, with Chaz mixing kir royales and Shari bossing everyone around and me making baguette-and-Hershey-bar sandwiches for everyone, and Luke in charge of the music, or something?

And it could really happen, because Shari and I have had no luck on the apartment front. I mean, we've answered about a thousand ads, and so far the places are either snapped up before one of us can get there to look at them (if they're at all decent), or they're so hideous no one in their right mind would want to live there (I saw a toilet that was balanced on wooden blocks over an OPEN HOLE in the floor. And that was in a studio apartment in Hell's Kitchen for *twenty-two hundred dollars a month*).

But it will be all right. We'll find a place eventually. Just like I'll find a job eventually. I'm not going to freak out.

Yet.

Oh! It's eight o'clock! I'd better wake up Luke. Today is his first day of orientation at New York University. He'll be attending the postbaccalaureate premedical program there, so he can study to be a doctor. He wouldn't want to be late.

But he looks so sweet lying there. With no shirt on. And his tan so dark against his mother's cream-colored, thousand-thread-count Egyptian cotton sheets (I read the tag). How can I—

Ack! Oh, my goodness!

Um, I guess he's already awake. Considering that he's now lying on top of me.

"Good morning," he says. He hasn't even opened his eyes. His lips are nuzzling my neck. And other parts of him are nuzzling other parts of me.

"It's eight o'clock," I cry. Even though of course I don't want to. What could be more heavenly than just lying here all morning making sweet sweet love to my man? Especially in a bed under a real Renoir, in an apartment across from the Metropolitan Museum of Art in NEW YORK CITY!

But he's going to be a doctor. He's going to cure children of cancer someday! I can't let him be late for his first day of orientation. Think of the children!

"Luke," I say, as his mouth moves toward mine. Oh! He doesn't even have morning breath! How does he *do* that? And why didn't I jump up first thing and hurry into the bathroom to brush my teeth?

"What?" he asks, lazily touching his tongue to my lips. Which I'm not opening, because I don't want him to smell what's going on inside my mouth. Which appears to be a small party given by the aftertaste of the chicken tikka masala and shrimp curry from Baluchi's that we had delivered last night, which was apparently impervious to both the Listerine and Crest with which I attempted to combat them eight hours ago.

"You have orientation this morning," I say. Which isn't an easy thing to say when you don't want to open your lips. Also when there are a hundred and eighty pounds of delicious naked man lying on top of you. "You're going to be late!"

"I don't care," he says, and presses his lips to mine.

But it's no good. I'm not opening my mouth.

Except to say, "Well, what about me? I have to get up and go look for a job and a place to live. I have fifteen boxes of stuff sitting in my parents' garage that they're waiting to send me as soon as I can give them an address. If I don't get it all out of there soon, I just know Mom's going to have a garage sale, and I'll never see any of it again."

"It would be more expedient," Luke says, as he plucks at the straps to my vintage teddy, "if you would just sleep naked, like I do."

Only I couldn't even get mad at him for not listening to a word I've said, because he manages to get the teddy off with an alacrity that really is breathtaking, and the next thing I know, his being late for orientation—my job and apartment search—and even those boxes sitting in my parents' garage are the last things on my mind.

A little while later he lifts his head to look at the clock and says, in some surprise, "Oh. I'm going to be late."

I am lying in a damp puddle of sweat in the middle of the bed. I feel like I've been flattened by a steamroller.

And I love it.

"I told you so," I say, mostly to the girl in the Renoir above my head.

"Hey," Luke says, getting up to head to the bathroom. "I have an idea."

"You're going to hire a helicopter to pick you up here and take you downtown?" I ask. "Because that's the only way you're going to make it to your orientation on time."

"No," Luke says. Now he's in the bathroom. I hear the shower turn on. "Why don't you just move in here with me? Then all you'll have to do today is look for a job."

He pops his head—his thick dark hair adorably mussed from our recent activities—around the bathroom door and looks at me inquisitively. "What do you think about that?"

Only I can't reply, because I'm pretty sure my heart has just exploded with happiness.

Lizzie Nichols's Wedding Gown Guide

There are many different styles and cuts of gowns for brides who choose a traditional long dress, but the five most common are:

The Ballgown

The Empire Waist

The Column or Sheath

The A-line

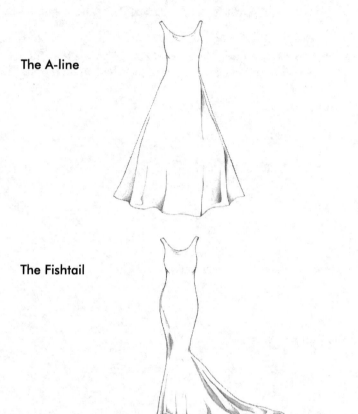

The Fishtail

LIZZIE NICHOLS DESIGNS™

But which shape gown is right for you?

That is the universal question, asked by every bride in the history of time.

• Chapter 2 •

A gossip goes about telling secrets, but one who
is trustworthy in spirit keeps a confidence.

—*Bible: Hebrew, Proverbs 11:13*

One Week Earlier

Well, at least you're not moving in with him," my older
sister Rose says, as ten shrieking five-year-old girls take
turns whacking a pony-shaped piñata hanging from a
tree limb behind us.

This stings. Rose's remark, I mean. The five-year-olds I can't do
anything about.

"You know," I say, irritated, "maybe if you had lived with Angelo
for a while before you got married, you'd have figured out he wasn't
your perfect soul mate after all."

Rose glares at me from across the picnic table.

"I was *pregnant*," she says. "It's not like I had much of a choice."

"Uh," I say, eyeing the five-year-old who is shrieking the loudest,
the birthday girl, my niece Maggie. "It's called birth control."

"You know, some of us actually take pleasure in the moment,"
Rose says, "instead of obsessing over the future all the time. So birth
control is not the first thing that springs to mind when a handsome
man begins making love to us."

I think of lots of ways to reply to this, as I sit there watching
Maggie decide that whacking the piñata with her stick is less inter-

esting than whacking her father with it. But for once, I keep my mouth shut.

"I mean, God, Lizzie," Rose goes on. "You go off to Europe for a couple of months and come back thinking you know everything. Well, you don't. Especially about men. He won't buy the cow if he can get the milk for free."

I blink at her. "Wow," I say. "Could you be getting more like Mom every day?"

My other sister, Sarah, can't keep from snorting into her plastic margarita glass at that one. Rose glares at her.

"Oh," she says. "You're one to talk, Sarah."

Sarah looks shocked. "Me? I'm nothing like Mom."

"Not Mom," Rose says. "But don't tell me that wasn't Kahlúa you were pouring into your coffee this morning. At *nine-fifteen*."

Sarah shrugs. "I don't like the taste of coffee straight."

"Oh, whatever, *Gran*." Then, narrowing her eyelids at me, Rose continues, "For your information, Angelo *is* my perfect soul mate. I didn't *have* to live with him before we got married to know that."

"Uh, Rose," Sarah says. "Your perfect soul mate is currently getting racked by your eldest."

Rose looks over and sees Angelo crumpled to the ground with his hands pressed between his thighs. Maggie, meanwhile, is now whacking the side of her parents' minivan, to the enthusiastic support of her birthday-party posse.

"Maggie!" Rose shrieks, leaping up from the picnic bench. "Not Mommy's car! Not Mommy's car!"

"Don't listen to Rose, Lizzie," Sarah says, as soon as Rose is out of earshot. "Living with a guy before you marry him is the perfect way to find out if you two are compatible in the ways that really count."

"Like what?" I ask.

"Oh, you know," Sarah says vaguely. "If you both like watching TV in the morning, or whatever. Because if one person wants to watch *Live with Regis and Kelly* in the morning, and the other person needs absolute silence in order to face the day, there can be fights."

Wow. I remember how mad Sarah used to get if any of us turned on the TV in the morning. Also, I had no idea Sarah's husband, Chuck, was a *Regis and Kelly* fan. No wonder she needed that Kahlúa in her coffee.

"Besides," Sarah says, running a finger along the side of what's left of Maggie's horse-shaped birthday cake, then sucking off the vanilla icing, "he hasn't asked you, right? To move in with him?"

"No," I say. "He knows Shari and I are getting a place."

"I just don't understand," Mom says, coming up to the picnic table with a new pitcher of lemonade for the kids, "why you have to move to New York City at all. Why can't you stay in Ann Arbor, and open a bridal gown refurbishment boutique here?"

"Because," I say, explaining for what has to be the thirtieth time alone since I got back from France a few days before. "If I really want to make a go of this, I need to do it in a place where I can have the broadest customer base possible."

"Well, I think it's just silly," Mom says, plunking down onto the picnic bench beside me. "The competition for affordable apartments and things like appointments to get cable installed in Manhattan are cutthroat. I know. Suzanne Pennebaker's oldest daughter—you remember her, Sarah, she was in your class. What was her name? Oh, right, Kathy—went to New York to try her hand at acting, and she was back in three months, it was so hard just to find a place to live. What do you think opening your own business is going to be like?"

I refrain from pointing out to Mom that Kathy Pennebaker also has a narcissistic personality disorder (at least according to Shari, based on the many, many boyfriends Kathy stole from girls we knew around Ann Arbor, then dumped as soon as the thrill of the chase was over). That kind of thing might not have made her too popular in a place like New York, where I understand heterosexual males are in somewhat short supply, and the womenfolk not opposed to using violence to make sure their man stays that way.

Instead, I say, "I'm going to start out small. I'm going to get a job in a vintage clothes shop, or something, and get to know my way around the New York City vintage clothing scene, save my money . . . and then open my own shop, maybe on the Lower East Side, where rents are cheap."

Well, cheaper.

Mom says, "What money? You aren't going to have any money left, once you've paid your eleven hundred dollars a month just for your apartment."

I say, "My rent isn't going to be that much, because I'll be splitting it with Shari."

"A studio—that is an apartment with no bedroom, just a single open space—costs two grand a month in Manhattan," Mom goes on. "You have to share it with multiple roommates. That's what Suzanne Pennebaker says."

Sarah nods. She knows about Kathy's boyfriend-stealing habit, too, which would have made getting along with roommates, at least of the female variety, difficult. "That's what they said on *The View,* too."

But I don't care what anyone in my family says. I am going to find a way to open my own shop somehow. Even if I have to live in Brooklyn. I hear it's very avant-garde there. All the really artistic people live there or in Queens, on account of being priced out of Manhattan by all the investment bankers.

"Remind me," Rose says, as she comes back to the picnic table, "never to let Angelo be in charge of the birthday-party planning again."

We look over and see that her husband is back on his feet, but limping painfully toward Mom and Dad's back deck.

"Never mind me," he calls to Rose, sarcastically. "Don't offer to help, or anything. I'll be fine!"

Rose looks heavenward, then reaches for the margarita pitcher.

"Perfect soul mate," Sarah says, chuckling to herself.

Rose glares at her. "Shut up." Then she plops the pitcher down. "Empty." There's growing panic in her voice. "We're out of margaritas."

"Oh, dear," Mom says, looking concerned. "Your father just mixed that batch—"

"I'll go in and make more," I say, hopping up. Anything to avoid having to hear more about how much of a failure I'm destined to be in New York.

"Make it stronger than Dad did," Rose advises, as a papier-mâché leg belonging to the piñata pony goes sailing past her head. "Please."

I nod and, seizing the pitcher, head toward the back door. I make it about halfway before I run into Grandma, who is just coming out of the house.

"Hey, Gran," I say. "How was *Dr. Quinn?*"

"I don't know." I can tell Gran's drunk, even though it's only one in the afternoon, because her housecoat is on backward again. "I fell asleep. Sully wasn't even in it. I don't know why they bother making episodes that don't have him in it. What's the point? No one wants to watch that Dr. Quinn run around in her gauchos. It's all about Sully. I heard them trying to talk you out of moving to New York."

I glance over my shoulder at my mother and sisters. They're all three of them running their fingers along the edge of the leftover cake, then sucking the frosting off the tips.

"Oh," I say. "Yeah. Well, you know. They're just worried I'm going to end up like Kathy Pennebaker."

Grandma looks surprised. "You mean a man-stealing whore?"

"Gran. She's not a whore. She just—" I shake my head, smiling. "How do you even know about that, anyway?"

"I keep my ear to the ground," Grandma says mysteriously. "People think because I'm an old drunk, I don't know what's happening. But I keep it real. Here. This is for you."

She shoves something into my hand. I look down.

"Grandma," I say, not smiling anymore. "Where did you get this?"

"Never you mind," Gran says. "I want you to have it. You're going to need it, moving to the city. What if you need to get out, and you need cash, fast? You never know."

"But, Grandma," I protest. "I can't—"

"For fuck's sake," Grandma yells at me. "Just take it!"

"Fine, I will," I say, and shove the neatly folded ten-dollar bill into the pocket of my black-and-white vintage Suzy Perette sleeveless day dress. "There. Are you happy now?"

"Yes," Grandma says, and pats me on the cheek. Her breath is pleasantly beery. It reminds me of all those times in grade school she helped me with my homework. Most of the answers were wrong, but I always got bonus points for imagination. "Good-bye, you rotten stinker."

"Grandma," I say, "I'm not leaving for three more days."

"Don't sleep with any sailors," Grandma says, ignoring me. "You'll get the clap."

"You know," I say with a smile. "I think I'm going to miss you most of all, Scarecrow."

"I don't know what you're talking about," Grandma huffs. "Scarecrow who?"

But before I can explain, Maggie, wearing the decapitated piñata pony's carcass on her head, marches silently past us, followed by her suddenly mute party guests, each wearing a piece of piñata—a hoofed foot here, a segment of the tail there—on their heads, and stepping in perfect formation.

"Wow," Gran says, when the last member of the macabre piñata-part parade has passed by. "I need a drink."

A sentiment I readily second.

~ Lizzie Nichols's Wedding Gown Guide ~

Which type of wedding gown best suits you?

If you are lucky enough to be tall and slender, you can pretty much get away with any type or shape of gown. That is why models are tall and slender—anything looks good on them!

But supposing you are one of the millions of women who aren't tall and slender? Which gown best suits you?

Well, if you are short, with a fuller figure, why not try a gown with an empire waist? The flowing silhouette will make your

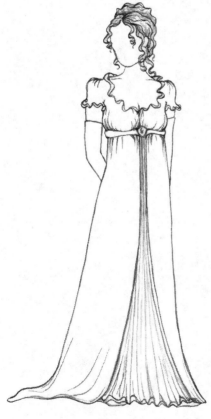

body look longer and more slender. That's why this style of gown was favored by both the ancient Greeks and the very fashion-conscious Josephine Bonaparte, Empress of France!

LIZZIE NICHOLS DESIGNS™

• Chapter 3 •

Great people talk about ideas, average people talk about things, and small people talk about wine.

—Fran Lebowitz (b. 1950), American humorist

I t's my own fault, really. For believing in fairy tales.

Not that I ever mistook them for actual historical fact, or anything.

But I did grow up believing that for every girl, there's a prince out there somewhere. All she has to do is find him. Then it's on with the happily ever after.

So you can only imagine what happened when I found out. That my prince really IS one. A prince.

No, I really mean it. He's an actual PRINCE.

And okay, he isn't exactly recognized, really, by his native land, since the French did a pretty thorough job of killing off most of their aristocracy over two hundred years ago.

But in the case of my particular prince someone in his family managed to escape Madame Guillotine by hotfooting it to England, and years later, even managed to get the family castle back, probably through intense and prolonged litigation. If they were anything like the rest of his family, I mean.

And okay, today owning your own château in the South of France means about a hundred grand a year in taxes to the French government, and nonstop headaches over roof tiles and renters.

But hey, how many guys do you know who actually own one? A château, I mean.

But I swear to you, that's not why I fell in love with him. I didn't know about the title or the château when I met him. He never bragged about it. If he had, I would never have liked him in the first place. I mean, what woman would? That you'd want to be friends with, anyway.

No, Luke acted exactly the way you'd expect a disenfranchised prince to act about his title—as if he were embarrassed by it.

And he IS embarrassed by it, a little. That he's a prince—an ACTUAL prince—and the only heir to a sprawling château (on a thousand-acre, sadly not very productive vineyard) a six-hour train ride from Paris. I only found out about it by accident, when I noticed this portrait of a very ugly man in the main hall at Château Mirac, and I noticed that on the nameplate, it said he was a prince, and he had the same last name as Luke.

Luke didn't want to admit it, but I finally pried it out of his dad. He says it's a lot of responsibility, being a prince, and running a château and all. Well, not the prince thing, so much, but the château part. The only way he can do it all—and turn enough of a profit to pay off their taxes every year—is by renting the place out to rich American families, and the occasional film studio, to shoot period movies in. God knows his vineyard doesn't turn much of a profit.

But by the time I found out about it—the prince stuff—I was already head over heels for Luke. I knew right away he was the guy for me, the minute I sat down next to him on that train. Not that I thought he'd ever, in a million years, feel the same way about me and all. He just had such a nice smile—not to mention really long eyelashes, the kind that Shu Uemura try so hard to emulate—I couldn't help falling for him.

So the fact that he has a title and an estate are really just frosting on what's already the most delicious cake I've ever tasted. Luke isn't like any of the guys I knew in college. He isn't the least bit interested in poker or sports. All he cares about is medicine—it's his passion—and, well, me.

Which suits me just fine.

So I guess it's only natural that I started planning my wedding immediately. Not that Luke's proposed—at least, not yet.

But, you know, I can still start PLANNING it. I know we'll be getting married SOMEDAY. I mean, a guy doesn't ask a girl he doesn't intend to marry to move in with him, right?

So, you know, WHEN we get married, it will be at Château Mirac, on the big grassy terrace there, overlooking the entire valley—over which the de Villiers at one time practiced their feudal lording. It will be in the summer, of course, preferably the summer right after my vintage bridal gown refurbishment shop—Lizzie Nichols Designs—is bought out by Vera Wang (another thing that hasn't happened yet. But it's bound to, right?). Shari can be my maid of honor, and my sisters can be my bridesmaids.

And unlike what they did for their bridesmaids (namely, me), I will actually choose tasteful gowns for them to wear. I won't force them to cram into any mint-green taffeta hoop skirts, the way they made me. Because unlike them, I am kind and thoughtful.

I suppose my whole family will insist on coming, even though none of them has ever been to Europe before. I'm a little worried my relatives won't be quite sophisticated enough for the cosmopolitan de Villiers.

But I'm sure they'll end up actually getting along like a house on fire, my father insisting on manning the firepit, Midwest-barbecue style, and my mother offering Luke's mother tips on how to get the yellow out of her nineteenth-century linen sheets. Gran might be a little bit trying, seeing as how they don't have *Dr. Quinn, Medicine Woman* in France. But after a kir royale or two, I'm sure she'll calm down.

I just know my wedding day will be the happiest day of my life. I can totally picture us standing in the dappled sunlight on the grassy terrace, me in a long white sheath, and Luke looking so handsome and debonair in an open-collared white shirt and black tuxedo pants. Like a prince is how he'll look, really . . .

I just have to figure out how I'm going to handle this next part, and I'm home free.

"Okay," Shari says, opening up the copy of the *Village Voice* she's just snagged, and turning it to the classifieds. "Basically, there's nothing out there that's worth looking at that isn't listed by a broker."

The thing is, this is going to take finesse. Not to mention subtlety.

"Which means we're just going to have to bite the bullet and pay one. It sucks," Shari goes on, "but in the long run, I think it's going to be worth it."

I can't just blurt it out. I have to lead up to it, slowly.

"I know you're short on cash," Shari says. "So Chaz says he can loan us what we need to pay the broker. We can pay him back when we get on our feet. Well, when *you* get on *your* feet." Because Shari has already landed a job at a small nonprofit, based on an interview she had last summer, before she left for France. She starts work tomorrow. "I mean, unless Luke is willing to front you. Is he? I know you probably hate to ask, but come on, the guy is loaded."

I can't just spring it on her out of nowhere.

"Lizzie? Are you even listening to me?"

"Luke asked me to move in with him," I blurt out before I can stop myself.

Shari stares at me across the booth's sticky tabletop. "And you were going to tell me this . . . when?" she asks.

Great. I've already blown it. She's mad. I knew she was going to get mad. Why can't I ever keep my big mouth closed. *Why?*

"Shari, he just asked me this morning," I say. "Just now, before I left to come meet you. I didn't say yes. I said I had to talk to you about it."

Shari blinks at me. "Which means you want to," she says. There's a definite edge to her voice. "You want to move in with him, or you'd have said no right away."

"Shari! No! I mean, well . . . yes. But think about it. I mean, face it, you're always going to be over at Chaz's place anyway—"

"Spending the night at Chaz's," Shari says acidly, "isn't the same as *living* with him."

"But you know he'd love you to," I say. "Think about it, Shari. If I move in with Luke, and you move in with Chaz, then we don't have to waste time looking for apartments anymore . . . or waste money on a broker and first and last month's rent. It will save us about five grand. Each!"

"Don't do that," Shari says sharply.

I blink at her. "Do what?"

"Make it about money," she says. "It's not about money. You know if you needed money, you could get money. Your parents would send you money."

I feel a spurt of irritation with Shari. I love her to death. I really do. But my parents have three kids, all of whom need money all the time. Supervisors at the cyclotron, which is what my dad is, make a comfortable living. But not enough to support their adult children in perpetuity.

Shari, on the other hand, is the only child of a prominent Ann Arbor surgeon. All she ever has to do when she needs money is ask her parents for some, and they fork over however much she wants, no questions asked. *I'm* the one who's been working in retail—and before that, babysitting every Friday and Saturday night throughout my teens, thus denying me anything resembling a proper social life—for the past seven years, scraping by on minimum wage, and denying myself life's more expensive pleasures (movies, eating out, shampoo other than Suave, a car, et cetera) in order to save enough to one day escape to New York, and pursue my dream.

I'm not complaining. I know my parents did the best they could by me. But it's annoying how Shari doesn't understand that not everyone's parents are as forthcoming with cash as hers are. Even though I've tried to explain it to her.

"We can't let ourselves become slaves of New York," Shari goes on. "We can't make major life decisions—like moving in with a boy-friend—be about the cost of rent. If we start doing that, we're lost."

I just look at her. Seriously, I don't know where she gets this stuff.

"If it's just about money," she says, "and you don't want to go to your parents, Chaz will float you a loan. You know that."

Chaz, who comes from a long line of fiscally thrifty lawyers, is loaded. Not just because his relatives keep dropping dead and leav-ing their financial assets to him, but because in addition to their cash, he's also inherited their frugality, and invests conservatively while living quite modestly—at least in comparison to his net worth, which is allegedly even more than Luke's. Not that Chaz has a châ-teau in France to show for it.

"Shari," I say. "Chaz is YOUR boyfriend. I'm not taking money from YOUR boyfriend. How is that any different than moving in with Luke?"

"Because you aren't having sex with Chaz," Shari points out with her usual asperity. "It would be a business arrangement, strictly impersonal."

But for some reason, the idea of asking Chaz for a loan—even though I know he'd think nothing of it, and say yes in an instant—isn't working for me.

Besides, it's not really about the money. It never was.

"The thing is," I say slowly. "It's not just about the money, Share."

Shari lets out a moan, and drops her face into her hands.

"Oh, God," she says to her lap. "I knew this was going to happen."

"What?" I don't understand what she's so upset about. I mean, I know Chaz is no prince and all, with his turned-around Michigan baseball hats and perpetual razor stubble. But he's really funny and sweet. When he isn't going on about Kierkegaard or Roth IRAs. "I'm sorry. But can't we make this work? I mean, what's the problem, exactly? Is it the triple stabbing? You don't want to live in Chaz's place because of the neighborhood? But the police told you, it was a domestic dispute. That will never happen again. I mean, unless they let Julio's dad out of Rikers—"

"It has nothing to do with that," Shari snaps. In the glow from the neon Pabst Blue Ribbon sign on the wall beside our booth, her wildly curling black hair has a bluish sheen. "Lizzie, you've known Luke a month. And you're going *to move in with him*?"

"*Two* months," I correct her, hurt. "And he's Chaz's best friend. And we've known Chaz for *years*. *Lived with* Chaz for years. Well, in the dorm, anyway. So it's not like Luke's this complete stranger, like Andrew was—"

"Exactly. What *about* Andrew?" Shari demands. "Lizzie, you just got out of a relationship. A completely fucked one, but a relationship, nonetheless. And look at Luke. Two months ago, he was living with someone else! And now he's just going to rush right in to live with someone new? Don't you think maybe you guys need to take it a little more slowly?"

"We're not getting *married*, Share," I say to her. "We're just talking about living together."

"Luke might be," Shari says. "But Lizzie, I know you. You're already secretly fantasizing about marrying Luke. Don't deny it."

"I am not!" I cry, wondering how she could possibly know the truth. And okay, she's known me for my whole life, practically. But come on. That's spooky.

She narrows her eyes at me. "Lizzie," she says, in a warning voice.

"Oh, all right," I say, slumping back against the bloodred vinyl booth. We're at Honey's, a seedy Midtown karaoke bar halfway between Chaz's apartment, where Shari is staying on East Thirteenth between First and Second Avenues, and Luke's mom's place, on East Eighty-first and Fifth Avenue, so it's equally difficult (or easy, depending on how you want to look at it) for us to get to.

Honey's may be a dive, but at least it's usually empty—at least before nine at night, when the serious karaoke practitioners show up—so we can talk, and the diet Cokes are only a dollar. Plus, the bartender—a punky Korean-American in her early twenties—doesn't seem to care if we order something or not. She's too busy fighting with her boyfriend over her cell phone.

"So I want to marry him," I say dejectedly, as the bartender yells, *"You know what? You know what? You suck,"* into her pink Razor. "I love him."

"It's fine that you love him, Lizzie," Shari says. "It's perfectly natural. But I'm still not convinced moving in with him is the best idea." Oh, great. Now she's chewing her lower lip. "I just . . ."

I look up from my diet Coke. "What?"

"Look, Lizzie." Her dark eyes seem fathomless in the dim light of the bar. Even though outside it's sunny, only being noon. "Luke's great and all. And I think what you did—getting his parents back together, and convincing Luke to go after his dream of pursuing a medical career—was really cool of you. But as far as you two long-term—"

I blink at her, totally stunned. "What about it?"

"I just," Shari says, "don't see it."

I can't believe she's saying this. My best friend—ALLEGEDLY.

"Why?" I demand, horrified to feel tears stinging my eyes. "Because he's a prince—sort of? And I'm just a girl from Michigan who talks too much?"

"Well," Shari says. "More or less. I mean, Lizzie . . . you like to watch *The Real World* marathons in bed with a pint of Coffee Heath Bar Crunch and the latest issue of *Sewing Today*. You like to listen to Aerosmith at full volume while you hem fifties cocktail dresses on your Singer 5050. Can you imagine ever doing either of those things in front of Luke? I mean, do you really act like yourself around him? Or do you act like the kind of girl you think a guy like Luke would want?"

I glare at her. "I can't believe you're even asking me that." I'm practically crying, but I'm trying to hide it. "Of *course* I act like myself around Luke."

Although it's true I've been wearing my control-top Spanx every day since I got to New York. And that they leave angry red lines along my waistline that I have to wait to fade before I let Luke see me naked after I've peeled them off.

But that's only because I started eating bread again when I was in France, and I gained back a little of the weight I lost over the summer! Just a little. Like fifteen pounds or so.

Oh, God. Shari's right!

"Look," Shari says, apparently noticing my stricken expression. "I'm not saying you shouldn't move in with him, Lizzie. I'm just saying you might want to cool it on the wedding-planning thing. Your wedding, anyway. With Luke."

I reach up to wipe the tears from my eyes. "If the next words out of your mouth are that he won't buy the cow if he can get the milk for free," I say bitterly, "I will seriously vomit."

"Of course I'm not going to say that," Shari says. "Just take things one day at a time, okay? And don't be afraid to be yourself in front of him. Because if he doesn't love the real you, he's not Prince Charming after all."

I can't help gaping at her a little. Because, really. It's like she's a mind reader.

"How," I ask tearfully, "did you get so smart?"

"I majored in psych," Shari said. "Remember?"

I nod. Her new job is counseling women at a nonprofit program that helps victims of domestic abuse find alternative housing, obtain orders of protection, and secure public benefits such as food stamps and child support. It's not a high-paying job, salarywise. But what Shari doesn't receive in financial compensation, she'll make up for in the knowledge that she is saving lives, and helping people—especially women—to attain better existences for themselves and their children.

Although if you think about it, those of us in the fashion industry do the same thing. We don't save lives, necessarily. But we help make lives better, in our own small way. It's like the song says . . . young girls, they do get weary, wearing that same old shaggy dress.

It's our job to get them into a new one (or a refurbished old one), so they can feel a little bit better about themselves.

"Look," Shari says. "The truth is . . . I don't know. I'm kind of bummed. I was really looking forward to us getting a place together. I even thought about how much fun it was going to be thrifting for old furniture and then fixing it up. Or borrowing a car and going to IKEA in New Jersey to buy a bunch of stuff. Now I'm going to have to live with Chaz's hand-me-down furniture from his family's law offices here in town."

I have to laugh. I've seen the elaborate gold-trimmed couches in Chaz's living room—the one with the wood floor that gently slopes south, and the windows with the folding gates over them because they look out over a fire escape . . . the same windows from which Shari saw Julio's dad go on his stabbing spree.

"I'll come over and see what I can do about the couches," I say. "I have a bunch of bolts of material I got when So-Fro Fabrics closed down. When my mom ships my boxes to me, I can make a slipcover for you. And some curtains," I add. "So you won't have to see any more stabbings."

"That'd be nice," Shari says, with a sigh. "Well. Here." She slides her copy of the *Village Voice* toward me. "You're going to need this."

I look down at it blankly. "Why? If Luke and I already have a place?"

"To *find a job*, dufus," Shari says. "Or is Luke going to support your thrifting habit as well as provide your housing?"

"Oh." I let out a tiny laugh. "Yeah. Thanks."

And I flip to the jobs section of the classifieds . . .

. . . just as a dwarf with a long, Gandalf-like staff opens the door to Honey's, ambles up to our table, looks at us, then turns around and leaves, all without uttering a word.

Both Shari and I glance at the bartender. She doesn't appear to have noticed the dwarf. Shari and I look back each other.

"This town," I say, "is very weird."

"Tell me about it," Shari says.

⟳ Lizzie Nichols's Wedding Gown Guide ⟲

Know your . . .

Wedding-gown sleeve lengths!

Strapless—no sleeves at all, of course!

Spaghetti strap—very thin straps

Sleeveless—wider straps

Cap—very, very short sleeves, usually just an extension of the shoulder. Not attractive in brides over forty (unless they work out. With weights).

Short—lower edge of the sleeve usually falls straight across the middle of the upper arm.

This length is generally considered too casual for a formal wedding.

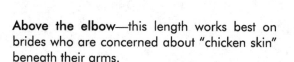

Above the elbow—this length works best on brides who are concerned about "chicken skin" beneath their arms.

Three-quarter—this sleeve ends three fourths of the way down the arm, midway between the elbow and the wrist. Flattering on nearly everyone.

Seven-eighth—ends two inches above the wrist. This is an awkward length for bridal gowns.

Wrist length—this length works nicely for more conservative brides, or those trying to hide unsightly eczema on their arms.

Full length—falls one inch below the wrist bone. This is the preferred length for brides favoring a "medieval" or "Renaissance" look to their gown.

Chapter 4

Gossip is the tool of the poet, the shop-talk of the scientist, and the consolation of the housewife, wit, tycoon and intellectual. It begins in the nursery and ends when speech is past.

—Phyllis McGinley (1905–1978), American poet and author

Maybe Shari's right. Maybe I do need to take things with Luke a little slower. There's no need to start planning our wedding now. After all, I only just got my degree . . . or not even, actually, since I just turned in my thesis, and my advisor says I won't technically graduate until January. Not that I'm changing my graduation date on my résumé, because, you know, who even checks that?

Besides, Mom and Dad would FLIP if they found out I took off for Europe—let alone accepted all those book lights as graduation gifts—without actually having finished my degree.

The same way they would FLIP if they found out I was moving in with a guy I met there. In Europe, I mean. I'm going to have to keep my living situation on the DL. Maybe I'll just tell them Shari and I are sharing a place . . . except what if they talk to Dr. Dennis? Dang . . .

Okay, I'll worry about that later.

Obviously, I need to use this time to concentrate on my career. I mean, how am I ever going to get interviewed by *Vogue* if I never actually *do* anything interview-worthy?

Although Shari would look really cute in a cap-sleeved dupioni silk bustier bridesmaid top, with a tea-length skirt in a sort
of antique-rose color, like that skirt on the mannequin in the
window . . .

Okay, stop it. Just stop. I'm not going to think about that now.
There'll be plenty of time to design a bridesmaid gown that will look
lovely on Shari and hideous on Rose and Sarah. Right now I need
to concentrate on getting a job. Because that's the most important
thing at the moment. What am I going to do with my life? I can't
just be someone's wife. Anybody can do that.

And okay, sure, I bet *Vogue* would interview me just for being
the wife of a prince. Well, a pseudoprince. They do interviews with
wives of pseudoprinces all the time. They call them "hostesses."

I don't want to be a "hostess." I don't even *like* parties.

No, I have to figure out a way to leave my mark on the world.
Something only I can do. Which appears to be refurbish vintage
wedding dresses.

Which you would think there'd be a huge demand for. Doesn't
everyone have an old wedding dress in the attic they'd like to have
fixed up? The trick is, how to reach all the women out there who
need my services, while at the same time being able to support
myself? Of course there's always the Internet, but—

Ooooh, that is the cutest Jonathan Logan red Spanish lace
dress . . . shame about the rip in the lace. Still, that's an easy fix. How
much—oh my God. Four hundred and fifty dollars? Are they insane?
We sold one just like this at Vintage to Vavoom in Ann Arbor for
one fifty. And this one is like a size two. Who can even fit into something this small?

"May I help you?"

Oh. Right. I'm not here to shop.

"Hi," I say, flashing what I hope is a dazzling smile in the direction of the clerk in the plaid pants (she's being ironic), with the multiple facial piercings. "I was wondering if the manager was around?"

"Why do you want to see the manager?"

Hmmm. Multiple Facial Piercings has a bit of an attitude, I see. Then again, seeing as how her shop is on a busy avenue in the Village, she probably sees all kinds. She probably has to be suspicious. Who knows what kind of crazy creepolas come in here? If they get a lot like that guy I just saw on the corner, with his pants down around his ankles, pawing through the trash can and muttering about Stalin, I can see why she might be a little standoffish with strangers.

"Actually," I say brightly, "I'm wondering if the store might be hiring. I've got years of experience in vintage retail, in addition to—"

"Leave your résumé at the counter," Multiple Facial Piercings says. "If she's interested, she'll call you."

But something tells me that the manager will never call. Just like the human resources representative from the costume department at the Metropolitan Museum of Art never called. Just like the head of the Museum of the City of New York's Costume and Textile Collection never called. Just like Vera Wang never called. Just like any of the gazillion places at which I've dropped off résumés haven't called.

Only in this case, I know the manager's not going to call because she's seen my résumé and she thinks I'm underqualified for the position, or because there aren't any openings, or because I don't have any local references, like all those other places. I know the manager's not going to call because she's never even going to *see* my résumé. Because Multiple Facial Piercings has already decided she doesn't like me, and is going to throw my résumé into the trash the minute I step out of her store.

"My hours are superflexible," I say, in a last-ditch effort. "And I have a lot of seamstressing experience. I'm great at alterations—"

"We don't do in-store alterations," Multiple Facial Piercings says with a sneer. "If people want something altered these days, they just take it to their dry cleaner."

I swallow. "Right. Well, I notice this Jonathan Logan you have here has some damage. I could easily repair this—"

"People who buy our clothes want to make repairs themselves,"

Multiple Facial Piercings says. "Leave your résumé at the counter, and we'll call you . . ."

Her heavily made-up eyes flick from the top of my head—my hair is pulled back in a wide, Jackie O–style scarf—to my dress, a rare 1950s Gigi Young blue and white polka dot with an accordion-pleated skirt—to my shoes—white ballet-style flats (because you can't wear heels when you're tromping around Manhattan). It is clear from her expression that Multiple Facial Piercings doesn't like what she's seeing.

". . . or not." Multiple Facial Piercings tosses her Mohawk, then lifts a hand to wave at me. I see that what I'd taken for festively colored sleeves is actually her bare arm, the skin of which is completely covered in tattoos. "Buh-bye."

"Um." I can't stop staring at the tattoos. "Bye."

Okay. Okay, so maybe the New York employment scene is a little . . . different from the one back in Ann Arbor.

Or maybe I just hit the wrong store on the wrong day.

Yeah, that's it. They can't all be like that one. Maybe heading to the Village first thing was a mistake.

Or maybe I shouldn't even be thinking retail. Maybe I should try hitting some bridal shops—not Vera Wang, obviously, since I already crashed and burned there (the woman who answered the phone at Vera Wang corporate, when I called to see if they'd received my résumé, made it more than clear that they would definitely be calling me—in ten years, when they managed to wade through all the other résumés aspiring wedding-gown designers had dropped off)—and leaving my résumé and some photos of some of the gowns I've worked on. Maybe that would make more sense. Maybe . . .

Oh God, what am I going to say to Luke? Shari's right, moving in with someone *is* a big deal, and not something you should just do because it's cheaper than paying a broker's fee.

Although of course that isn't why I'm doing it. I love Luke, and I think living with him would be totally dreamy.

So long as, you know, I enter into it without any expectations—

like Shari said—of marriage. Just take things one day at a time. Because we're both in transitional stages of our lives right now, Luke in school, and me . . . well, doing whatever it is I'm going to do. We can't be thinking of marriage. That's years away.

Although not too many years, I hope. Because I'd really like to go sleeveless on my wedding day and God only knows how long it's going to be before I lose all the elasticity in my arms and get that jiggle thing which can be so unattractive in a bride. Or anyone.

Okay, this isn't working. This traipsing around, dropping my résumé off at vintage clothing stores. I need to regroup. I need to get out the phone book or go online and really concentrate my efforts on places that fit my style. I need to—

Ooooh, look at those steaks. Maybe that's what I need to do. Pick up something for dinner. I mean, Luke isn't going to feel like going out after a long day of orientation.

And okay, I'm not the world's best cook. But anyone can grill a steak. Well, I guess broil it, since we have no grill.

That's what I'll do. I'll get some steaks, and a bottle of wine, and I'll make dinner. Then Luke and I can have a discussion about our living together, and what it means. And then I'll go back to job hunting tomorrow after we've got it all straightened out.

Perfect. Okay.

Only maybe I'll shop in Luke's neighborhood, instead of down here, since I don't want to have to carry a lot of stuff uptown on the subway. Where *is* the subway, anyway?

"Um, excuse me. Can you tell me how to get to the six train?"

Oh! How rude!

And I'm *not* an asshole. How can someone be an asshole just for asking where the subway is? God, is it really true what they say about New Yorkers? So far they *do* seem kind of rude. Is this why Kathy Pennebaker came back home? I mean, besides the whole other-people's-boyfriend addiction thing?

Or was she driven to steal even *more* boyfriends by the uncaring attitude of her New York neighbors?

Okay, where am I? Second Avenue and Ninth Street. East Ninth Street, because the east and west sides are divided by Fifth Avenue (where Luke's mother's apartment is. Overlooking Central Park . . . and the Met). Luke told me that to get to Fifth Avenue, if you're heading west from the East River, you have to cross First, Second, and Third avenues, and then Lexington, Park, and finally Madison (to remember the order in which these nonnumbered avenues go, Luke told me to "Look Past My Face"— or *Lexington, Park, Madison, Fifth*).

The streets—East Fifty-ninth Street, home to Bloomingdale's, and East Fiftieth Street, where Saks is, for instance—run perpendicular to the avenues. So Bloomingdale's is on Fifty-ninth and Lexington Avenue, Saks on Fiftieth and Fifth Avenue. Luke's mother's place is on Eighty-first and Fifth . . . around the corner from the Betsey Johnson on Madison between Eighty-first and Eighty-second.

Then of course there's the West Side. But I'll have to learn that later because right now I'm having a hard enough time figuring out the side I'm actually living on.

Okay, so the subway up and down the East Side runs along Lexington Avenue. So all you have to do when you're lost, Luke said, is find Lexington, and you'll eventually find the subway.

Unless of course you're in the Village, like I am, where Lexington suddenly turns into something called Fourth Avenue, then Lafayette, and finally Centre Street.

Again, not something I'm going to worry about right now. I'm just going to head west from Second Avenue, hoping to find Lexington in one of its many forms, and a subway stop home, somewhere around here . . .

Home. Wow. I'm already calling it home.

Well, isn't that what any place is? Any place that you share with someone you love, I mean?

Maybe that's why Kathy left New York. Not the rude people or the incomprehensible street layout or the whole boyfriend-stealing thing, but because there just wasn't anybody here that she loved.

Who loved her back, anyway.

Poor Kathy. Chewed up by the big city, then spat out again.

Well, that's *not* going to be me. I'm not going to be the next Kathy Pennebaker of Ann Arbor. I am *not* going back home with my tail between my legs. I am going to make it in New York City if it kills me. Because if I can make it here, I can make it any—

Oooh, a cab! And it's vacant!

And okay, cabs are expensive. But maybe just this once. Because I'm so tired, and it's so far to the subway, and I want to get back in time to start making Luke dinner, and—

"Eighty-first and Fifth, please."

—oh, look, there's the Astor Place subway stop right there. If I had just walked one more block, I could have saved myself fifteen bucks . . .

Well, that's okay. No more cabs this week. And this is so nice, sitting in this clean air-conditioned cab, instead of fighting my way down the stairs to the smelly platform to wait for a supercrowded train where I won't even be able to get a seat. And then there are the panhandlers in every car, asking for money. I can never seem to say no. I don't want to turn into one of those hardened, jaded New Yorkers, like Multiple Facial Piercings, who seemed to find my Gigi Young dress so amusing. When you can't empathize with another's hardship—or realize how hard it is to even FIND a Gigi Young dress in wearable condition—what's the point of even being alive?

So I end up getting off the subway five dollars poorer every time I ride it, not even counting the fare. It's practically cheaper to take a cab. Sort of.

Oh God. Shari's right. I have to get a job—and a life.

And fast.

If you are on the petite side, why not try an A-line gown? Full skirts can make a short bride look as if she is being swallowed up by material—unless she opts for a ballgown or fishtail cut . . . but this does not flatter every petite bride universally, so tread with caution when trying on "princess" or "mermaid" gowns!

Off-the-shoulder and scoop necklines—even thin straps—are recommended for the petite bride. Column or sheath skirts are not. Remember, you are getting married, not working behind the counter at Ann Taylor Loft!

LIZZIE NICHOLS DESIGNS™

Chapter 5

'm marinating the steaks when the phone rings. Not my
cell, but the apartment phone—Luke's mother's phone.

I don't answer it because I know it's not for me.
Besides, I'm busy. It's no joke trying to prepare a semigourmet meal
in a New York–style galley kitchen, which is basically about as big
as the inside of the cab I took to get back uptown this afternoon.
Luke's mom's apartment is really nice, as one-bedroom Manhattan
apartments go. It's still got its original prewar crown molding and
gold fixtures and parquet floors, and all.

But the kitchen seems to have been built more for unpacking
take-out than preparing eat-in.

Mrs. de Villiers's answering machine kicks on after about five
rings. I hear her voice—her Southern accent exaggerated for dramatic effect—drawl, "Hello, you've reached Bibi de Villiers. I'm
either on the other line or nappin' at the moment. Please leave a
message, and I'll get right back to y'all."

I giggle. Napping. *Vogue* should do a spread on Bibi. Talk about
professional hostesses. Plus, she's married to a prince. Well, a pseudo-

prince. And she's got great—if slightly conservative—taste in clothes. I've never seen her in anything but Chanel or Ralph Lauren.

"Bibi." A man's voice fills the apartment . . . which is also filled with the smell of freshly chopped garlic, which I'm using in the marinade, along with soy sauce, honey, and olive oil, all of which I picked up at Eli's over on Third Avenue . . . which is quite a hike from Fifth. "I haven't heard from you in quite a while. Where have you been?"

Clearly, this friend of Bibi's does not know she reconciled with her husband during her niece's wedding in the South of France, and that the two of them—Luke's parents—were still in Dordogne, tripping the light *fantastique* . . . as the French would say. Or not, actually.

"I will be waiting for you in the usual place," the man goes on, "this weekend. I only hope I do not wait in vain."

Wait a minute. The usual place? Waiting for her? Who the heck is this guy? And how come, if he and Bibi are so close, he doesn't even know which country she's in?

"Good-bye for now, *chérie*," the man says. And then he hangs up.

Chérie? Was this guy for real? Who goes around leaving messages on people's machines, calling them *chérie*? Except maybe gigolos.

Oh God. Did Luke's mother employ a gigolo?

No, of course not. She wouldn't have to. She's a vital, beautiful woman—and obviously loaded, as one can tell merely by glancing at the art on the walls of her Manhattan pied-à-terre. The Renoir is the crown jewel of her collection, of course. But she has no shortage of Mirós and Chagalls and even a tiny Picasso sketch that hangs in the bathroom.

And I'm not even going to mention her shoe collection, which crowds the entire top shelf of the bedroom closet . . . box after box marked Jimmy Choo, Christian Louboutin, and Manolo Blahnik.

What would a woman like that be doing with a gigolo?

Unless . . . unless he's not a gigolo, but a lover! It would make sense for Bibi de Villiers to have taken a lover. She was, after all, in divorce proceedings with Luke's father . . . until I came along, that is.

Why wouldn't a sophisticated woman of the world like Luke's mom have a boyfriend . . . a boyfriend she's forgotten all about since getting back together with Luke's dad?

At least, I assume she's forgotten about him. Obviously she has, if he doesn't even know where she is . . .

Oh God. This is so . . . awkward. Why did he have to call now, tonight, when Luke and I have to have our Moving in Together talk? I can't say to Luke, "Hey, this random guy left a message for your mom, calling her *chérie* . . . and we need to figure out how I can move in with you without losing my identity as an individual."

Maybe if I check the caller ID I can figure out where this guy called from. That, at least, might give me a clue as to—

Oh. Oh, great. I erased the message. At least if that flashing Delete sign is any indication.

Okay. Well, that solves that.

Besides, it's probably better this way. It's not like the guy left his name. I can't be all, "Um, hi, Mrs. de Villiers? Yeah, a random dude with a French accent who isn't your husband called and asked if you're going to meet him at the usual place, at which he will be waiting." Because that could embarrass her.

And I'm all about trying not to embarrass my future in-laws.

Dang. I just did it again, didn't I? I have to get marriage off my brain. I think I'll go set the dining table. With the beautiful silver that one day might be mine if—

Ack! Okay, maybe I need to turn on the TV. The news should be on. That will distract me.

"Police made a gruesome discovery in the backyard of a house the media is now calling the Harlem House of Horror. Human remains— six complete skeletons so far, with more expected to be uncovered—"

Oh my God, what kind of place is this? A backyard filled with human skeletons? No. Just no. Changing the channel.

"—seventh hit-and-run at that corner in the past month alone. This time it was a young mother killed as she was attempting to walk her small children to school—"

Good Lord! Maybe I'll try reading the want ads instead. Oooh, Page Six, the gossip section! I'll just take a quick look before I get to the job listings—

—New York high society is all abuzz about the impending nuptials of John MacDowell, sole heir to the MacDowell real estate fortune. The bride, Jill Higgins, is an employee at the Central Park Zoo. The couple met at the Roosevelt Hospital emergency room, where Miss Higgins was being treated for a back injury she received while lifting a seal that had escaped its enclosure, and where John MacDowell was having an ankle wrapped after twisting it during a polo match—

Oh! How romantic! And what a fun job, working with seals! If only I could—

Luke's key is turning in the lock! He's home!

Thank God I peeled off my Spanx two hours ago. The red marks must have faded by now.

And I'm not wearing them anymore. Luke is going to have to love me for me—the real me—or it's over.

Except . . . look how adorable he is, in those faded jeans and that nice button-down shirt I picked out for him to wear! Maybe it's all right to wear my Spanx just a little longer . . . until I've lost those fifteen extra pounds I brought home from France. Which I'm sure to do soon, given all the walking you have to do in this town. Plus, I completely ignored the baguettes at Eli's . . .

"Hey," he says. There's a big smile on his face. "How's it going?"

Hey, how's it going. This is what my boyfriend says to me, ten hours after asking me to move in with him. It's clear he hasn't exactly been agonizing over my answer.

Or maybe he has and is trying to play it casual.

"What's that smell?" he asks.

"Garlic," I say. "I'm marinating a couple of steaks."

"Great," he says, putting down his keys on the little marble-topped console table by the door. "I'm starved. How was your day?"

Wow. How was your day? This is what it's like to live with someone. I mean, a guy. It's a lot like living with a girl, really.

Except that instead of waiting around for my answer, the way Shari used to when we were roommates, Luke comes over, puts his arms around my waist, and gives me a kiss.

Okay. Not so much like living with a girl. At all.

"So," Luke says, grinning down at me. "When are you going to break the news to your parents?"

Oh, okay. The reason he hasn't been agonizing over my answer to his question is that he already knew what my answer was going to be.

I drop my arms from around his neck, stunned.

"How did you know?"

"Are you kidding me?" He's laughing now. "The Lizzie Broadcasting System has been hard at work all day."

I glare at him. "That's impossible. I haven't told anyone! Anyone except—" I break off, flushing.

"Right," Luke says, playfully flicking the tip of my nose with one long index finger. "Shari told Chaz, who called to demand my intentions."

"Your—" Now I'm not just flushing. I'm blushing. "He had no right to do that!"

But Luke is still laughing. "He thinks he does. Oh, don't look so mad. Chaz thinks of you as the little sister he never had. I think it's sweet."

I didn't. In fact, I was going to give Chaz a very unsisterly piece of my mind next time I saw him.

"What did you say?" I can't help asking, curiosity overcoming my anger.

"About what?" Luke's found the bottle of wine I'd bought and opened to let breathe, and is pouring us each a glass.

"Your, um, intentions."

I'm trying to keep it casual. And light. Guys don't like it when you get too heavy, I've noticed. They especially don't like it when you try to talk too much about the future. They're like little woodland animals. Everything's well and good when you're just doling out the nuts and everything's cool.

But the minute you bring out the net to try to catch them—even if it's for their own good, like to help them escape a forest fire—all hell breaks loose. No WAY was I bringing up the C word with Luke. Two months into a relationship might be early enough to consider moving in together. But it was WAY too early to start bandying about the word "commitment."

Even if one of us did have wedding dresses permanently on the brain.

"I told him not to worry," Luke says, handing one of the wine-glasses to me. "That I would do everything in my power not to sully your reputation." Luke clinks the edge of his glass to mine. "Also that he should be thanking me," he adds with a wink.

"Thanking you?" I echo. "Why?"

"Well, because now Shari can move in with him. He'd asked her to before, but she said she couldn't abandon you."

"Oh." I blink a few times. I hadn't known that. Shari had never said a word.

But if she'd only been moving in with me out of pity, why had she reacted the way she did when I'd told her about Luke's offer?

"Anyway, I was thinking we could go out to celebrate," Luke was going on. "The four of us. Not tonight, obviously, because you picked up steaks. But maybe tomorrow night. There's this fantastic Thai place downtown I know you're going to love—"

"We need to talk," I hear myself saying. Whoa. Where did that come from?

Luke looks surprised, but not offended or anything. He sinks down onto his mother's white couch—I am so not sitting there with food or drink in my hands—and looks up at me with a grin.

"Sure," he says. "Of course. I mean, there's a lot of stuff we need to figure out. Like where you're going to put all your clothes." His grin gets broader. "I gather from Chaz that your collection of vin-tage wear is somewhat impressive."

Except it isn't my clothes I'm worried about. It's my heart.

"If I'm going to live with you," I say, moving to sit on the arm of the couch . . . there's less chance of catastrophic results if a spill occurs there. Plus, I'm far enough away from him that he can't distract me with his manliness. "I want to split the cost—utilities, groceries, all of that—fifty-fifty. You know. So it's fair. To both of us."

Luke isn't grinning now. He's sipping his wine and shrugging. "Sure," he says. "Whatever you want."

"And," I say, "I want to pay rent."

He looks at me oddly. "Lizzie. There's no rent to pay. My mother owns this place."

"I know," I say. "I mean I want to pay something toward the mortgage."

Luke's grinning again. "Lizzie. There's no mortgage. She paid cash for the place."

Wow. This is way harder than I thought it would be.

"Well," I say. "I have to pay *something*. I mean, I can't just sponge off you for free. That's not fair. And if I'm paying to live here, then I get some say in what goes on with the place. Right?"

Now one of his dark eyebrows has slid up. "I see what you mean," he says. "And are you planning on doing some redecorating?"

Oh God. This is not going at all the way I'd hoped it would. Why did Chaz have to call him? I get accused all the time of having a big mouth. But if you ask me, guys gossip way more than girls do.

"Not at all," I say. "I love what your mother's done to the place. But I'm going to have to move some stuff to make room." I clear my throat. "For my sewing machine. And things like that."

Now both of Luke's eyebrows are up. "Your *sewing* machine?"

"Yes," I say, a little defensively. "If I'm going to start my own business, I'm going to need my own space in here to do that. And I want to pay for that space. It's only fair. What about . . . is there a monthly maintenance fee? You know, that the building charges for upkeep?"

"Sure," Luke says. "It's thirty-five hundred dollars."

I nearly choke. It's a good thing I've sat on the arm of the couch, or I'd have spat all over it, and not the parquet floor, which is the recipient of a mouthful of red wine.

"*Thirty-five hundred dollars?*" I cry, jumping up and hastening to the kitchen for a dish towel. "A *month*? Just for *maintenance*? I can't afford that!"

Luke is laughing now. "How about a portion of it, then," he says, as he watches me clean up my mess. "A thousand a month?"

"Deal," I say, relieved. Although only slightly, since I have no idea how I'm even going to come up with a thousand dollars a month.

"Fine," Luke says. "Now that we've got that settled—"

"We don't," I say. "Have it settled, I mean."

"We don't?" He doesn't look alarmed, though. He looks more amused. "We've covered groceries, utilities, your need for space for your sewing machine, and rent. What more is there?"

"Well," I say. "Us."

"Us." He isn't running like a frightened woodland creature. Yet. He simply looks mildly curious. "What about us?"

"If I move in," I say, summoning all my courage, "it would only be on a trial basis. To see how it works out. Because, you know, we've only known each other for two months. What if it turns out, I don't know. In the winter I become a real crab or something?"

Both of Luke's eyebrows go up again. "Do you?"

"I don't know," I say. "I mean, I don't think so. But there was this girl, Brianna, from our floor in McCracken Hall? And she used to turn into a total psychopath when it got cold outside. Not that she was particularly stable when it was warm out. But she got way worse when it was cold. So, you know. I think we should reserve the right to call off the whole living-together thing if one or the other of us feels like it isn't working out. And since it's your mother's apartment, I'll be the one who moves out. But you have to give me thirty days to find a new place before you change the locks. That's only fair."

Luke is still grinning. But now the grin is slightly whimsical.

"You're very concerned," he says, "about fairness, aren't you?"

"Well," I say, feeling slightly deflated that this is his only response to my long speech. "I guess I am. I mean, there's so little justice in the world. Young mothers get killed by hit-and-run drivers, and people's skeletons turn up in backyards, and—"

Now Luke's frowning. And reaching for me.

"I have no idea what you're talking about," he says, pulling me down onto his lap. Fortunately, I've put down my wineglass. "But I'm awfully glad we've had this little chat. Is it over?"

I quickly run through all the things I'd hoped to cover with him. Splitting the rent and utilities, making room for my sewing machine, and a Get Out of Jail Free card in case either of us (him more than me, since I didn't plan on going anywhere) needed it. Yes. Done.

I nod. "It's over."

"Good," Luke says, and bends me back against the couch. "Now how do you get this thing off?"

Lizzie Nichols's Wedding Gown Guide

Pear-shaped girls, don't despair! True, according to the band Queen, fat-bottomed girls make the rockin' world go round. But often, we can't find a thing to wear!

Pear-shaped girls are in luck when it comes to wedding gowns, however. The A-line cut flatters by drawing attention away from the lower half of the body, and up toward the bustline.

This can be emphasized even more by going with an off-the-shoulder or deeply V'ed neckline, but stay away from halter-neck gowns and full or pleated skirts, as these looks can add bulk to the hips. The bias or straight-cut look is deadly to any pear-shaped bride . . . they cling to exactly what you're trying to draw attention away from!

Lizzie Nichols Designs™

• Chapter 6 •

Three may keep a secret, if two of them are dead.

—Benjamin Franklin (1706–1790), American inventor

Wedding Gown Restoration Specialists.

That's what the sign on the door says.

Well, that's certainly me. I mean, that's what I *do.* Not just wedding gowns, of course. I can restore—or refurbish—just about any garment. But wedding gowns are where the real challenges lie. And where the money is, too, of course.

Only I'm trying not to obsess about money. Even though it's really hard not to obsess about something that you seem to need so much of just to *exist* in this town. I mean, I have seen what some of the other tenants of Luke's mom's building are wearing when they come down the elevator. I never saw so much Gucci and Louis Vuitton in my life.

Not that you need Gucci and Louis to exist. But you need money—a lot of it—to lead anything like a normal life in Manhattan. If by normal you mean no splurges on cabs, movies, or lattes, and that you make your own breakfast, lunches, and dinners.

And okay, I can easily live without the latest monogram-canvas Louis Vuitton tote.

But it seems kind of harsh that I can't even pop into the nearby falafel place for a quick bite. Not that I am eating carbs, thanks to the size of my butt, or that there is a falafel place anywhere near the vicinity of the Met, which there most definitely is not, residences on Fifth Avenue being almost literally MILES from any affordable eateries and/or grocery stores. In fact, Fifth Avenue is like a wasteland, nothing but million-dollar apartments, museums, and the park.

I actually envy Shari her walk-up with Chaz. Sure, there are no Renoirs in it, and the floors slope toward the windows, and there's only a portable stand-up shower that leaks and the enamel on the claw-foot tub is so stained it looks as if someone might have been murdered in it.

But there's a totally cheap sushi place right across the street! And a bar with dollar Bud Lights at happy hour like two steps from their stoop! And a grocery store half a block away that delivers . . . for FREE!

I know I shouldn't complain. I mean, I have a doorman. AND a guy who runs the elevator. And a view of the Metropolitan Museum of Art, and Luke's mother's windows are all double-paned, so you can't even hear all the horns and sirens on Fifth Avenue.

And I'm only paying a thousand dollars a month for it. Plus utilities.

But I'd give it all up in a minute if I could just have a freaking *caffè misto* every now and then and not feel racked with guilt about it.

Which is what brings me to Monsieur Henri's, not four blocks from Mrs. de Villiers's pied-à-terre. It's one of Manhattan's premier wedding-gown restoration and preservation hot spots. Anybody who is anybody has Monsieur Henri restore, refurbish, and preserve her wedding gown. At least according to Mrs. Erickson from 5B, whom I met in the laundry room last night (the plumbing in Mrs. de Villiers's building is too old to allow each apartment to have its own individual washer and dryer, and the cost of renovating would raise the maintenance fees even higher). Anyway, she told me that adding half a cup of vinegar to the rinse cycle saves you from having to spend extra money on fabric softener. And she should know. I mean, she had on a cocktail ring with a diamond about as big as a golf ball. She said she was only doing her own laundry because she'd had to fire her maid due to drunkenness, and the service hadn't found her a new one yet.

So when I ring the bell to Monsieur Henri's place, I am fairly confident that for once, I won't be completely wasting my time. Mrs. Erickson had looked to me as if she'd know about wedding-gown restorers—the angle I am now pursuing, since the whole costume-restoration and vintage thing wasn't working out. I have, in the past two weeks, been to every vintage clothing store in the five boroughs . . . none of which was hiring.

Or so the managers claimed. Several saw my college degree on my résumé, and said I was overqualified. Only one of them was interested in looking at my portfolio of refurbished vintage clothes, and when he was through, he said, "This might impress people back in Minnesota, but around here our customers are a little more sophisticated. Suzy Perette just doesn't cut it."

"Michigan," I corrected him. "I'm from Michigan."

"Whatever," the manager said, rolling his eyes.

Seriously? I had no idea people could be so mean. Especially people in the vintage-clothing community. I mean, back home, thrifters are very supportive of and caring for one another, and it's about quality and originality—not the label. Here, in the words of one of the store managers I met, "If it's not Chanel, no one cares."

Wrong! So wrong!

And, in the words of Mrs. Erickson, "What do you want to work in one of those filthy shops for, anyway? Believe me, I know. My friend Esther volunteers at a thrift shop for Sloan-Kettering. She says the catfights over a simple Pucci scarf are not to be believed. Go see Monsieur Henri. He'll set you straight."

Luke suggested that taking career advice from a woman I met in a basement laundry room wasn't the soundest thing he'd ever heard of.

But Luke has no idea just how desperate things have gotten. Because I haven't told him. I am trying to appear sophisticated and full of savoir-faire where Luke is concerned. It's true he was kind of shocked when all my boxes from home arrived, and we realized there was nowhere to put them. Fortunately, Luke's mom's apartment comes with its own lockable storage unit in the basement garage, where I've stashed all my bolts of material and most of my sewing supplies.

The clothes, however, went straight to a portable hanging rack I bought at Bed Bath & Beyond and installed in the bedroom, under the Renoir girl's disapproving gaze. Luke seemed kind of shocked when he saw it—"I had no idea anyone owned more clothes than my mother," he said—but he recovered himself and even asked me to model some of the slinkier ensembles (as well as, for some reason, my Heidi outfit, which he seemed to get an enormous kick out of).

But what Luke doesn't know is that if something doesn't give soon, that outfit, as well as the rest of the collection, are going up onto eBay. Because I am down to my last few hundred dollars.

And though it will break my heart to have to sell the clothes I've been collecting for so many years, it would break my heart more to have to admit to Luke that I don't have the money for next month's rent.

And while I know he'll only laugh and say it's all right and not to worry about it, I can't *help* worrying about it. I don't want to be his live-in mistress or whatever. I mean for one thing that is hardly an effective career path, as we know from Evita Perón. But also, I want to go *shopping*! I want to add new things to my collection so badly!

Only I can't. Because I'm broke.

So Monsieur Henri is my only hope. Because if he doesn't work out, I'm totally selling off the Suzy Perettes for sure, and maybe even the Gigi Youngs.

Either that, or I'm signing up for a temp agency. I will fax and file for the rest of my life, so long as SOMEONE will hire me.

But as soon as Monsieur Henri (or whoever the guy is who buzzes me in when I press on the bell to Monsieur Henri's shop) ushers me into the waiting area of his shop, all smiles and graciousness—until I tell him I'm not getting married (yet), I'm there to ask about employment opportunities—I have a pretty good idea it's going to be the temp agency for me.

Because the middle-aged, mustached man's face falls, and he demands, in a suspicious, heavily French-accented voice, "Who sent you? Was it Maurice?"

I blink at him. "I have no idea who Maurice is," I say, just as a tiny, birdlike Frenchwoman comes out of the back with a big smile plastered on her face . . . until I say the word "Maurice."

"You think she is a spy from Maurice?" the woman asks the man, in rapid French (which I now understand—well, mostly—on account of having spent a summer in that country, and a semester before that learning it in class).

"She has to be," the man replies in equally rapid French. "What else would she be doing here?"

"No, honestly," I cry. I know enough French to understand it, but not enough actually to speak it myself. "I don't know anybody named Maurice. I'm here because I understand you're the best wedding-gown restorer in town. And I want to be a wedding-gown restorer. Well, I mean, I *am* one. Here, look at my portfolio—"

"What is she talking about?" Madame Henri (because that's who she has to be, right?) asks her husband.

"I have no idea," he replies. But he takes my book, and begins thumbing through it.

"That's a Hubert de Givenchy gown I found in an attic," I tell them, when they get to the page showing Bibi de Villiers's wedding gown. "It had been used to wrap a hunting rifle, which had rusted all over it. I was able to get the rust stains out by soaking it overnight in cream of tartar. Then I handstitched repairs to the straps and hem—"

"Why are you showing this to us?" Monsieur Henri demands, shoving my book back at me. Behind his head is a wall full of framed photographs of before-and-after shots of wedding gowns he's restored. It's pretty impressive. Some of them were so yellowed with age, they looked as if they'd fall apart at the merest touch.

But Monsieur Henri had managed to get them back to their original snowy-whiteness. He either had a way with fabrics, or some kind of wicked chemicals in his back room.

"Because," I say slowly. "I just moved here to New York from Michigan, and I'm looking for a job—"

"Maurice didn't send you?" Monsieur Henri's eyes are still narrowed suspiciously.

"No," I say. Really, what is going on here? "I don't even know what you're talking about."

Madame Henri—who has stood at her much taller husband's side, peeking around his arm at my portfolio—gives me the once-over, her gaze taking in everything from my perky ponytail (Mrs. Erickson advised me to keep my hair out of my eyes), to the Joseph Ribkoff sheath dress I'm wearing beneath a vintage beaded cardigan (it's gotten chillier outside since I arrived in New York. Summer isn't quite gone, but fall is definitely in the air).

"Jean, I believe her," she says to her husband in French. "Look at her. Maurice would not send someone as stupid as she is to trick us."

I want to yell "Hey!" in an enraged voice and stomp out of their shop in a huff, since I perfectly understood that she'd just called me stupid.

But on the other hand, I can see that Monsieur Henri has turned the page and is looking at the before-and-after shots I took of Luke's cousin Vicky's hideous self-designed wedding gown, which I managed to salvage into something semidecent (though in the end she chose the Givenchy I repaired instead). He actually seems interested.

So instead I say, "I had to do all that by hand," referring to the stitching on Vicky's dress. "Because I was traveling at the time, and didn't have my Singer."

"This is hand-done?" he asks, squinting at the photo, then reaching for a pair of bifocals tucked away in his shirt pocket.

"Yes," I say, trying hard not to look at his wife. Stupid! Well, what does *she* know? She obviously can't read. Because it says right on my résumé that I'm a University of Michigan grad. Or I will be in January, anyway. The University of Michigan doesn't accept stupid people . . . even if their fathers *are* supervisors at the cyclotron.

"You took out the rust stains," Monsieur Henri says, "without chemicals?"

"Just cream of tartar," I say. "I soaked it overnight."

Monsieur Henri says, somewhat proudly, "Here we too do not use chemicals. That is how we received our endorsement from the Association of Bridal Consultants and became Certified Wedding-Gown Specialists."

I don't know how to reply to that. I didn't even know there was such a thing as certified wedding-gown specialists. So I just say, "Sweet."

Madame Henri elbows her husband.

"Tell her," she says in French. "Tell her the other thing."

Monsieur Henri peers down at me through the lenses of his eyeglasses. "The National Bridal Service gave us their highest recommendation."

"That is more than they have ever given that *cochon* Maurice!" Madame Henri cries.

I think calling this poor Maurice guy—whoever he is—a pig might be a bit much.

Especially since I've never heard of the National Bridal Service, either.

But again I manage, for once in my life, to keep my mouth shut. There are two wedding gowns on dressmaker's dummies in the window of the tiny shop. They're restoration refurbishments, according to the placard in front of them . . . and they're exquisite. One is covered in seed pearls that dangle like raindrops, glistening in the sun. And the other is a complicated confection of lacy ruffles that my fingers itch to touch, in order to figure out how they were created.

Mrs. Erickson was right. Monsieur Henri knows his stuff. I could learn a lot from him—not just about sewing, either, but about running a successful business.

Too bad Madame Henri is such a—

"This is a very stressful job," Monsieur Henri goes on. "The women who come to us . . . to them, this is the most important day of their lives. Their gown must be absolutely perfect, and yet delivered on time."

"I'm a total perfectionist myself," I say. "I've stayed up all night to finish gowns when I didn't even *have* to."

Monsieur Henri doesn't even appear to be listening. "Our clients can be very demanding. One day they want one thing. The next day, something else—"

"I'm completely flexible," I say. "And I'm also very good with people. You might even say I'm a people person." Oh, God. Did I just say that? "But I would never let a client pick something that isn't flattering."

"This is a family-run business," Monsieur Henri says with sudden—and alarming—finality, closing my portfolio with a loud snap. "I am not looking to hire outsiders."

"But—" No. He is *not* turning me away. I *have* to know how he made those ruffles. "I know I'm not family. But I'm good. And what I don't know—I'm a very quick learner."

"*Non,*" Monsieur Henri says. "It is no use. I built this business for my sons—"

"Who want nothing to do with it," his wife says bitterly in French. "You know that, Jean. All those lazy pigs want to do is go to the discotheque."

Hmmm. Her own sons are pigs, too? Also . . . discotheque?

"—and I do all my own work," Monsieur Henri continues loftily.

"Right," Madame Henri snorts. "That's why you have no time for me anymore. Or your sons. They run so wild because you are always here at the shop. And what about your heart? The doctor said you've got to reduce your stress levels, or you'll have a stroke. You keep saying you want to work less, leave the shop to someone else to run sometimes, so we can spend more time in Provence. But do you do anything about this? Of course not."

"I live right around the corner," I say, trying not to let them catch on that I understand every word they're saying. "I can be here whenever you want me. If, you know, you want to spend more time with your family."

Madame Henri's gaze locks onto mine. "Perhaps," she murmurs, in her native tongue, "she is not so stupid after all."

"Please," I say, fighting down an urge to yell, *If I'm so stupid, would I be living on Fifth Avenue?* Because, of course, people who judge you by what avenue you live on *are* stupid. "Your gowns are so beautiful. I want to open a shop of my own someday. So it only makes sense that I'd want to learn from the best. And I have references. You can call the manager of the last shop I worked in—"

"*Non,*" Monsieur Henri says. "*Non,* I am not interested."

And he shoves my résumé back at me.

"Who's stupid now?" his wife demands tartly.

But Monsieur Henri—perhaps because he's seen the tears that have suddenly sprung up in my eyes . . . which, I know. Crying! At a job interview!—seems to soften.

"Mademoiselle," he says, laying a hand on my shoulder. "It is not that I don't think you have talent. It is that we are a very small shop. And my sons, they are in college now. This is very expensive. I cannot afford to pay another person."

And then I hear four words come trickling out of my mouth—like spit does, while I sleep—that I never in a million years would have guessed I'd ever say. And immediately after I've spoken, I want to shoot myself. But it's too late. They're already out there.

"I'll work for free."

God! No! What am I saying?

Except that it's seemed to work. Monsieur Henri looks intrigued. And his wife is smiling as if she's just won the lottery or something.

"An internship, you mean?" Monsieur Henri lowers his bifocals to look at me more closely.

"I . . . I . . ." Oh God. How am I going to get out of this one? Especially since I'm not even sure I want to. "I guess so. And then when you see how hard I work, maybe you could consider promoting me to a paid position."

Okay. There, that sounds better. That's exactly what I'll do. I'll work like a dog for him, make myself indispensable. And then, when he can't do without me, I'll threaten to walk away unless he pays me.

I'm pretty sure this is not the most effective strategy for getting a job. But it's the only one I've got at the moment.

"Done," Monsieur Henri says. Then he whips off his bifocals and holds out his hand for me to shake. "Welcome."

"Um." I slip my hand in his, feeling all the calluses on his fingers and palm. "Thanks."

About which Madame Henri observes in smug French, "Ha! She really is stupid after all!"

~ Lizzie Nichols's Wedding Gown Guide ~

Know your . . .

Wedding-gown train lengths!

The three basic wedding-dress train lengths are:

The Sweep Length
Barely touches the floor

The Chapel Length
Trails on the floor about four feet
out from the dress

The Cathedral Length
Trails six feet out from the dress (or more . . . but only if you're royalty!)

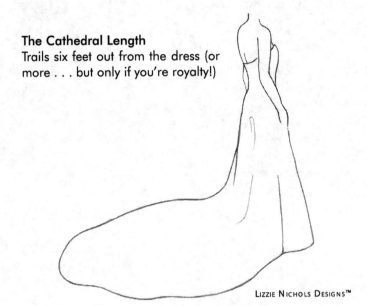

Lizzie Nichols Designs™

Chapter 7

I'm crying as I measure.

I can't help it. I'm just so screwed.

And it's not like I know anyone is home.

So when Chaz comes out of his bedroom, holding a tattered paperback and looking sleepy, and goes, "Holy Christ, what are *you* doing here?" I let out this little shriek and fall over, sending the measuring tape flying.

"Are you all right?" Chaz reaches for my arm, but it's too late. I'm already flat on my butt on his living room floor.

I blame the sloping parquet. I really do.

"No," I sob. "No, I'm not all right."

"What's wrong?" Chaz isn't quite laughing. But there is a definite upward curl to the corners of his lips.

"It's not funny," I say. Life in Manhattan has completely robbed me of my sense of humor. Oh, sure, it's all fine and good when Luke and I are in bed together, or curled up on his mom's couch, watching *Pants Off/Dance Off* on her plasma screen (artfully hidden from view beneath a genuine sixteenth-century tapestry depicting a lovely pastoral scene when not in use).

But the minute he walks out the door to go to class—which is basically from nine to five every weekday—and I'm left on my own, all of my insecurities come rushing back, and I realize that I'm as close to striking out in Manhattan as Kathy Pennebaker did. The only difference between us, really, is that I don't have a personality disorder.

That's been clinically diagnosed, anyway.

"Sorry," Chaz says. He's trying not to smile as he looks down at me. "Do you want to tell me what you're doing sneaking into my apartment in the middle of the afternoon? Luke won't let you cry in his mom's place, or something?"

"No." I stay where I am on the floor. It feels good to cry. Also, Shari and Chaz keep the place pretty clean, so it's not like I'm worried about getting my dress dirty or anything. "Shari gave me your spare key so I could come in and measure for the slipcovers and curtains I'm making you."

"You're making us slipcovers and curtains?" Chaz looks pleased. "Cool." He stops looking pleased when I keep on crying. "Or maybe not cool. If it's making you cry."

"I'm not crying because of the slipcovers," I say, reaching to dab at my eyes with the backs of my wrist. "I'm crying because I'm such a loser."

"Okay. I'm going to need a drink for this one," Chaz says with a sigh. "You want one?"

"Alcohol won't solve anything," I wail.

"No," Chaz agrees. "But I've been reading Wittgenstein all afternoon, so it might make me feel less suicidal. You in or you out? I'm thinking gin and tonics."

"I'm i-in," I hiccup. Maybe a little gin is what I need to buck myself up. It always seems to work for Grandma.

Which is how, a little while later, I find myself sitting next to Chaz on his gold-trimmed couches (the cushions are gold, too. If I didn't know they came from a law office, I'd swear his couches came from a Chinese restaurant. An upscale one. But still), telling him the wretched truth about my finances.

"And now," I conclude, holding on to my tall, frosty drink glass, the contents of which are mostly consumed, "I have a job—I'm not going to say it's my dream job, or anything, but I think I could learn a lot—but it doesn't pay, and I have no idea how I'm going to get rent money for next month. I mean, I can't even temp now, because I don't have my days free, on account of having to be at Monsieur Henri's. And you know how much I suck at bartending and food service. Honestly, unless I sell off my vintage clothing collection, I don't think I'm going to make it. I don't even know how I'm going to get the subway fare to get back home from *here*. And I *can't* tell Luke, I just can't, he'll just think I'm stupid, like Madame Henri does, and it's not like I can ask my parents for money, they don't have any, and besides, I'm an adult, I should be supporting myself. So clearly I'm going to have to tell Monsieur Henri that I'm very sorry, but I made a mistake, and then head down to the closest temp agency and hope they have something—*anything*—for me."

I draw in a deep, shuddering breath. "It's either that, or go back to Ann Arbor and hope my old job at Vintage to Vavoom is still available. Except that if I do that, everyone will go around saying how Lizzie Nichols tried to make it in New York but struck out, just like Kathy Pennebaker."

"She the one who used to steal everyone's boyfriend?" Chaz asks.

"Yes," I say, thinking how nice it is that Shari's boyfriend already knows all the important people and references from our lives, so I don't have to explain them to him, the way I do Luke.

"Well," he says. "They won't compare you to her. She's got a personality disorder."

"Right. She has more of an excuse for striking out in New York than I do!"

Chaz considers this. "She's also a big whore. I'm just quoting Shari, here."

I think I'm getting a migraine. "Can we leave Kathy Pennebaker out of this?"

"You brought her up," Chaz points out.

What am I doing here? What am I doing, sitting on my best friend's boyfriend's couch, telling him all my problems? Worse, he's my boyfriend's best friend.

"If you tell Luke," I growl, "anything about what I said here today, I'll kill you. I really mean it. I'll—I'll kill you."

"I believe you," Chaz says gravely.

"Good." I climb to my feet—not very steadily. Chaz didn't skimp on the gin. "I've got to go. Luke'll be home soon."

"Hold on there, champ," Chaz says, and pulls me back down to the couch by the back of my beaded cardigan.

"Hey," I say. "That's cashmere, you know."

"Simmer down," Chaz says. "I'm going to do you a solid."

I hold up both hands, palms out, to ward him off. "Oh no," I say. "No way. I do not want a loan, Chaz. I'm going to do this on my own, or not at all. I'm not touching your money."

"That's good to know," Chaz says dryly. "Because I wasn't planning on offering you any of my money. What I'm wondering is if you could do the wedding-gown thing part-time. Like, afternoons only."

"Chaz," I say, putting my hands down. "I'm not getting *paid* to do the wedding-gown thing. When you aren't getting paid, you can pretty much make your own hours."

"Right," he says. "So you have your mornings free?"

"Regrettably," I say.

"Well, it just so happens," he says, "that Pendergast, Loughlin, and Flynn just lost their morning receptionist to a touring company of *Tarzan*, the musical."

I blink at him. "Your dad's law firm?"

"Correct," Chaz says. "The receptionist position there is apparently so demanding that it has to be split into two shifts, one from eight in the morning until two in the afternoon, and the other from two in the afternoon until eight in the evening. The afternoon shift is currently held by a young woman with modeling aspirations, who needs her mornings free for go-sees . . . or to recover from her hangover from partying the night before, whichever you care to believe. But they're looking for someone to fill in for the morning shift. So, if you're serious about wanting a job, it might not be a bad gig for you. You'd have your afternoons free for Monsieur Whatsisname, and you wouldn't have to sell off your Betty Boop collection, or whatever it is. It only pays twenty bucks an hour, but it comes with benefits like major medical and paid vaca—"

But he doesn't get to go on. Because I've already thrown myself at him when I hear the words "twenty bucks an hour."

"Chaz, are you serious?" I cry, grasping big handfuls of his T-shirt. "Will you really put in a good word for me?"

"Ow," Chaz says. "That's my chest hair you're pulling."

I let go of him. "Oh God. Chaz! If I could work all morning, then go to Monsieur Henri's in the afternoons . . . I might be able to make it. I might actually be able to make it in New York City after all! I won't have to sell my stuff! I won't have to go home!" More important, I won't have to admit to Luke how much of a failure I am.

"I'll call Roberta in human resources and set up an appointment for you," Chaz says. "But I'm warning you, Lizzie. It's not easy work. Sure, all you're doing is transferring phone calls. But my dad's law firm specializes in divorces and matrimonial planning—in other words, prenups. Their clients are pretty demanding, and the lawyers are pretty uptight. Things can get really tense. I know, my dad had me work in the mailroom one summer when I was just out of high school. And it sucked."

I'm barely listening. "Is there a dress code? Do I have to wear panty hose? I hate panty hose."

Chaz sighs. "Roberta can tell you all about that. Listen. Not to make it not all about you for a change, or anything, but do you know what's up with Shari?"

That gets my attention. "Shari? No. Why? What are you talking about?"

"I don't know." For a minute, Chaz looks younger than his twenty-six years—which is only three years older than Shari and I are, and yet in so many ways, light-years older than that, even. I personally think that's what comes of sending your kid off to boarding school during those integral tween and teen years. But maybe that's just me. I can't imagine having a kid and purposely sending him away, the way Chaz's parents did, just because he was a little ADD. "She just can't seem to stop talking about this new boss of hers."

"Pat?" I've heard the Pat stories ad nauseum myself. Every time I talk to Shari, it seems like she has another story about her intrepid new boss to share.

But it isn't a wonder, really, that Shari's impressed by the woman. She has, after all, been instrumental in saving hundreds, maybe even thousands of women's lives by getting them out of their abusive family situations and into new safe environments.

"Yeah," Chaz says, when I mention this. "I know all that. And I'm glad Shari likes her job, and all. It's just . . . I hardly ever see her anymore. She's always working. Not just nine to five, but evenings and some weekends, too."

"Well," I say. Regrettably, I'm beginning to sober up already. "I'm sure she's just trying to keep afloat. From what she says, the girl who had the job before her kind of left everything in a huge mess. She told me it would be months before she got it all straightened out."

"Yeah," Chaz says. "She told me that, too."

"So," I say. "You should be proud of her. She's helping to make a difference." Unlike me. And, I want to add, Chaz, who is only working on his Ph.D., after all. Although when he gets it, he intends to teach. Which is admirable. I mean, molding young minds, and all. Certainly more than I can say I'll ever be doing.

But young girls, they do get weary . . .

Okay, I totally have to stop thinking of that song all the time.

"I *am* proud of her," Chaz says. "I just wish she could help make a difference fewer hours of the day, is all."

"Aw." I smile at him. "You're sweet. You wuv your girlfriend."

He shoots a sarcastic look at me. "Maybe you *do* have a personality disorder," he says.

I laugh and take a swing at him, but he ducks.

"What about you and Luke?" he wants to know. "I mean, aside from the shameful secret you're keeping from him—about your abject poverty—how are you two getting along?"

"Great," I say. I think about asking him what I should do about Luke's mom. The guy who'd called—the one with the accent—had left another message, sounding wounded that Bibi hadn't shown up to their meeting. Again, he didn't leave a name, but again, he'd mentioned their standing appointment, and that he'd be waiting.

I'd erased the message before Luke got home from class. It just didn't seem to me like the kind of thing a guy would want to listen to. About his mother, that is.

Of course, I was considering the fact that I hadn't blabbed the whole thing out to Luke anyway the minute he walked through the door a sign of my newfound maturity and ability to keep my mouth shut.

The fact that I'm not blabbing it to Chaz now is even further proof of my incredible New York sangfroid.

Instead I say to Chaz conversationally, "I'm still doing the tiny woodland creature thing, and it seems to be working."

Chaz blinks at me. "The *what*?"

And I realize, belatedly, that I've been lulled into a false sense of comfort by his easygoing nature . . . so much so that I've started talking to him about stuff I normally reserve for Shari's ears only! What am I doing, talking about my woodland creature theory with another GUY? Worse than just another guy—my boyfriend's *best friend*?

"Uh, nothing," I say quickly. "Things are fine with Luke."

"What's the tiny woodland creature thing?" he wants to know.

"Nothing," I say again. "Just—nothing. It's a girl thing. It's not important."

But Chaz totally won't let it go. "Is it a sex thing?"

"Oh my God!" I cry. "No! It's not a sex thing! God!"

"Well, what is it then? Come on, you can tell me. I won't tell Luke."

"Oh, right," I say with a laugh. "I've heard that before—"

Chaz looks wounded. "What? Have I ever ratted you out to any of your boyfriends before?"

I glare at him. "I've never had a boyfriend before. At least, not one who wasn't gay or using me for my money. Back when I had some money, I mean."

"Come on, just tell me," Chaz says. "What's it mean to do the tiny woodland creature thing? I swear I won't tell anyone."

"Just . . ." I can see I have no choice but to tell him. Otherwise, he's never going to let it go. And with my luck, he'll bring it up in front of Luke. "It's just this theory I have, all right? That guys are like tiny woodland creatures. And to lure them in, you can't make any sudden moves. You have to be subtle. You have to be cool."

"Lure them in to do what?" Chaz asks, seeming genuinely not to know. "You've already got Luke. I mean, you're living together. Although I still don't understand why you can't tell your parents that's what you're doing. They're going to find out it isn't Shari you're sharing your place with eventually. Don't you think the fact that you have an address on Fifth Avenue is going to make them a *little* suspicious?"

I roll my eyes. "Chaz. My parents don't know from Fifth Avenue. They've never been to New York. And you know what I'm talking about."

"No, I really don't. Enlighten me?"

"You know," I say. Because he's clearly never going to let it go. "Get them to commit."

"Get them to . . ." Comprehension dawns across Chaz's face. Comprehension combined with what appears to be a healthy dose of horror. "You want to *marry* Luke?"

I have no choice but to lift up one of the gold cushions and hurl it at him in fury. "Don't say it like that!" I yell. "What's wrong with it? I love him!"

This time Chaz is too stunned to duck. The cushion bounces off him, nearly overturning his empty gin and tonic glass, already teetering precariously on the uneven floor.

"You've only known the guy like three months," he cries. "And you're already thinking about *marriage?*"

"Oh, what?" I can't believe this is happening. Again. Why did I open my big mouth? Why can't I ever keep *anything* to myself? "Like there's some kind of correct time frame in which you're supposed to decide these kinds of things? Sometimes you just *know,* Chaz."

"Yeah, but . . . *Luke?*" Chaz is shaking his head in disbelief. This is not a good sign. Considering Luke is his best friend. And he probably has insider information.

"What *about* Luke?" I demand. But I'll admit it, even though I sounded cool about it—to my own ears, anyway—my heart was beginning to race. What was he talking about? Why did he have that expression on his face? Like he'd just smelled something bad?

"Look, don't get me wrong," Chaz says. "I think Luke's a great guy to hang out with and all. But I wouldn't *marry* him."

"No one is asking you to," I point out. "In fact, in most states, that would be illegal."

"Ha, ha," Chaz says. Then he clams up. "Listen. Never mind. Forget I said anything. You go on forest-creaturing him, or whatever it is. Have fun."

"Woodland," I say. Now my heart isn't just racing. It feels like it's about to explode out of my chest. "Woodland creature. And tell me what you mean. Why wouldn't you want to marry Luke? I mean, aside from the fact that you're not gay." And that he hasn't asked. Me, I mean.

"I don't know." Chaz looks uncomfortable. "I mean, marriage is pretty final. You have to spend the rest of your life with the person."

"Not necessarily," I say. "I think your father's built himself a pretty lucrative career proving that this isn't always the case."

"That's what I mean, though," Chaz says. "If you pick the wrong person, it can end up costing you hundreds of thousands of dollars. If my dad's firm represents you, I mean."

"But I don't think Luke is the wrong person," I explain to him patiently. "For me. And I'm not saying I want to get married to him tomorrow. I'm not an *idiot*. I want to be established in my career before I start having kids and all of that. And I told him the whole moving-in-together thing was on a trial basis and all of that. I'm just saying that, if things work out, when I'm thirty or so, marrying Luke would be very nice."

"Well," Chaz says. "That's fine, I guess. But *I'm* just saying, a lot of stuff can happen in the six years before you turn thirty—"

"Seven," I correct him.

"—and that if you guys were horses, and I were a betting man, Luke's not the horse I would bet on to come in first. Or at all, for that matter."

I shake my head. My heart has slowed down. It's clear Chaz doesn't have the slightest idea what he's talking about. Not bet on Luke? What is he talking about? Luke is the most fantastic person I've ever met. What other guy does Chaz know who's memorized every song on the Rolling Stones' *Sticky Fingers* album by heart—and frequently sings them in the shower—on *key*? What other guy does Chaz know who can take oil, vinegar, some mustard, and an egg, and make the most delicious salad dressing I've ever tasted? What other guy does Chaz know who was willing to give up his lucrative salary as an investment banker to go back to school to become a doctor, and *help heal sick children*?

"That's not a very nice thing to say about your friend," I point out.

Chaz looks defensive. "I'm not saying he's a bad person. I'm just saying that I've known him a lot longer than you have, Lizzie, and he's always had a problem with—well, let's just say when the going gets tough, Luke has a habit of getting going. As in quitting."

I'm appalled. "Because he put off medical school to become an investment banker, then realized he made a mistake? People do that, you know, Chaz. People make mistakes."

"You don't," Chaz says. "I mean, you make mistakes. But not that kind. You've known what you've wanted to do since the day I met you. You've also known it was going to be hard, and that it would take a lot of sacrifice, and that you probably wouldn't make a lot of money at it right away. But that never stopped you. You never gave up on your dream when the going got tough."

I gape at him. "Chaz, have you even been in the same room with me for this entire conversation? I just got through telling you how I'm about to give up on my dream."

"You just got through telling me how you were going to move home and figure out some other way to pursue it that doesn't include New York City," Chaz corrects me. "That's different. Listen, Liz, don't get me wrong. I'm *not* saying Luke's a bad guy. I'm just saying I wouldn't—"

"Bet on him to finish first if he were a horse and you were a betting man," I finish for him impatiently. "Yes, I know, I heard you the first time. And I get what you're saying, I guess. But you're talking about the OLD Luke. Not the Luke he's turned into, now that he has me to support him. People change, Chaz."

"Not that much," Chaz says.

"Yes," I say. "They do. That much."

"Can you give me empirical data to support that statement?" Chaz asks.

"No," I say. Now I'm really getting impatient. I don't know how Shari puts up with Chaz sometimes. Oh, sure, he's cute, in a jockish kind of way. And he totally adores her, and is supposedly fantastic in bed (sometimes I think Shari shares a little too much). But what's with the turned-around baseball caps? And the *Can you give me the empirical data to support that statement?*

"Then that," Chaz goes on, "is a specious argument—"

What's that Shakespeare saying? *The first thing we do, let's kill all the lawyers?* It should be, *The first thing we do, let's kill all the graduate students getting a Ph.D. in philosophy.*

"Chaz!" I cut him off. "Do you want to help me measure your windows so I can go home and start on your curtains, or what?"

He glances at the windows. They are covered with hideous folding metal gates, in order to keep out the few remaining crackheads in the city, all of whom seem to live in his neighborhood, for some reason.

They are terrifically ugly. Even a guy should be able to see that.

"I guess," he says, looking deflated. "It's more fun arguing with you, though."

"Well, *I'm* not having any fun," I inform him.

He grins. "Okay. Curtains it is. And Lizzie."

I've scooped up the measuring tape and am slipping off my shoes so I can climb up onto the radiator to measure. "What?"

"About the job. In my dad's office. There's one more thing."

"What?"

"You're going to have to keep your mouth shut. I mean, about who you see and what you overhear in there. You're not supposed to talk about it. It's a law office. And they promise their clients total discretion—"

"God, Chaz," I say, irritated all over again. "I can keep my mouth shut, you know."

He just looks at me.

"If it's important, I *can*," I insist. "Like, if my paycheck depends on it."

"Maybe," Chaz says, almost as if to himself, "recommending you for the job isn't the best idea . . ."

I throw the measuring tape at him.

~ Lizzie Nichols's Wedding Gown Guide ~

Yes, I know. Everybody's doing it. Well, if everyone jumped off the Brooklyn Bridge, would you do it, too?

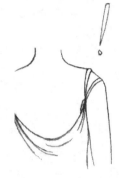

So stop letting your bra straps show!

I don't care how much you paid for your over-the-shoulder-boulder-holder, it's uncouth to force us to look at it (especially if the straps are graying or frayed—and ESPECIALLY on your wedding day)!

Keep your girls where they should be by having your wedding-gown specialist attach about an inch and a half of seam binding or a thread chain under the shoulder seam of your sleeve or strap. Then have her sew a ball snap to the free end of the guard, and a socket snap toward the neck edge.

Then snap your strap. It will be out of sight . . . and so will you!

LIZZIE NICHOLS DESIGNS™

Chapter 8

If an American was condemned to confine his activity to his own affairs, he would be robbed of one half of his existence.

—Alexis de Tocqueville (1805–1859), French politician and historian

New York is a strange place. Things here can change in the blink of the eye. I guess that's what they mean when they say a New York minute. Everything just seems to go faster here.

Like, you can be walking down a street that seems perfectly tree-lined and pleasant, and not even one block later, you suddenly find yourself in a trash-filled, graffitied seedy underbelly of a neighborhood, resembling something out of a crime scene on one of the *Law and Orders*. And all you've done is crossed a street.

So I guess, considering all this, I shouldn't have been so amazed that in a forty-eight-hour period, I went from having no job in New York City to being the proud owner of *two* of them.

The interview with the human resources division of Chaz's dad's office is going well. *Really* well. It's like a joke, actually. The harried-looking woman whose office I'm escorted into after waiting for nearly half an hour in the fancy lobby (they'd upgraded from gold-trimmed couches to deep-brown leather ones, which blended nicely with the dark wood paneling on the walls and rich green carpeting) asks me one or two pleasant questions about how I know

Chaz—"From the dorm we all lived in in college," I say, not mentioning that Shari and I had met him at an outdoor movie night sponsored by the student government of McCracken Hall, at which Chaz had been the one who'd started passing around a joint, causing us to refer to him for days afterward as the Joint Man . . . until Shari spied him eating breakfast in the dining hall by himself one morning, plunked herself down beside him, asked him his name, and by that evening had slept with him in his single in McCracken's tower suites. Three times.

"Great," Roberta, my interviewer, says, apparently not realizing she's getting a less than complete relationship history from me. "We all love Charles. The summer he worked here in the mailroom, he had us all in stitches the whole time. He's so funny."

Yeah. Chaz is hilarious.

"It's just too bad," Roberta goes on wistfully, "that Charles didn't choose the law. He has his dad's same brilliant academic mind. When either of them starts arguing a point—well, get out of the way!"

Yeah. Chaz likes to argue a point, all right.

"So, Lizzie," Roberta says pleasantly. "When can you start?"

I gape at her. "You mean I got the job?"

"Of course." Roberta looks at me strangely, as if any other turn of events would be unthinkable. "Could you start tomorrow?"

Can I start tomorrow? Is there a grand total of three hundred and twenty-one dollars in my checking account? Are my credit cards maxed out to their limits? Am I fifteen hundred dollars in debt to MasterCard?

"I can *definitely* start tomorrow!"

Oh, Chaz, I take it all back. I love you. You can say whatever you want about Luke. You can be as pessimistic as you choose about the wisdom of my wanting to marry him. For this, Chaz, I owe you. Big time.

"I love your boyfriend." I call Shari on my cell to tell her as I come out of the skyscraper on Madison Avenue in which the offices of Pendergast, Loughlin, and Flynn take up the entire thirty-seventh floor.

"Really." Shari sounds, as always when I call her at her office these days, a little frantic. "You can have him."

"Taken," I say. I'm on Fifty-seventh Street between Madison and Fifth. It's such a nice fall day—just warm enough that you don't need a coat, and just cool enough that you don't feel sweaty—I decide to walk to Monsieur Henri's, just thirty blocks north, instead of taking the subway, saving myself a whopping two bucks. Hey, every little bit counts. "Chaz got me a job in his dad's office."

"A job?" I hear computer keys clacking. Shari is talking and e-mailing at the same time. But that's okay. I'll take whatever I can get, it's so hard to reach her these days. "I thought you already had a job. At that wedding-gown place."

"Yeah," I say, realizing I hadn't been quite as upfront with my friends about my deal with Monsieur Henri as I ought to have been. "That's not really a paying gig—"

"WHAT?" I realize by her tone—and the cessation of clacking keys—that I now have Shari's undivided attention. "You took a *non-paying* job?"

"Right," I say. It's kind of hard to walk down a busy sidewalk like the one I'm currently hurrying along and talk on your cell at the same time. There are so many businesspeople rushing back to their offices, street vendors hawking Prada knockoffs, tourists stopping to gawk at the tall buildings, and homeless people asking for spare change that it's as hard to navigate as the Indy 500 Speedway during the race. "Well, it's not easy to find a paying fashion gig in this city when you're just starting out."

"I can't believe that," Shari says, sounding incredulous. "What about *Project Runway*?"

"Shari," I say. "I'm not going on a *reality show*—"

"No, I just mean . . . they make it seem like it's all so easy—"

"Well," I say. "It's not. Anyway, I want us to get together to celebrate—you and me and Chaz and Luke. So what are you doing tonight?"

"Oh," Shari says. I hear the clacking start up again. Which isn't easy, considering the fact that there are cars honking and people talking loudly all around me. And yet, I can still hear the fact that my best friend is only half paying attention to me. "I can't. Not tonight. We're getting slammed here today—"

"Fine," I say. I understand that Shari's new job is the most important thing in the world to her right now. Which is as it should be. I mean, she is, after all, saving women's lives. "How about tomorrow night, then?"

"This week is really bad for me, Lizzie," Shari says. "I'm going to be working late just about every night."

"What about Saturday?" I inquire patiently. "You aren't working on Saturday night, are you?"

There's a pause. For a second or two, I think Shari's going to say that she does, indeed, plan on working through Saturday night.

But then she says, "No, of course not. Saturday it is."

"Great," I say. "We'll hit Chinatown. And then Honey's. On Saturday night the serious karaoke players come out. And, Shari?"

"What, Lizzie? I really have to go, Pat's waiting—"

"I know." There's always someone waiting for Shari these days. "But I wanted to ask you—are things okay between you and Chaz? Because he asked me about you."

I have her full attention again. "He asked you *what* about me?" Shari demands, somewhat sharply.

"Just if I thought you were all right," I say. "I said I thought you were. I guess he misses you as much as I do." I think about this as I wait for the light to change before crossing the street. "Actually, he probably misses you more . . ."

"I can't help it," Shari snaps, "if I'm too busy helping victims of domestic violence find safe places to live to worry about my boyfriend. This is part of the problem, you know. I mean, men think the entire world revolves around them. And so when the woman in his life finds herself thriving—excelling, even—in the workplace, a man naturally feels threatened, and eventually leaves her for someone who has more time to give to him."

I am, to put it bluntly, stunned by this speech. So stunned I actually stop walking for a second, and am bumped from behind by an irritated-looking businessman. "Excuse you," the businessman mutters before hurrying along.

"Shari," I say into the phone. "Chaz does *not* feel threatened by your new career. He loves that you love your job. He just wants to know when he's ever going to see you again. He isn't leaving you."

"I know," Shari says, after a pause. "I just—sorry. I didn't mean to lay all that on you. I'm just having a bad day. Forget I said anything."

"Shari." I shake my head. "This sounds like something more serious than just a bad day. Are you and Chaz—"

"I really have to go, Lizzie," Shari says. "I'll see you Saturday."

And then she hangs up.

Wow. What was *that* about? I wonder. Chaz and Shari have always had something of a stormy relationship, full of bickering and even some fights (the most serious of which was the one stemming from Shari's decision to kill and dissect her lab rat, Mr. Jingles, even after Chaz had found an identical replacement rat at PetSmart for whom none of us had developed the kind of affection we all felt for Mr. Jingles).

But they'd always made up quickly (except for the two weeks after Mr. Jingles's death that Chaz wouldn't speak to Shari). In fact, the fantastic makeup sex was one of the reasons Shari cited for picking so many fights with Chaz in the first place.

So is that what's going on now? Just an elaborate ploy on Shari's part to inject a little more excitement into their relationship?

Because, as I'm discovering myself, it's not easy to keep the flame alive when you're living together. Mundane everyday things can totally get in the way of blissful cohabitation. Like whose turn is it to do the dishes, and who gets control of the remote, and who unplugged whose cell phone charger to plug in the hair dryer instead then forgot to plug the cell phone charger back in.

Those kinds of things are real romance killers.

Not that I don't love every minute of living with Luke. I mean, from the moment I wake up to see the Renoir girl's smiling face above my head, to the moment I fall asleep, listening to Luke's gentle breathing beside me (he always falls asleep before I do. I don't know how he does it. The minute his head touches the pillow, he's out like a light. Maybe it's all that boring reading for his Principles of Biology and General Chemistry that he does before bed in order to keep up with his homework), I thank my lucky stars that I made the decision to leave England and go to France. Because otherwise I would never have met him, and I wouldn't be as happy as I am now (worries about finances aside).

Still, I guess I can understand it if Shari is trying to get a rise out of Chaz just to shake things up a little. Because I've watched television with Chaz before, and the way he flips up and down the channels instead of just leaving it on one semiinteresting program and then going to the onscreen guide to see what else is on can be almost as annoying as the way Luke, it turns out, considers really upsetting documentaries about things like the Holocaust suitable viewing for a fun Friday night at home.

But I don't have time to worry about Shari and Chaz—or even Luke's aversion to romantic comedies—because when I get to Monsieur Henri's that afternoon and ring the bell to be let in (he hasn't given me a key, and probably won't, I fear, until I've proved myself capable of doing something other than a cross-stitch), I find bedlam.

An older woman with big hair and the kind of brightly colored clothing that I've already learned pegs her as "bridge and tunnel" (someone who lives outside Manhattan, and has to take a bridge or tunnel to get to it) is holding this enormous white box and shouting, "Look! Just look!" while a girl who could only be her daughter (even though she's more stylishly attired in black and a blowout) stands nearby, looking sullen, and not a little rebellious.

Monsieur Henri, in the meantime, is saying, "Madame, I know. This is not the first time. I see this often."

I try to keep out of the way, and sidle up to Madame Henri, who is watching the drama unfold from the curtained doorway to the workroom at the back of the shop.

"What's happening?" I ask her.

She shakes her head. "They went to Maurice" is all she says in way of reply.

Which of course tells me nothing. I still don't have the slightest idea who Maurice is.

But then Monsieur Henri reaches into the box, and carefully pulls out a long-sleeved, virginal, fragile-as-gossamer-looking white gown.

At least, it used to be white. The lace has turned a sickening shade of yellow.

"He promised!" the woman is saying. "He promised the preservation box would keep it from yellowing!"

"Of course he did," Monsieur Henri says, in a dry tone. "And when you took it back to show him, he told you that the reason it turned this color was because you broke the preservation seal."

"Yes!" The woman's chin is trembling, she's so upset. "Yes, that's exactly what he said! He said it was my fault, for allowing air inside the box!"

I let out an involuntary sound of protest. Monsieur Henri glances in my direction. I immediately blush, and take a quick step backward.

But Monsieur Henri has fastened his blue-eyed gaze at me and isn't looking away.

"Mademoiselle?" he asks. "There is something you wish to say?"

"No," I say quickly, aware that Madame Henri is staring daggers at me. "I mean, not really."

"I think there is." Monsieur Henri's eyes are very bright. He can't see anything close up without his glasses. But his farsightedness is uncanny. "Go on. What is it that you wish to say?"

"Only," I begin reluctantly, fearing I might be saying something he won't like, "that storing textiles in a sealed container can actually harm them, especially if moisture gets in. It can cause the material to mildew."

Monsieur Henri, I see, looks pleased. This gives me the courage to continue. "Not one of the historic costumes at the Met is stored in an airtight room," I go on. "And they're doing just fine. It's important to keep old fabric out of direct sunlight—but there's no way breaking the seal on a preservation box caused the yellowing on that dress. That was caused by improper cleaning before storage . . . most likely the result of the gown not having been cleaned at all, and stains from champagne or perspiration being left untreated."

The smile Monsieur Henri bequeaths me upon my concluding this recitation is dazzling enough to cause his wife to suck in her breath . . .

. . . and throw me a look of surprise. It's clear she's reassessing her "stupid" remark from earlier in the week.

"But how can that be?" the woman asks, her brow furrowed. "If the gown was cleaned before it was put in storage—"

"God, Mom," the girl interrupts, sounding disgusted. "Don't you get it? That Maurice guy didn't clean it. He just stuck it in there, put the lid on, and gave it back, *saying* he'd cleaned it."

"And told you never to open the box," Monsieur Henri adds. "That breaking the seal would cause the material to yellow—and void your money-back guarantee." Making a tsk-tsking noise, Monsieur Henri looks down at the dress he's holding. Which, I have to say, is not the nicest gown I've ever seen. I mean, it's okay.

But if the reason the older woman broke the seal on the box in which the gown had been preserved was so that her daughter could wear it to *her* wedding, well, she was in for a surprise. Because I couldn't see Miss Blowout putting on that high-necked, Victorian-looking thing for all the Suzy Perettes in the world.

"I have seen this a thousand times," Monsieur Henri says sadly. "It is such a shame."

The older woman looks alarmed. "Is it ruined?" she wants to know. "Can it be saved?"

"I don't know," Monsieur Henri says dubiously. I can see that he's playing them. All the dress needs is a nice white-vinegar soak and maybe a cold-water wash with some OxiClean.

"Gee, that's too bad," Blowout says, before Monsieur Henri can say anything more. "I guess we'll just have to get a new dress."

"We are not getting you a new dress, Jennifer," Big Hair snaps. "This dress was good enough for me, and good enough for each of your sisters. It's good enough for you!"

Jennifer looks mutinous. Monsieur Henri doesn't need to put on his glasses to see this. He hesitates, and it's clear he's not certain how to proceed. Madame Henri clears her throat.

But I jump in, before she can say a word, with, "The stains can be removed. But that's not the real problem, is it?"

Jennifer is looking at me suspiciously. So, actually, is everyone in the shop.

"Elizabeth," Monsieur Henri says, using my first name for the first time in our acquaintance—and in a sugary-sweet voice I know is completely fake, too. He clearly wants to kill me. "There is no problem."

"Yes, there is," I say, in a voice just as fakey as his. "I mean, look at that dress, and then look at Jennifer here." Everyone in the shop glances at the dress, then at Jennifer, who preens a little, sweeping back the stick-straight ends of her blowout. "Do you see the problem now?"

"No," Jennifer's mother says bluntly.

"This dress was probably very flattering on you, Mrs.—" I pause and look questioningly at Jennifer's mom, who says, "Harris."

"Right," I say. "Mrs. Harris. Because you're a statuesque woman, with excellent carriage. But look at Jennifer. She's very petite. A dress with this much material will overwhelm her."

Jennifer narrows her eyes and scissors a glance in her mother's direction. "See?" she hisses. "I told you."

"Er, uh," Monsieur Henri blusters uncomfortably, still looking as if he wants to kill me. "In point of fact, Mademoiselle Elizabeth is not, er, technically speaking, an employee of—"

"But this gown could easily be altered to flatter someone of Jennifer's proportions," I say, pointing to the high neckline, "merely by opening up this area here, giving it more of a sweetheart neckline, and maybe getting rid of the sleeves—"

"Absolutely not," Mrs. Harris says. "It's a Catholic ceremony."

"Then tightening the sleeves," I go on smoothly, "so that they don't bell. A girl with a figure as good as Jennifer's shouldn't hide it. Especially on a day when she wants to look her best."

Jennifer has been listening to all of this intently. I can tell because she's stopped fiddling with her hair.

"Yeah," she says. "See, Mom? That's what I *told* you."

"I don't know," Mrs. Harris murmurs, chewing her lower lip. "Your sisters—"

"Are you the youngest?" I asked Jennifer, who nodded. "Yeah, I thought so. Me, too. It's hard being the youngest, always getting your big sisters' hand-me-downs. You get to a point where you'd just die to have something—*anything*—new, something all your own."

"*Exactly!*" Jennifer explodes.

"But in the case of your mother's wedding gown, you *can* have that," I say, "and still observe family tradition by wearing it . . . you just have to give it a few tweaks to make it uniquely your own. And we can easily do that here—"

"I want that," Jennifer says, turning to her mother. "What she said. That's what I want."

Mrs. Harris looks from the gown to her daughter and then back again. Then she lets out a little laugh and says, "Fine! Whatever you want! If it's cheaper than a new gown—"

"Oh," Madame Henri steps forward to say, "it will be, of course. If the young lady would like to come with me to change, we can begin measuring for the alterations right away . . ."

Jennifer flicks her blowout back and, without another word, follows Madame Henri to the dressing room.

"Oh," Mrs. Harris cries, after glancing at her watch. "I have to go put money in the meter if we're staying. Excuse me—"

She hurries out of the shop. As soon as the door eases shut behind her, Monsieur Henri turns to me and, indicating the yellowed dress he's still holding, says hesitantly, "You are quite adept with the, er, customer."

"Oh," I say modestly. "Well, that one was easy. I know exactly how she felt. I have older sisters myself."

"I see." Monsieur Henri's gaze is shrewd as he looks down at me. "Well, I will be interested to see if you can work a needle as well as you work your mouth."

"Watch me," I say, plucking the gown from his hands. "Just watch."

Lizzie Nichols's Wedding Gown Guide

If you are top-heavy, or have an hourglass figure, I have one word for you: strapless!

I know what you are thinking . . . strapless, at a wedding? But strapless is no longer considered immodest in most churches!

And with the right support in the bodice, this look can be extremely flattering on a top-heavy bride, especially when paired with an A-line skirt. V-necklines are also terrific on large-on-the-top women, as are off-the-shoulder and scoop-neck designs.

Just remember that the higher the neckline, the bigger the boobs look!

Lizzie Nichols Designs™

Chapter 9

Nothing travels faster than light, with the possible exception of bad news, which follows its own rules.

—Douglas Adams (1952–2001), British author and radio dramatist

receptionist?"

That's what Luke says when I tell him the news. For once, he's gotten home before I have, and is making dinner—coq au vin. One of the many advantages of having a boyfriend who is half French is that his culinary repertoire extends beyond mac and cheese. Plus, there's the kissing.

"Right," I say. I'm sitting on a velvet-cushioned stool in front of the granite-topped bar beneath the pass-through between the kitchen and dining/living room.

"But." Luke is pouring us each a glass of cabernet sauvignon, then hands me mine through the pass-through. "Aren't you . . . I don't know. A little overqualified to be a receptionist?"

"Sure," I say. "But this way I'll be able to pay the bills and still do what I love—for part of the day, anyway. Since I haven't had any luck finding a paying fashion gig."

"It's only been a month," Luke says. "Maybe you just need to give your job search a little more time."

"Um." How can I explain this to him without revealing the fact that I am flat busted broke? "Well, I am. If something better comes along, of course I can always quit."

Except I don't want to. Quit Monsieur Henri's, anyway. Because I'm starting to like it there. Especially now that I know who Maurice is: a rival "certified wedding-gown specialist" who owns not one but four shops throughout the city, and who has been stealing away Monsieur Henri's clientele with his promise of a new chemical treatment to combat cake and wine stains (no such treatment exists), and who overcharges his customers for even the simplest alterations, and underpays his vendors and employees (although I don't see how he could underpay them more than Monsieur Henri is underpaying me).

Worse, Maurice has been bad-mouthing Monsieur Henri, telling every bride in town that Jean Henri is retiring to Provence and could pick up and leave at any time, due to his business falling off—which is apparently true, judging from the Henris' private conversations, which they aren't aware I completely understand. Well, almost completely.

As if all of that were not bad enough, the Henris have heard a rumor that Maurice is planning on opening up another one of his shops . . . DOWN THE STREET FROM THEIRS! With his glitzy red awning and matching signature red carpet (yes!) outside the front door, the Henris don't have a chance of competing . . . not with their subtle yet tasteful front window display and modest brownstone.

No, even if the Costume Institute calls tomorrow, I plan on sticking around at Monsieur Henri's. I'm in too deep to get out now.

"Well," Luke says, sounding dubious, "if it makes you happy . . ."

"It does," I say. Then I clear my throat. "You know, Luke, not everyone is cut out for the traditional nine-to-five thing. There's nothing wrong with taking on a job you're maybe overqualified for if it pays the bills and allows you to do the thing you really love in your spare time. As long as you really do the thing you love, and don't spend all your free time watching television."

"Good point," Luke says. "Taste this and tell me what you think." He holds out a spoon containing some of the juice from the coq au vin. I lean over the bar to taste it.

"Delicious," I say, thinking my heart just might bubble over with joy. I have a boyfriend who loves me . . . and is a terrific cook. I have a job I love. And I have a way to pay the rent on the kick-ass apartment I'm living in.

New York isn't working out so badly after all. Maybe I won't be Ann Arbor's next Kathy Pennebaker.

"Oh, hey," I say. "We're going out Saturday night with Chaz and Shari. To celebrate my new job. And because we haven't seen them in forever. Is that okay?"

"That," Luke says, stirring, "sounds great."

"And you know?" I'm still leaning across the pass-through. "I think we should really try to make it a fun night. Because I think Chaz and Shari are going through a tough time."

"You get that feeling, too?" Luke shakes his head. "Chaz seems pretty miserable these days."

"Really?" I raise my eyebrows. I can't exactly say Chaz seemed miserable when I saw him. But then maybe I was too busy bawling my eyes out to notice. "Wow. Well, I'm sure it's just a transitional thing. Once Shari settles into her new job, they'll be fine."

"Maybe," Luke says.

"What do you mean, maybe?" I ask. "What do you know that I don't know?"

"Nothing," Luke says innocently. *Too* innocently. He's smiling, though, so I know whatever it is, it can't be that bad.

"What is it?" I'm laughing now. "Tell me."

"I can't tell you," Luke says. "Chaz made me swear not to tell. *You*, of all people, especially."

"That's not fair," I say, pouting. "I won't tell. I swear."

"Chaz said you'd say that." Luke is grinning, so I know whatever it is he's not supposed to tell me, it isn't something bad.

"Just tell me," I whine.

And then, just like that, I know. Or think I know, anyway.

"Oh my God," I cry. "He's going to propose!"

Luke stares at me over his bubbling chicken. "What?"

"Chaz! He's going to ask Shari to marry him, isn't he? Oh my gosh, that is so great!"

And I can't believe I didn't figure it out sooner. Of *course* that's what's going on. That's why Chaz asked me those searching questions about Shari in their place the other day. He was feeling me out to see if Shari had said anything about how living with him was going!

Because he wants to make it permanent!

"Oh, Luke!" I have to hold on to the counter to keep from falling off my stool, because I'm practically swooning, I'm so excited. "This is so fantastic! And I have the best idea for a dress for her . . . it's like a bustier, you know, but with off-the-shoulder capped sleeves, in dupioni silk, and with little pearl buttons down the back, totally fitted through the waist, and then pooching out into this totally elegant belled skirt—not a hoop skirt, she wouldn't like that . . . Oh, you know, she might not even want a belled skirt. Maybe I should make it more—well, here, this is what I mean."

I reach for a notepad that his mother has left lying around—Bibi de Villiers, it says on the top of each page, in cursive—and scribble out the design I'm thinking of with a pen from the bank we both use.

"See, something like this?" I hold up the sketch, and see that Luke is staring at me with a mingled expression of horror and amusement.

"What?" I ask, shocked by the look on his face. "You don't like it? I think it'll be cute. In ivory? With a detachable train?"

"Chaz isn't asking Shari to *marry* him," Luke says, half grinning and half frowning. It's clear he can't tell which to do, so he's doing both.

"He isn't?" I put down the notepad and stare at my sketch. "Are you sure?"

"I'm *positive*," Luke says. Now he's completely grinning. "I can't even believe you'd think that!"

"Well." I am so crestfallen, I can't hide it. "Why not? I mean, they've been going out forever—"

"Right," Luke says. "But he's only twenty-six. And he's still in school!"

"*Graduate* school," I point out. "And they *are* living together."

"So are we," Luke says with a laugh, "but we're not getting married anytime soon."

I force a laugh along with him, although the truth is, I don't see anything funny about the situation. No, we may not be getting married anytime soon. But the *possibility* is still there, isn't it?

Isn't it?

But of course I don't ask him this out loud. Because I'm still woodland-creaturing him.

"Chaz and Shari have known each other for a lot longer than we have," I settle for saying instead. "It wouldn't be the weirdest thing if they got engaged."

"I guess not," Luke admits—but grudgingly. "Still, I don't exactly see either of them as the marrying kind."

"What's the marrying kind?" I ask . . . sort of hating myself even as the words are coming out of my mouth. Because it's totally obvious from this conversation that marriage is the last thing on Luke's mind.

And it's ridiculous that it's on my mind. At all. I mean, I have so many other things to worry about besides getting married. Like making a name for myself in my chosen field. Or even getting a *paying job* in my chosen field.

Plus, I'm supposed to be playing it cool. We're living together on a trial basis. Like Shari said, Luke and I haven't known each other that long . . .

But I can't help it . . . maybe because my chosen field is all about helping women who have someone who is willing to make a commitment to them do so in the most perfect gown imaginable.

And I can't help thinking that if I could get my love life in order, I'd have more time to concentrate on the career thing.

So, really, the only reason I want to get married—or even just engaged—is so I can be better at my job.

Plus the fact that Luke is . . . well. Luke de Villiers, the hottest, coolest guy I've ever known. And he picked me—ME.

"You know what I mean," Luke is saying. "The marrying kind. People who don't have anything else going for themselves. So they just get married, because they don't know what else to do."

I blink at him. "I don't know anybody like that," I say. "I don't know anybody who just got married because they had nothing else going for them."

"Oh, yeah?" Luke eyes me. "What about your sisters? I mean, no offense or anything, because my cousin Vicky's no different. But from what you've said . . ."

"Oh," I say. I'd forgotten about Rose and Sarah. Who actually got married because they got pregnant. It's like no one in my house ever heard of birth control. Except for me. "Yeah."

"I actually know plenty of couples like that," Luke assures me. "You know, from school . . . people who just don't have a life, so they glom on to someone else's—be it for money, or stability, or just because they think that's what they're supposed to do straight out of college. And trust me . . . they're insufferable."

"Yeah," I say. "I'm sure they are. But . . . some of them must really be in love."

"They probably think they are," Luke says. "But when they're that young, how do they even know what love is?"

"Um," I say. "The way I know I love you?"

"Ah." He reaches out to cup my cheek in his hand, smiling tenderly down at me. "That's sweet. But I'm not talking about us. Hey, I almost forgot." He raises his glass. "To the new job."

"Oh," I say, a little surprised. My new job is the last thing on my mind at the moment. "Thanks."

We clink rims.

I'm not talking about us, he'd said. That's something, isn't it? That he believes we're different. Because we *are* different.

"Want to set the table?" Luke asks, as he checks the coq au vin—which is filling the apartment with such delicious aromas that I suspect Mrs. Erickson, from 5B, will be knocking soon, to ask if she can have a bite. "I think this is going to be ready in a minute or two."

"Sure," I say—then, with elaborate casualness as I hop down from the stool and walk over to the case on the sideboard where Mrs. de Villiers keeps her silver—not her silverWARE. Her silver. Which has to be hand-washed after use, and put back in its special antitarnish cloth-lined case—so I can set the table, "So if he isn't proposing, what is it?"

"What is what?" Luke wants to know.

"What Chaz told you not to tell me," I say.

"Oh." Luke laughs. "You promise not to say anything to Shari?"

I nod.

"He's thinking about surprising her with a cat. From the animal shelter. You know. For the two of them. Because Shari loves animals so much."

I blink at him. Because Shari doesn't love animals. Chaz does. Chaz must be thinking about getting a cat for himself. Which isn't a wonder. I mean, he's alone so much, with Shari working all the time, he probably just wants some company. I kind of know the feeling, with Luke in classes all day.

But I don't say this out loud. Instead I smile and say, "Oh."

"Remember, don't tell her," Luke warns me. "You'll ruin the surprise."

"Oh, don't worry," I lie. "I won't tell her."

Because you *have* to tell your best friend when her boyfriend is planning on surprising her with a pet. Any other course of action is unthinkable.

Jeez. Guys really *are* weird.

Know your . . .

Bridal-gown necklines!

Halter neck—This cut features straps of material that join at the back of the neck. While it looks great on women with nice shoulders, it is usually cut low in back, making finding a bra difficult.

Scoop or round neckline—U-shaped neckline, often cut similarly low in both front and back. Flattering on just about anyone!

Sweetheart neckline—A heart-shaped neckline that is low in front and high in back.

Queen Anne neckline—This is a more accentuated version of the sweetheart neckline.

Off-the-shoulder neckline—This style features small sleeves or straps which actually sit just below the shoulder, leaving the shoulders and collarbone bare. This is not an ideal look for brides with wide shoulders, but it works nicely for curvy brides with full or medium-sized bosoms.

Strapless—This figure-hugging bodice has no straps or sleeves. Fuller-figured or broad-shouldered brides often look best in this style.

V-neck—Just like it sounds! This neckline dips to a V shape in front, which deemphasizes a large bustline.

Square—Again, just like it sounds. A neckline shaped like a square, and one that looks good on nearly everyone!

Bateau—This wide-necked look follows the collarbone to the edge of the shoulders, where the front and back panels join.

Jewel—Round and high cut, this style is good for small-busted brides, or those who belong to churches that frown on showing the upper chest and collarbone area for reasons of modesty.

Asymmetrical—This neckline, different on one side than it is on the other, often precludes its wearer from being able to find a suitable bra. Unless your dressmaker can put in built-in support, you're going to have to wear a strapless bra or go braless if you choose this design . . . and is that really the first impression you want to give your future in-laws?

Chapter 10

Officially, the office of Pendergast, Loughlin, and Flynn doesn't open for business until nine A.M.

Unofficially, the phones start ringing at eight sharp. Which is why they need the receptionist there early, ready to transfer calls.

I'm in the fancy black leather swivel chair (with wheels on it) behind the reception desk, trying to grasp what Tiffany, the afternoon receptionist (no, really. That's her name. I thought she was making it up, but when she got up to get us coffee from the high-tech kitchen in the back, I peeked in the drawers on either side of the desk, and I saw that, in addition to twenty different shades of fingernail polish and about thirty different samples of lipstick, she's crammed all her pay stubs in there, and I read one, and it said, right there, in pink and black, "Tiffany Dawn Sawyer"), is explaining to me.

"Okay," Tiffany says. She is supposed to be a model when she isn't working behind the reception desk at Pendergast, Loughlin, and Flynn, and I believe it, because her skin is as clear and as smooth as porcelain, her hair is a lustrous shoulder-length curtain of tawny gold, she's six feet tall, and she looks as if she weighs about a hundred and twenty pounds—especially after a big breakfast like the one she's enjoying at the moment, courtesy of Pendergast, Loughlin, and Flynn's kitchens, black coffee and a pack of cherry Twizzlers.

"So, like, when you get a call," Tiffany explains, her carefully made-up eyes heavy-lidded, because, as she's already explained to me, she drank "way too many mojitos" last night, and she's "still wasted," "you ask who's calling, and then you tell them to hold, and then you press the transfer button, and then you put in the person's extension, and then when that person picks up, you say who's calling, and if the person says he'll talk to whoever is calling, you press send, and if the person says he doesn't want to talk to whoever is calling, or if he doesn't pick up, you hit the line the caller is on, and you take a message."

Tiffany takes a deep breath, then adds gravely, "I know it's rilly complicated. That's why they asked me to come in early today so I could sit here with you and make sure you get the hang of it. So don't, like, panic, or anything."

I look at the two-sided typed list of extensions that Roberta from human resources has helpfully shrunk down to palm size, then sealed in clear contact paper, so I can't stain or tear it. There are over a hundred names on it.

"Transfer, extension, say who's calling, send or take a message," I say. "Right."

Tiffany's ocean-blue eyes widen in surprise. "Good. You got it. God. It took me like a week to get that."

"Well," I say, not wanting to hurt her feelings. Tiffany has already told me her life story—she left her home in North Dakota right after high school graduation to come to the big city to model; in the four years since, she's done a lot of print work, including the annual fall Nordstrom catalog; lives with a photographer she met in a bar, who's promised to get her more print work and is "like, married, but, like, she's a total bitch. Only he can't divorce her 'cause he's from, like, Argentina, and the INS is breathing down his neck, so he's got to, like, pretend the whole thing is for real for a while longer. As long as he keeps paying for her place in Chelsea she'll lie that they're still together, but really she's living with her personal trainer. But as soon as he gets his green card, it's over. Then he's going to marry me"; and dislikes the flavor grape—and I don't want to make her feel bad, on account of the fact that she only has a high school diploma, and I'm a college graduate (well, practically), and so naturally I'm going to catch on to things a little faster than she is. "It *is* hard."

"Ooooh, here's a call," Tiffany says, as the phone chirps softly. The ringers in the offices of Pendergast, Loughlin, and Flynn are kept at a very low volume, so as not to annoy the partners—who, according to Tiffany, are extremely high-strung, due to their demanding hours and jobs—or the clients, who are extremely high-strung due to the hourly rates they are paying for legal help from Pendergast, Loughlin, and Flynn. "So, answer it, just like I told you."

I pick up the receiver and say confidently, "Pendergast, Loughlin, and Flynn, how may I direct your call?"

"Who the hell is this?" the man on the other end of the line demands.

"This is Lizzie," I say, as pleasantly as I can, considering his tone.

"You the temp?"

"No, sir," I say. "I'm the new morning receptionist. How may I direct your call?"

"Get me Jack" is the terse reply.

"Certainly," I say, frantically scanning my little shrink-wrapped list. Jack? Which one is Jack? "Who may I say is calling?" I ask, stalling for time as I look for the name Jack.

"Jesus Christ," the man on the other end of the line yells. "This is Peter fucking Loughlin, for fuck's sake!"

"Of course, sir," I say. "Please hold."

"Don't you fucking—"

I press hold with trembling fingers, then turn toward Tiffany, who is dozing in her seat, her lusciously long black eyelashes perfectly curled against her high cheekbones.

"It's Peter Loughlin," I cry, waking her up. "He wants someone named Jack! He swore at me! I think he's mad I put him on hold . . ."

Tiffany is on it like a frat boy on a pizza, snatching the receiver from me and muttering, "Shit. Shit shit shit," beneath her breath before leaning over me to press the hold button, then saying smoothly, "Hi, Mr. Loughlin, it's me, Tiffany . . . Yes, I know. Well, she's new . . . Yes, I will . . . Of course. Here he is."

Then her long, manicured fingers fly over the keypad, and the call—and Peter fucking Loughlin—is gone.

"I'm sorry," I say tremulously, as Tiffany hangs up. "I just couldn't find anyone named Jack on the list!"

"Stupid bitch," Tiffany says, pulling out a ballpoint pen and scribbling something on the list Roberta gave me. Passing the list back to me, she sees my alarmed expression, and laughs. "Not you. That whore, Roberta. She thinks she's so great, because she went to an Ivy League college. Like, so what? All it got her was a job scheduling people's vacations. A monkey could do that. Big fuckin' whoop."

I blink down at the change Tiffany's made on my list. She's crossed out the first name "John" in front of the last name "Flynn" and written "Jack" over it. Because she'd used a ballpoint to write over clear contact paper, the change is barely legible.

"John Flynn's real name is Jack?" I ask.

"No. It's John. But he calls himself Jack, and so does everybody else," Tiffany assures me. "I don't know why Roberta put his real name instead of what people actually call him. Maybe because she wants to fuck with you. Roberta's totally jealous of girls who are better looking than she is. You know, since she looks like a horse-faced troll."

"Oh, there you are!" Roberta cries, as she pushes open the glass door from the elevator lobby and steps into the reception area. She's wearing a trench coat—from the lining, I can tell it's Burberry—and carrying a briefcase. For someone who only "schedules people's vacations," she looks superbusinesslike. "Everything all right? Tiffany showing you the ropes?"

"Yes," I say, throwing Tiffany a panicky look. What if Roberta overheard her calling her a horse-faced troll?

But Tiffany doesn't look the least bit worried. She's fished a nail file from one of the many drawers into which she's crammed her personal belongings, and is working on one of her gel tips.

"How are you this morning, Roberta?" Tiffany inquires sweetly as she files.

"I'm great, Tiffany." Roberta, now that I look at her, does sort of resemble a horse. She has a really long face, and superbig teeth. And she's kind of short and has terrible posture, making her, truth be told, a little bit troll-like. "Thanks so much for helping us out by pulling a double today in order to train Lizzie. We really appreciate it."

"I'm making time and a half after two o'clock, right?" Tiffany wants to know.

"Of course," Roberta says, her smile tightening perceptibly. "Just like we discussed."

Tiffany shrugs. "Then it's all good," she says in a syrupy-sweet voice.

Roberta's smile tightens even more. "Great," she says. "Lizzie, if you—"

The phone chirps. I leap upon it. "Pendergast, Loughlin, and Flynn," I say into the receiver. "How may I direct your call?"

"I have Leon Finkle for Marjorie Pierce," a woman's voice purrs.

"One moment please," I say, and press the transfer button. Then, highly aware that Roberta is watching my every move, I find Marjorie Pierce's extension on my cheat sheet, press the numbers, then say, when a voice on the other end picks up, "Leon Finkle for Marjorie Pierce?"

"I'll take the call," the voice says. And I press send and watch as the little red light by the transfer buttons disappears. Done. I hang up.

"Very nice," Roberta says, looking impressed. "It took Tiffany weeks to even learn that much."

The look Tiffany darts Roberta would have frozen the hottest mochaccino. "I didn't have as good an instructor as Lizzie does," she says coldly.

Roberta gives us another brittle smile and says, "Well, carry on. And, Lizzie, I'll need you to stop by my office before you leave so you can fill out those forms to get you on our insurance."

"I'll do that," I say, and since the phone is chirping again, leap to seize the receiver. "Pendergast, Loughlin, and Flynn," I say.

"Jack Flynn, please," a voice on the other end of the phone says. "Terry O'Malley calling."

"One moment, please," I say, and press transfer.

"Stupid fucking bitch," Tiffany is muttering beneath her breath, as she nibbles a Twizzler.

"Terry O'Malley for Mr. Flynn," I say, when a woman picks up Mr. Flynn's line.

"Her vagina has cobwebs from lack of use," Tiffany says.

"Send the call, please," the woman says. I press send.

"You know she had the nerve to tell me not to paint my nails at the desk?" Tiffany is rolling her eyes in the direction Roberta has just disappeared. "She said it wasn't *professional*."

I refrain from pointing out that I don't think it's very professional to paint your nails at your job in a law office, either.

The phone chirps again. I answer it. "Pendergast, Loughlin, and Flynn," I say. "How may I direct your call?"

"To yourself," Luke says. "I just called to wish you luck on your first day."

"Oh." I feel my knees melt as they always do when I hear his voice. "Hi."

I've gotten over the thing from last night. The thing where he'd said people our age are too young to know what love really is. Because he said he didn't mean us. Obviously he was just making a generalization. Most people our own age probably don't know what love is. Tiffany, for instance, probably doesn't know what love really is.

Besides, after dinner, he illustrated *very* competently that he knows what love is. Well, making love, anyway.

"How's it going?" Luke wants to know.

"Great," I say. "Just great."

"You can't talk because there's someone sitting right next to you, right?" Which, of course, is one of the reasons that I love him so much. Because he's so perceptive. About most things, anyway.

"Right," I say.

"That's okay, my first class starts in a minute anyway," he says. "I just wanted to see how things were going."

As he's speaking, the glass door to the reception area opens and a blond, slightly stocky-looking young woman comes in. She's dressed in jeans and a white turtleneck sweater that does nothing to flatter her, along with a pair of Timberland boots. You don't really expect to see a lot of these kinds of boots in the Pendergast, Loughlin, and Flynn offices. The woman looks familiar for some reason, but I can't place her.

I do notice, however, that Tiffany has looked up from the nail she is repolishing and that her jaw has fallen.

"Uh, I gotta go," I say to Luke. "Bye."

I hang up. The young woman is approaching the reception desk. I see that she's pretty, in a healthy, all-American-girl kind of way, although she wears very little makeup and doesn't seem to mind that a layer of belly fat is resting gently across the waistband of her too-low low-rise jeans, instead of being safely tucked away inside the waistband of jeans with a slightly higher rise, as would be more flattering.

"Hi," the woman says to me. "I'm Jill Higgins. I have a nine o'clock appointment with Mr. Pendergast?"

"Of course," I say, quickly scanning my cheat sheet for Chaz's dad's extension. "Have a seat and I'll let him know you're here."

"Thank you," the woman says with a smile that reveals a lot of healthy-looking white teeth. While she goes to sit down on one of the leather couches, I punch in Mr. Pendergast's extension.

"Jill Higgins is here for her nine o'clock appointment with Mr. Pendergast," I say to Esther, Mr. Pendergast's attractive, fortyish assistant, who'd stopped by to introduce herself upon arriving at work.

"Shit," Esther says. "He's not in yet. I'll be right up."

I hang up just as Tiffany pokes me in the shoulder.

"Do you know who that is?" she whispers, nodding at the young woman on the couch.

"Yes," I whisper back. "She told us her name. It's Jill Higgins."

"Yeah, but, like, do you know who Jill Higgins is?" Tiffany wants to know.

I shrug. The woman's face looks familiar, but I'm pretty sure she isn't a television or movie star, because she's too normal-size.

"No," I whisper back.

"She's only marrying, like, the richest bachelor in New York," Tiffany hisses. "John MacDowell? His family owns more Manhattan real estate than the Catholic church. And the church *used* to own the most of anyone in the city . . ."

I swivel my head to look at Jill Higgins with renewed interest.

"The girl who works in the zoo?" I whisper, remembering the Page Six article I read about her. "The one who threw her back out lifting the stranded seal?"

"Exactly," Tiffany says. "The MacDowell family's trying to get her to sign a prenup. Basically, they're trying to make it so she doesn't see, like, a dime unless she pushes out an heir. But the groom wants to make sure her rights are protected, so he's hired Pendergast, Loughlin, and Flynn to represent her."

"Oh!" I am struck by the pathos of this. Jill Higgins looks so nice and normal! How could anyone be so mean as to think she might be a gold digger? "That's so sweet of him. I mean, John MacDowell, to hire lawyers for her."

Tiffany grunts. "Yeah, right. He's probably only doing it so that later on, when things go, like, south, she can't say she was swindled."

This seems like a very cynical take on it to me. But then what do I know? This is only my first day. Tiffany's been working here for two years, the longest any receptionist has stayed with Pendergast, Loughlin, and Flynn so far.

"Did you hear what they call her?" Tiffany whispers.

"Who?"

"The press. What they call Jill?"

I look at her blankly. "Don't they just call her Jill?"

"No. They're calling her 'Blubber.' Because she works with seals, and she's got that tummy."

I frown. "That's mean!"

"Also," Tiffany goes on, clearly enjoying herself, "because she cried when one of them asked her if it makes her insecure to know there are so many women out there who are way more attractive than she is, dying to get their hands on her fiancé."

"That's horrible!" I glance over at Jill. She looks remarkably calm for someone dealing with all of that. Lord knows how I'd react in the same situation. The press would probably call me Niagara—because I'd never *stop* crying.

"Miss Higgins!" Esther appears in the lobby, looking trim in a houndstooth skirt suit. "How are you? Won't you come on back? Mr. Pendergast is running a little late, but I've got coffee for you. Cream *and* sugar, right?"

Jill Higgins smiles and gets up. "That's right," she says, following Esther down the hall. "How nice of you to remember!"

After she's out of earshot, Tiffany snorts and goes back to painting her nails. "You know, that MacDowell guy may be rich and all," she says. "And yeah, okay, she gets to quit her job throwing fish to those nasty seals. But I wouldn't marry into that family for less than twenty mil. And she'll be lucky if she sees a few hundred thousand."

"Oh," I say, thinking Tiffany should be an actress *and* a model, she has so much flair for the dramatic. "They can't be *that* bad—"

"Are you kidding?" Tiffany rolls her eyes. "John MacDowell's mom is such a battle-axe, she isn't letting that girl plan one single part of her own wedding. Which I guess makes sense, since she's from Iowa or something, and her dad's, like, a mailman or something. But still . . . Blubber doesn't even get to choose her own wedding gown! They're making her wear some old monstrosity they've had moldering around the mansion for a million years. They say it's 'tradition' that MacDowell brides wear it . . . but if you ask me, they're just trying to make her look bad so that John MacDowell has second thoughts and dumps her for some society bitch his mom's got all picked out for him."

My ears have perked up at this. Not the part about the society girl John MacDowell's mom wishes he were marrying instead of Jill, but the other part. "Really? Who is she using as her wedding-gown specialist? Do you know?"

Tiffany blinks at me. "Her what?"

"Her wedding-gown specialist," I say. "I mean, she *has* one . . . right?"

"I don't have the slightest idea what you're talking about," Tiffany says. "What's a wedding-gown specialist?"

But at that moment the reception area doors open again and a man I recognize as Chaz's father—basically an older, grayer version of Chaz, only without the turned-around baseball cap—walks in . . . then stops when he sees me.

"Lizzie?" he asks.

"Hi, Mr. Pendergast," I say brightly. "How are you today?"

"Well, I'm just great," Mr. Pendergast says with a smile, "now that I've seen you. I'm really happy you've joined us here at the firm. Chaz couldn't seem to say enough good things about you when I spoke to him the other day."

This is high praise, considering the fact that Chaz, so far as I know, goes out of his way to avoid speaking to his parents whenever possible. The fact that he called them on my behalf is enough to make my eyes fill with tears. He really is the greatest guy in the world. Aside from Luke, of course . . .

"Thank you so much, Mr. Pendergast," I say. "I'm so happy to be here. It's so nice of you to—"

But at that moment the phone chirps.

"Well, duty calls," Mr. Pendergast says with a twinkle. "See you later."

"Sure," I say. "And Miss Higgins is already here . . ."

"Great, great," Mr. Pendergast calls, as he hurries back to his office.

I pick up the phone. "Pendergast, Loughlin, and Flynn," I say. "How may I direct your call?"

After I send the caller successfully on his way, I hang up and look at Tiffany. "I'm starving," she says. "Want to order from Burger Heaven downstairs?"

"It's not even ten," I point out.

"Whatever, I'm so hungover I could die. I need some grease in my stomach or I'll york."

"You know what?" I say to Tiffany. "I really think I'm getting the hang of this. You can leave if you want."

But Tiffany doesn't take the hint. "And give up time and a half? No, thanks. I'm getting a double cheeseburger. You want one?"

I sigh . . . and give in. Because it looks like it's going to be a long day. And the truth is, I can tell I'm going to need the protein.

Lizzie Nichols's Wedding Gown Guide

Okay, big girls, don't think I've forgotten you! Designers may have—so many dressmakers seem scared to take on those of us who are size sixteen or higher.

But there's really no need, because large-size women CAN look great in a wedding gown . . . if they pick the right one! The best option is to go for a fitted bodice with an A-line skirt.

Full skirts are out on the plus-side bride, as they tend to make wide hips look even wider, as do column or sheath

skirts. But an A-line skirt that gently skims the contours is a flattering look on a larger girl. Strapless gowns are not usually recommended for very large brides as they require a very fitted bodice that can be unflattering to someone with a sizable belly. But this varies from body shape to body shape.

Plus-size brides, more than anyone, can benefit from the help of a certified wedding-gown specialist, since we can really help them find a style that is both flattering *and* appropriate for their special day.

LIZZIE NICHOLS DESIGNS™

Chapter 11

To find out a girl's faults, praise her to her girlfriends.

—*Benjamin Franklin (1706–1790), American inventor*

The dwarf is singing "Don't Cry Out Loud."

"I don't know about anyone else," Chaz says, "but I find his performance exceptionally moving. I give it an eight."

"Seven," Luke says. "I find the fact that he's *actually* crying a little distracting."

"I give it a ten," I say, blinking back tears of my own. I don't know if it's that all Melissa Manchester songs make me a little nostalgic, or if it's the fact that this particular one is being sung so poignantly by a weeping dwarf dressed like Frodo from *Lord of the Rings,* complete with a Gandalf staff. Maybe it's the three Tsingtaos I had with dinner, and the two Amaretto sours I've downed since, here in the booth. But I'm gone.

The same can't be said of my best friend Shari, however. She's picking at the label of her Bud Light, looking distracted—pretty much how she's been all night.

"Hey," I say, nudging her with my elbow. "Come on. How do you rate his performance?"

"Uh." Shari sweeps some of her curly dark hair from her eyes and peers at the man on the little stage at the back of the bar. "I don't know. A six."

"Harsh," Chaz says, shaking his head. "Look at him. He's singing his guts out."

"That's just it," Shari says. "He's taking it too seriously. It's *karaoke.*"

"Karaoke is an art form in many cultures," Chaz says. "And, as such, should be taken seriously."

"Not," Shari says, "at a dive bar called Honey's in Midtown."

The tenor of Shari's voice has changed. Chaz is just being playful, but she sounds genuinely annoyed.

Then again, she's seemed that way ever since she and Chaz arrived at the Thai place downtown where we met to have dinner. No matter what Chaz says, Shari either disagrees or ignores him. She even berated him for ordering too much food . . . as if there *is* such a thing.

"It's probably just stress," I had said to Luke, as the two of us walked slightly behind Chaz and Shari on our way toward Canal Street, dodging fish guts that had been tossed into the gutters by the Chinese markets on either side of the street. "You know how hard she's been working lately."

"You've been working pretty hard yourself," Luke had replied. "And *you* aren't acting like a grade-A—"

"Hey, now," I'd interrupted. "Come on. Her job is slightly more stressful than mine. She's dealing with women whose *lives* are at stake. The only thing the women I work with have at stake is whether or not their butt is going to look big on their wedding day."

"That can be stressful," Luke had insisted with touching loyalty. "You shouldn't put yourself down."

But the truth is, I don't actually believe what's bothering Shari is work stress. Because if it was just that, the delicious piles of pad thai and beef satay we'd just consumed—not to mention all that beer—would have helped. But it hadn't. She's as cranky now, after dinner, as she'd been before dinner. She hadn't even wanted to come to Honey's. She'd wanted to go straight home to bed. Chaz had practically forced her into the cab with us, instead of letting her find a separate one to take her back to their place.

"I just don't get it," Chaz had said to us after Shari excused herself to go to the bathroom between courses at dinner. "I know she's unhappy. But when I ask her what's wrong, she says everything's fine and that I should leave her alone."

"That's the same thing she says to me," I'd said with a sigh.

"Maybe it's hormonal," Luke had suggested. Which, considering all the bio he was taking, was a natural leap.

"For six weeks?" Chaz had shaken his head. "Because that's how long it's been. Ever since she started that job . . . and moved in with me."

I'd swallowed. It was all my fault. I just knew it. If I had just moved in with Shari like I'd promised, instead of ditching her to live with Luke, none of this would have happened . . .

"If you think you can do so much better," Chaz is saying now, shoving the songbook across the table of the booth we're sitting in, "why don't you give it a whirl?"

Shari looks down at the black binder in front of her. "I don't do karaoke," she says coldly.

"Um, that's not what I recall," Luke says, waggling his dark eyebrows. "At least, not from a certain wedding I remember . . ."

"That," Shari says dourly, "was a special occasion. I was just trying to help out Big Mouth over there."

I blink. *Big Mouth?* I mean, I know it's true and all . . . but I've been getting better. Really. I haven't told ANYONE about meeting Jill Higgins. And I've managed to keep from Luke the fact that his mother's lover (if that's who the guy even is . . . which, more and more, I'm starting to suspect) has called the *apartment yet again.* I'm a veritable vault of incendiary information!

But I decide to cut Shari some slack. Because I did leave her in the lurch and all.

"Come on, Shari," I say, reaching for the binder. "I'll find us something fun to sing. What do you say?"

"Count me out," Shari says. "I'm too tired."

"You can never be too tired for karaoke," Chaz says. "All you have to do is stand up there and read from a teleprompter."

"*I'm too tired,*" Shari says again, this time more adamantly.

"Look," Luke says, "somebody has to get up there and sing something. Otherwise, Frodo is going to perform another ballad. And then I'll have to slit my wrists."

I've started flipping through the binder. "I'll do it," I say. "I can't let my boyfriend commit suicide."

"Thanks, honey," Luke says, winking at me. "That's so nice of you."

I've found the song I want and am filling out the little slip of paper you're supposed to give to the waitress if you want to sing. "If I do this," I say, "you guys have to do one, too. Luke and Chaz, I mean."

Chaz looks solemnly at Luke. "'Wanted Dead or Alive'?"

"No," Luke says, shaking his head vehemently. "No way."

"Come on," I say. "If I'm doing it, you guys have to—"

"No." Luke is laughing now. "I do not do karaoke."

"You have to," I say gravely. "Because if you don't, we'll be subjected to more of that." I nod toward a group of giggly twenty-somethings, each wearing the light-up penis necklaces and slackly drunken expressions that give away the fact that they are part of a bachelorette party—as if the fact that they're screeching "Summer Lovin'" from *Grease* into a single microphone is not evidence enough.

"They are making a mockery of the karaoke," Chaz agrees, pronouncing "karaoke" with the correct Japanese inflection.

" 'Nother round?" the waitress, wearing an adorable red silk mandarin dress, with a not-so-adorable metal bar through her lower lip, wants to know.

"Four more," I say, sliding two song slips toward her. "And two songs, please."

"No more for me," Shari says. She holds up her mostly full beer bottle. "I'm good."

The waitress nods and takes my song slips. "Three more, then," she says, and goes away.

"What did you mean, *two* songs?" Luke asks me suspiciously. "You didn't—"

"I want to hear you sing that you're a cowboy," I say, my eyes wide with innocence. "And that on a steel horse you ride . . ."

Luke's mouth twists with suppressed mirth. "*You*—" He lunges at me, but I shrink against Shari, who goes, "Stop it."

"Save me," I say to Shari.

"Seriously," she says. "Cut it out."

"Oh, come on, Share," I say, laughing. What's wrong with her? She used to love goofing around in dive bars. "Sing with me."

"You're so annoying," she says.

"Sing with me," I beg. "For old times' sake."

"Get out," Shari says, giving me a shove toward the end of the bench we were sitting on. "I have to go pee."

"I won't get out," I say, "unless you sing with me."

Shari pours her beer over my head.

Later, in the ladies' room, she apologizes. Abjectly.

"Seriously," she says, sniffling as she watches me stick my head beneath the hand dryer. "I am so, so sorry. I don't know what came over me."

"It's okay." I can barely hear her above the roar of the hand dryer—not to mention the keening of the bachelorettes onstage. "Seriously."

"No," Shari says. "It's not okay. I'm a terrible person."

"You're not a terrible person," I say. "I was being a jerk."

"Well." Shari is leaning against the radiator. The ladies' room at Honey's is not what anyone would call the height of chic decor. There is one sink and one toilet, and the walls have been covered in vomit-beige paint that does little to hide the layers of graffiti beneath it. "You *were* being a jerk. But not any more than usual. I'm the one who's turned into such a massive bitch. I seriously don't know what's wrong with me."

"Is it your job?" I ask. The hand dryer is solving the problem of my wet hair. But it isn't doing much for the beery smell coming from my Vicky Vaughn Junior minidress. That's something I'm going to have to tackle with the Febreze bottle when I get home.

"It's not my job," Shari says mournfully. "I love my job."

"You do?" I can't hide my surprise. All Shari ever seems to do is complain about her hours and workload.

"I do," she says. "That's the problem . . . I'd rather be there than at home, any day."

I open my double-flap seventies Meyers handbag (in stunning lime-green vinyl, only thirty-five dollars with my Vintage to Vavoom employee discount) to look for something—anything—that I could spray on myself to get rid of the beery smell. "Is that because you love your job so much?" I ask carefully. "Or because you don't love Chaz anymore?"

Shari's face crumples. She puts her hands over it to hide her tears.

"Oh, Share." My heart twisting, I step away from the hand dryer to put my arms around her. Through the door, I can hear the thump-thump-thump of the bass as the bachelorettes shriek that it's up to you, New York, New York.

"I don't know what happened," Shari sobs. "I just feel like whenever I'm with him, I'm suffocating. And even when he's not around . . . it's like he's smothering me."

I am trying to be understanding. Because that's how best friends are with each other.

But I've known Chaz for a long time. And he has so never been the suffocating or smothering type. In fact, it would be hard to find a more happy-go-lucky guy. I mean, except when he's jabbering on about Kierkegaard.

"What do you mean?" I ask her. "How is he smothering you?"

"Well, like he calls me all the time at work," Shari says, furiously wiping away her tears. Shari hates it when she cries . . . and consequently doesn't do so very often. "Sometimes even twice a day!"

I blink down at her. "Calling someone twice a day at work isn't all that much," I say. "I mean, I call you that many times a day. A lot more than that, actually." I don't even mention how many times a day I've started e-mailing her, now that I spend so many hours at a workstation with an actual computer, on which I'm supposed to record any notes and messages for the lawyers I work for.

"That's different," Shari says. "Besides, it's not just that. I mean, there's the whole cat thing." My revealing to Shari that Chaz was thinking about adding a four-legged friend to their domicile had resulted in her being "diagnosed" with a previously unknown dander allergy, and the sad admittance that she would never, alas, be able to live in a house or apartment with anything furry. "There's also the fact that when I get home from work, he wants to know how my day went! After already having talked about it on the phone."

I drop my arms from her. "Shari," I say. "Luke and I talk to each other about a million times a day." This is a slight exaggeration. But whatever. "And we always ask each other how our day went when we get home."

"Yeah," Shari says. "But I bet Luke doesn't spend the whole day you're gone lying around the apartment reading Wittgenstein, then going grocery shopping, cleaning the apartment, and making oatmeal cookies."

My jaw drops. "Chaz goes grocery shopping, cleans, and makes oatmeal cookies while you're at work?"

"Yes," Shari says. "And does the laundry. Can you believe that? He does the laundry while I'm at work! And folds everything up into these perfect squares! Even my underwear!"

I am looking at Shari with suspicion now. Something is wrong. Very wrong.

"Share," I say. "Are you even listening to yourself? You're mad at your boyfriend because he calls you regularly, cleans your apartment, does the grocery shopping, makes you cookies, and does your laundry. Do you realize that you've basically just described the most perfect man in the world?"

Shari scowls at me. "That may sound like the perfect man to some people, but it isn't to me. You know what would be the perfect man to me? One who was around less. Oh, and get this: he wants sex. *Every day.* I mean, that was all right back when we were in France. But we were on *vacation.* Now we've got responsibilities—well, some of us do, anyway. Who has time for sex *every day?* Sometimes he even wants it twice a day, morning and then again at night. I can't take it, Lizzie. That's just . . . that's just too much. Oh my God . . . can you believe I just said that?"

I'm glad she asked that, because the answer is no, I can't. Shari's always been more sexually aggressive—and adventurous—than me. It looks like the tables have finally turned. I have to keep myself from blurting out that Luke and I often have sex twice a day—and that I quite enjoy it.

"But you and Chaz used to, um, do it that much all the time," I say. "I mean, when you first started going out. And you liked it then. What's changed?"

"That's just it," Shari says. She looks truly upset. "I don't know! God, what kind of counselor am I, when I can't even figure out my own problems? How can I help people with theirs?"

"Well, sometimes it's easier to help other people with their problems than deal with your own," I say in what I hope is a soothing voice. "Have you talked about all of this with Chaz? I mean, maybe if you told him what was bothering you—"

"Oh, right," Shari says sarcastically. "You want me to tell my boyfriend that he's too perfect?"

"Well," I say. "You don't have to put it quite like that. But maybe if you—"

"Lizzie, I am perfectly aware that I sound like a lunatic. There's something wrong with me. I know it."

"No," I cry. "Shari, it's just . . . it's hard. It's my fault, really. Maybe you guys weren't ready to move in together. I should never have bailed on you like I did and moved in with Luke. I deserved to have beer poured on me. I deserve to have a lot worse than that done to me—"

"Oh, Lizzie," Shari says, looking up at me with her dark eyes filled with tears again. "Don't you get it? It has nothing to do with you. It's me. There's something wrong with *me*. Or at least with the concept of Chaz and me. The truth is . . . I just don't know anymore, Lizzie."

I stare at her. "Know what?"

"I mean, I look at you and Luke, and how perfect you two are together—"

"We're not perfect," I interrupt quickly. I don't want to remind her about the woodland creature thing. Or the fact that I'm pretty sure Luke's mom is having—or was having, anyway—an affair, and I haven't told him. "Seriously, Shari. We—"

"But you seem so happy together," Shari says. "The way Chaz and I used to be . . . but for some reason, it's gone."

"Oh, Shari." I chew my lower lip, frantically trying to think of the right thing to say. "Maybe if you two got couples counseling . . ."

"I don't know," Shari says. She looks—and sounds—hopeless. "I don't know if it would even be worth it."

"Shari!" I can't believe she would say that. About Chaz, of all people!

"Lizzie?" Someone bangs on the door. A woman's voice calls my name again. "You're up!"

I realize it's the waitress and that my song's waiting to be played—and performed.

"Oh no," I say. "Shari, I . . . I don't know what to say. I really think maybe you and Chaz are just going through a weird phase right now. I mean, Chaz is a great guy, and I know he really loves you . . . I'm sure things will get better with time."

"They won't," Shari says. "But thanks for letting me unload on you. Literally. Sorry about the beer."

"It's okay," I say. "It was kind of refreshing, in a way. It was getting hot out there."

"Are you coming?" the waitress demands. "Or not?"

"Coming," I call. Then I appeal to Shari. "Will you sing with me?"

"Not a chance," she says with a smile.

Which is how I find myself all alone on the stage at Honey's, assuring the bachelorettes, who are drunkenly catcalling me, the dwarf, who is glaring at me angrily for robbing him of yet more time in the spotlight, and Chaz, Shari, and Luke that young girls do get weary of wearing that same old shaggy . . . and that when they get weary, it would behoove everyone to try a little tenderness.

A piece of advice that, sadly, Chaz seems to have already employed . . . with less than satisfying results.

Fittings

Ensuring that your gown fits properly is one of the many duties of your certified wedding-gown specialist. You can help by bringing with you to your fittings the shoes, the headdress, and the kind of support or undergarments you plan on wearing on your special day. Too often a bride has not tried on her gown with the bra or shoes she plans to wear at her wedding, only to discover her straps are showing or that her gown is too long or short!

It's important as well to be at or very close to whatever weight you want to be on your wedding day at your first fitting. Gowns can of course be taken in . . . but the less your seamstress has to do so, the better. And don't even talk about letting gowns out . . . that's a whole other story, and you don't want to go there.

Generally only two fittings are necessary, but of course more can be scheduled if necessary . . . so long as you don't wait too long! Not even the most brilliant certified wedding-gown specialist can work wonders overnight. Plan on having your last fitting about three weeks prior to your wedding day—and lay off the Krispy Kremes!

LIZZIE NICHOLS DESIGNS™

Chapter 12

A rumor without a leg to stand on will get around some other way.

—John Tudor (b. 1954), American Major League baseball player

S o what are you doing for Thanksgiving?" Tiffany wants to know.

Even though her shift doesn't start until two, Tiffany has been showing up every day at noon, and hanging out with me at the reception desk until I go home . . . sometimes even bringing lunch for both of us to nibble on surreptitiously beneath the desktop, since food is banned in the reception area ("Highly unprofessional," is what Roberta called it the day she caught me innocently nibbling on a bag of microwave popcorn I filched from the office kitchen).

At first I just thought this was an odd habit of Tiffany's—showing up two hours early to work every day, I mean. Until Daryl, the "fax and copy supervisor" (he's in charge of making sure all the office fax and copy machines are fully stocked and in working order, and the faxes delivered promptly to their addressees), informed me that I had only myself to thank for Tiffany's new and improved work ethic.

"She likes hanging out with you," he said. "She thinks you're funny. And she doesn't have any friends except that nasty-ass boyfriend of hers."

I was touched but surprised when I heard this. The truth is that Tiffany and I have little in common (save the desk chair we sit in, and a love for fashion, of course), and her potty mouth can be a little alarming at times. And I have never, for instance, seen her outside of work . . . hardly surprising, since we work completely different shifts. But not exactly what I'd call a true bond.

On the other hand, we're both regularly screamed at by Peter fucking Loughlin. And that's something that scars someone for life and therefore cemented our friendship.

Still, when Tiffany asks the Thanksgiving question, I'm afraid. Afraid that she's about to follow it with an invitation to join her and the "nasty-ass boyfriend" (so called by Daryl for no other reason—that I can ascertain, anyway—than that he is keeping Tiffany from being available for Daryl to date) for their holiday meal.

Which I'm sure would be fun and all of that, but not something I think Luke is quite ready for—to be subjected to my coworkers, I mean. So far, I've managed to keep him a safe distance from both Monsieur and Madame Henri, and the fine folks of Pendergast, Loughlin, and Flynn.

Although, considering that I still haven't told my family he and I are living together, you might say I'm keeping him from my family, as well.

"Luke's parents are coming to town," I say truthfully.

"Rilly?" Tiffany looks up from the nail she's filing. "They're coming all the way from France?"

"Uh, no, Houston," I say, after a slight pause during which I pick up, answer, and transfer a call for Jack Flynn. "They only spend part of the year in France, and the rest in Houston, where Luke's from. They're coming here for Thanksgiving so his mom can do some holiday shopping and his dad can go to some Broadway shows."

"So they're taking you out for Thanksgiving dinner?" Tiffany looks impressed. "Sweet."

"Uh," I say. "Not exactly. I mean, I'm cooking the dinner. Luke and I are. For the two of them, and Shari and Chaz, too."

Tiffany stares at me. "Have you ever cooked a turkey before?" she wants to know.

"No," I say. "But I'm sure it won't be hard. Luke's a really good cook, and I printed out a bunch of recipes from the Food Network's Web site."

"Oh yeah," Tiffany says, her voice tinged with sarcasm. "That'll work out great, then."

But I don't let her negativity get me down. I'm convinced our Thanksgiving is going to work out great. Not only will Luke's parents—whom we'll be giving up our bed to, since it is, technically, his mom's bed—have a great time, but so will Chaz and Shari. In fact, if everything goes as planned, Chaz and Shari will be so moved by the example of loving bliss Luke and I (and his parents) make, that they'll start getting along again.

I'm sure of it. More than sure. I'm *positive*.

"Your own family must miss you," Tiffany says casually. "Are they mad you aren't coming home for Thanksgiving?"

"No," I say, glancing at the clock. Four more minutes before I can leave . . . and be rid of Tiffany for another day. Not that I mind her that much, she's just . . . well, wearing. "I'm going home for Christmas."

"Oh? Luke going with you?"

"No." I'm having to hide my annoyance now. Luke's parents spend Christmas and New Year's at their château in France. They'd asked him to join them this year.

And yeah, I was disappointed about this. Not that he hadn't asked me to come with him. He had. Although he'd preceded the invitation with the words, "I suspect you'll want to spend the holidays with your own family, but . . ."

Which he had actually suspected wrongly.

But not completely. I DID want to spend the holidays with my own family . . . *and* with Luke. I'd wanted him to come back to Ann

Arbor with me to meet my parents. This didn't seem like an unreasonable expectation to me, either. I'd met his family, after all. It seemed to me that if Luke really wanted to make a long-term thing out of our relationship, he'd want to meet my family.

But when I'd asked him if he wanted to fly home with me, he'd winced and said, "Oh hey, I'd love to. But, you know, I already got my ticket to France. I got a really excellent deal on it. And it's nontransferable and nonrefundable. I could check and see if they have any left for you, though, if you want to come with me . . ."

But the truth is, I only get three days off work at Pendergast, Loughlin, and Flynn (Monsieur Henri's is shutting down for the entire week between Christmas and New Year's), not exactly enough time to fly to France and back. But—lucky me—plenty of time to visit Ann Arbor. When I get back, I'll be stuck working—and living—alone until Luke gets back after New Year's.

That's right. *After* New Year's. I get to ring in the New Year solo here in Manhattan while he's off whooping it up in the South of France. Happy New Year to me!

Not that I shared any of this with Tiffany. It wasn't any of her business. Besides, I knew what she'd say. *Her* boyfriend had come out to meet *her* parents in North Dakota the first year they'd started dating.

"Well." Tiffany is heaving a sigh. "I guess Raoul and I will just hang out at home and have take-out or something. Since neither of us cooks."

I am *not* going to ask Tiffany and her boyfriend to join us for our Thanksgiving meal. It's just going to be me and Luke, his parents, and Chaz and Shari. A nice, civilized meal, like the ones we all used to have over the summer at Château Mirac.

One fifty-nine. I am so close to being out of here.

"The Chinese place near us does a kind of turkey dumpling on Thanksgiving," Tiffany goes on. "It's pretty good. Though of course I miss sweet potatoes. And pecan pie."

"Well, there are lots of restaurants in my neighborhood that are serving three- and even four-course Thanksgiving meals that day," I say cheerfully. "Maybe you guys could make a reservation at one of those."

"It's not the same as being in someone's home," Tiffany says. "Restaurants are so cold. For Thanksgiving, you want cozy. There's nothing cozy about a *restaurant*."

"Well," I say. Two o'clock. I'm done. I'm out.

I stand up. "I'm sure you can find a restaurant that delivers Thanksgiving dinner."

"Yeah," Tiffany says with a sigh, getting up to take my chair. "But it's not the same as home-cooked."

"That's true," I say. *Don't do it, Lizzie,* I'm telling myself. *Do not fall for it. No pity invitations.* "Well, I have to run—"

"Yeah," Tiffany says, not looking at me. "Good luck with the wedding dresses thing."

I am halfway out the door, my coat over my arm, when I feel myself pulled back, as if by some kind of tracking device.

"Tiffany," I hear my mouth saying, even though my brain is shrieking *Nooooo!*

She glances up from the computer screen, which she's using, I know, to check her horoscope. "Yeah?"

"Would you and Raoul like to come over for Thanksgiving dinner?" *Nooooo!*

Tiffany does a good job of dissembling indifference. She really would make a terrific actress.

"I don't know," she says with a shrug. "I'll have to check with Raoul. But, like . . . maybe."

"Well," I say. "Just let me know. Bye."

I curse myself in the elevator the whole ride down to the lobby. What is the *matter* with me? Why did I invite her? She can't cook so it's not like she's going to bring anything.

And she certainly isn't going to be able to add anything to the table conversation. All Tiffany Sawyer knows anything about is the latest pump from Prada and which Hollywood celebrity is sleeping with which Hollywood producer's son . . .

And I've never even met this Raoul character, her married—married!—lover. Who knows what *he's* like. From what Daryl says, nothing that great (though Daryl is admittedly biased).

Oh, why do I let my big mouth get me into these things?

I try to cheer myself up, however, with the thought that Raoul might balk at the idea of coming to Thanksgiving dinner at a perfect stranger's place.

Although considering that this perfect stranger has an apartment on Fifth Avenue, this seemed unlikely. Having a Fifth Avenue address, I'm finding out, is like living in Beverly Hills or something. New Yorkers—even transplanted ones—are insane about real estate . . . maybe because there's so little of it actually available, and what there is is prohibitively expensive.

So whenever I tell people where I live, their eyes bulge out a little. And without my even mentioning the Renoir.

Oh well. I'm doing a kind thing. It's not like Tiffany has anyone else, not being particularly close to her ultraconservative parents, who don't approve of her relationship with Raoul. And Lord knows Roberta isn't likely to have her over for dinner anytime soon. My doing so will score me some bonus karma points, which I really need, given the amount of trouble my big mouth is always getting me into . . .

. . . a fact driven home harder than ever when the elevator doors open on the lobby level and I step out to see a familiar face at the security desk. Jill Higgins, on her way up to another appointment with Chaz's dad. Today she's wearing her usual ensemble of jeans, sweater, and Timberlands—even though the *Post* did a whole makeover spread about her this weekend, where they had a paper-doll cutout of Jill with all these different outfits to put on her, including her zoo uniform and a tacky bridal gown.

I hesitate. I've been thinking about Jill a lot—every day, practically. Well, it's kind of hard not to, considering there always seems to be some story or other about "Blubber" in the local rags. It's like New Yorkers can't seem to believe that someone as rich as John Mac-Dowell could fall in love with a woman who isn't as stereotypically beautiful as . . . well, Tiffany.

And the fact that Jill's a working girl—and works with *seals,* no less—seems to have made her an even bigger target for acid-tongued New York society. Apparently, she'll be the first MacDowell wife ever to hold a job (aside from volunteer work for charity that is).

And the fact that Jill has said she intends to keep her job working with the seals even after she's married has the matrons of Fifth Avenue (I know. My own street!) cringing.

All of which has me worried. Seriously. And okay, not as worried as I am about Shari and Chaz (naturally). But still. I can't stop thinking about what Tiffany told me my first day of work—that John MacDowell's family is making that poor girl wear some ancestral bridal gown that's been in their family for a million years on her big day.

I'm willing to bet that ancestral gown's a size two, at the largest.

And Jill's a size fourteen or twelve, at the smallest.

How's she going to fit into a dress like that? And she has to—she *has* to wear it. That whole thing about the dress . . . that is a clear challenge by her fiancé's mother. It's like Mrs. MacDowell is saying, "Do this . . . or you'll never fit in with the rest of us. *Literally.*"

Jill has got to rise to the challenge, or she'll never have any peace from her in-laws. And the press'll certainly never stop calling her Blubber.

And okay. Maybe I'm projecting. But from what I've read—and what I know, from working at Pendergast, Loughlin, and Flynn—I'm not far off.

So what's Jill going to do? She has to be taking that dress to *someone* for alterations . . . but who? Is it someone who understands the urgency of the situation? Is it someone who is going to tell her the truth—that there is no way you can squeeze a size-twelve body into a size-two gown without using a lot of hideous panels?

Oh God. Just the thought of panels is making me shudder.

And as I stand there, watching Jill show her driver's license so that the security guard can make her a pass, I realize that I want her to come to me. I know it sounds crazy. But I don't want anybody else working on Jill's dress. Not because I'm afraid of her falling prey to a huckster like Maurice . . . although I am. But because I want her to look beautiful on her wedding day. I want John's family to gasp as she comes down the aisle, because she looks so beautiful. I want that dress to be an in-your-face to her mother-in-law. I want the New York press to take back that "Blubber," and substitute it with "Beautiful."

And I know I can make that happen. I just know it. Doesn't Jennifer Harris *love* what I—under Monsieur Henri's watchful eye, of course—have done so far to her mother's bridal gown? Even her mother grudgingly admitted during her daughter's latest fitting that the gown looks "better" on Jennifer than it ever did on any of her other girls.

There's only one reason for that: my hard work.

I want to do the same for Jill. I mean, she threw out her back *lifting a seal*! A girl like that deserves the very best in certified wedding-gown specialists.

And okay, I don't quite have my certification yet. But it's really only a matter of time . . .

Only how? How can I let Jill know I'm here for her if she needs me? I can't very well slip her my business card (oh yes. I'd had business cards made up, with Monsieur Henri's address and my cell number on them), while also maintaining the level of "discretion and professionalism" Roberta told me Pendergast, Loughlin, and Flynn expects from its employees. I'm pretty sure something like that could get me fired . . . and I still need this job.

But not as much, I realize all at once, as Jill moves toward the security gate, and I spot the most hideous of all fashion faux pas— VPLs, or visible panty lines—below her waist. Oh God! VPLs! Someone must help her!

And, by God, that someone is going to be me. Which is more important anyway, my making rent or this poor, put-upon girl looking the best she possibly can on her wedding day? That's a no-brainer. I'm just going to go up to her and offer my services. We're not in the office now, I'm on my own time. And maybe she won't even remember where she's seen me before. No one ever remembers receptionists . . .

"Excuse me—"

Oh! Too late! She's going through the security gate. Dammit! I've missed her.

Well, that's okay. No, really, it's fine. I'll get her next time. If there *is* a next time . . .

There *has* to be a next time.

"So." A lanky guy in gray cords that I'd noticed hanging around one of the magazine stands in the lobby is sidling up to me.

Great. This is all I need. To be hit on by yet another guy who thinks from my clothes that I'm some midwestern rube who is going to fall for his line about how he's a photographer for a modeling agency, and do I want to go back to his studio with him so he can take some pictures of me? Because he wants to make me a star. Yawn.

"Sorry," I say, turning around and heading toward the lobby doors. "Not interested."

This, of course, is why New Yorkers have a reputation for rudeness. But it's not our fault! It's guys like this who make New Yorkers so suspicious of any stranger who tries to speak to them on the street!

"Wait." Gray Cords is following me. Oh no! "Was that Jill Higgins you were waving to just then?"

I stop. I can't help myself. The words "Jill Higgins" have this magic effect on me. That's how much I want to get my hands on her wedding dress.

"Yes," I say. Who *is* this guy? He certainly doesn't look like a pervert . . . but then, how do I know what a pervert looks like?

"So, you're a friend of hers?" Gray Cords wants to know.

"No," I say. And suddenly—just like that—I know who he is. It's amazing how hardened you can become after just a few months in Manhattan. "What paper are you with?"

"The *New York Journal,*" he says matter-of-factly, taking a PDA from one of his pockets and turning it on. "Do you know what she's doing here? Jill, I mean? There are a lot of law firms in this building. Was she headed up to one of them? Would you happen to know which one . . . and why?"

I can feel my face turning bright red. Not because I'm embarrassed for having said something indiscreet. Because for once I haven't. My face is getting red because I'm angry.

"You people—" I want to hit him. I really do. "You should be ashamed of yourself! Following that poor girl around, calling her 'Blubber'—what gives you the right to judge her? Huh? What makes you think you're so much better than she is?"

"Relax," Gray Cords says, looking bored. "Why do you feel so sorry for her, anyway? She's gonna be richer than Trump in a couple of months—"

"Get away from me!" I shout. "And get out of this building, before I notify security!"

"Okay, okay." Gray Cords slinks away, muttering the four-letter word for the female sex organ that I apparently remind him of.

But I don't care.

And just to ensure he stays away from Jill when she comes out, I march up to the security desk, point Gray Cords out to Mike and Raphael, and inform them that he just exposed himself to me. The last I see of Gray Cords, he is being chased out of the building by two men wielding billy clubs.

There are times when having a big mouth and no great reservations about telling outright lies really comes in handy.

⟶ Lizzie Nichols's Wedding Gown Guide ⟶

The last thing anyone wants on her wedding day is to end up on prime-time television—you know, with one of those moments where the bride slips and a dominolike effect causes everyone she comes into contact with to fall as well, until the last person lands with his face in the wedding cake, like something on *America's Funniest Home Videos* (although there is really nothing funny about wasted cake).

So be sure to break in your wedding shoes before the big day . . . not just to save yourself from blisters, but to keep yourself from slipping, as well. Women's shoes have notoriously slick soles. You can avoid having your feet slide out from under you at an inopportune moment by applying no-skid stickers to the bottom of your shoes (on the outside, not the inside, silly).

Forget to buy stickers? Never fear! By carefully (so as not to cut yourself) running a knife blade across the sole of your shoe in a hatchmark pattern, you can also prevent slipping on just about any surface (save ice. But if you're getting married on ice, you have a completely different set of problems).

Lizzie Nichols Designs™

• Chapter 13 •

Gossip is dying out because fewer and fewer people care to talk about anything besides themselves.

—Mason Cooley (1927–2002), American aphorist

By the time I finally get to Monsieur Henri's shop later that afternoon, I'm no longer freaking out about having invited Tiffany and her boyfriend to dinner. It was the right thing to do. Thanksgiving is about family, and Tiffany is certainly part of mine.

Well, my work family, anyway. Sure, she can be annoying—she's still only cleared one drawer in the reception desk for me, and she leaves sticky, half-gnawed Twizzlers *everywhere*. Plus, she's repeatedly erased my wedding-gown site bookmarks on our shared computer.

But she's been pretty nice to me, as well. I mean, she leaves all her fashion magazines behind for me to read (since I can't exactly afford to buy my own), and almost always has some little beauty tip to give me—like that Vaseline works just as well for dry skin as expensive moisturizers, or that putting deodorant on your bikini line after shaving prevents ingrown hairs.

Which is more than I can say for Madame Henri. Not about the deodorant (not that I've ever gone up to her and taken a big whiff) but about being nice to me. Oh, sure, she tolerates me.

But only because I take on a significant portion of her husband's workload, leaving him free to spend more time at home . . . a fact about which I'm not entirely sure he's that happy.

When I walk through the door that afternoon, in fact, Monsieur Henri and his wife are having a violent argument—only in French, of course, so that Jennifer Harris and her mother, who are there for Jennifer's final fitting, can't understand what they're saying.

"We've got to do it," Madame Henri is saying viciously. "I don't see how we're going to manage otherwise. Maurice has sucked away every last bit of our business with those newspaper ads of his. And when he opens up that new shop of his down the street—well, I don't need to tell you, that will be the nail in our coffin!"

"Let's wait," her husband says. "Things might pick up."

Then, noticing me, he says in English, "Ah, Mademoiselle Elizabeth! Well, what do you think?"

As if he has to ask. I'm standing there staring at Jennifer Harris, who has come out of the dressing room in her gown, and looks . . .

Well, like an angel.

"I love it," Jennifer says.

And anyone could see why. The gown—now with an open, Queen Anne–style neckline, and tight, over-the-wrist lace sleeves (with loops that go over the middle finger, to keep the lace in place)—looks fantastic.

But it's Jennifer herself who's the most beautiful of all. She's glowing.

Of course, she's glowing because I did a kick-ass job on her dress.

But that's beside the point.

"Are you wearing the shoes you're going to have on for the ceremony?" I ask, Monsieur and Madame Henri's latest tiff forgotten as I hurry forward to fuss with her skirt. I've added a lace drape—to match the sleeves—at the waist, giving her more of a Renaissance-style look. Which, with her long neck and stick-straight hair, really works.

"Of course," Jennifer says. "You told me to, remember?"

The hem is the perfect length—just sweeping the floor. She looks like a princess. No, like a fairy princess.

"Her sisters are going to kill me when they see her," Mrs. Harris says—but not unpleasantly. "Because she looks so much better than any of them ever did."

"Mom!" Jennifer knows she looks fantastic, so she can afford to be gracious. "You know that's not true."

But the fact that she can't take her gaze off her own reflection illustrates that she knows it *is* true.

Pleased with the results of my labor—and Monsieur Henri's, as well. He did, after all, provide the lace—I help Jennifer remove the gown and am packing it up for her while her mother pays the not insignificant bill (although it's a lot less than if they'd bought a whole new dress, even if they'd gone to—shudder—Kleinfeld's).

I've given Jennifer her garment bag with instructions on how to steam any creases out (by hanging the gown in the bathroom with a hot shower going). Whatever happens, I inform her, DO NOT IRON it. Jennifer is so high on how pretty she looks in her dress that she just says "Okay" in a daze, and runs out to where her mother has parked the car without another word.

Her mother, however, is more circumspect, stopping beside me after paying Monsieur Henri to squeeze my hand and say, while looking into my eyes, "Lizzie. Thank you."

"Oh, no problem, Mrs. Harris." I'm a little embarrassed. It's weird to be thanked for doing something you love and would have done in any case, whether or not anyone was paying you (which, in this case, no one was).

But when Mrs. Harris takes her hand away from mine, I see that I'm wrong. Because she's surreptitiously pressed a bill into my hand.

Reminded immediately of Grandma and her emergency sawbuck (which I still have in my handbag), I look down and am surprised to see two zeroes after the number one on the bill Mrs. Harris has given me.

"Oh, I can't accept this," I start to say.

But Mrs. Harris has already swept out the door, with a promise that she's going to tell all her friends with daughters of marriageable age about Monsieur Henri. "And I'll make sure they stay away from that horrible Maurice!" is her parting cry.

The second she's gone, Madame Henri starts in again on her husband.

"And as if things were not bad enough, those boys of yours stayed in the apartment again last night!"

"They're your sons, too," Monsieur Henri points out.

"No," Madame Henri corrects him. "Not anymore. If all they are going to do is come into the city to go to the clubs, then dirty up my perfectly clean apartment—which they know they are not supposed to stay in—they are *your* boys. Because you will not discipline them."

"What do you want me to do?" he demands. "I want them to have the advantages I did not have growing up!"

"They have had enough advantages," says Madame Henri emphatically. "Now is the time to let them fend for themselves. Let them see what it is like in real life, to have to earn a paycheck."

"You know it's not that easy," Monsieur Henri says.

Has he got that right. I look down at the hundred-dollar bill in my hand. It's the first "found" money I've had since moving to this city. Everything here is so expensive! It seems like no sooner do I get a paycheck than it's gone again, first to rent, then to Con Ed, then to food, then to cable (because I can't live without the Style channel), and then, if there's anything left over, to my cell phone bill.

"Well," Madame Henri says with a sniff. "I am having the apartment locks changed. And I am keeping the key here in the shop. Hidden."

And what about FICA taxes? FICA—Federal Insurance Contributions Act (or as Tiffany insists the letters really stand for, Fucking Idiots taking my Cash Assets)—seems to eat up more of my paychecks than anything.

"How much is *that* going to cost me?" Monsieur Henri wants to know.

"However much it is, it will be worth it," Madame Henri declares. "If it means those pigs will be kept out of the place. You should see what I found in the bedroom wastebasket. A condom! Used!"

It's impossible to pretend I don't understand French when I hear this. I can't help making a face . . . especially when Madame Henri brandishes a plastic trash bag that apparently holds the evidence of her claim.

"Ew!" I cry.

When both Henris look at me curiously, I quickly wrinkle my nose and say, "That garbage smells." Because, truthfully, it totally does. "Do you want me to take it out for you?"

"Er, yes, thank you," Madame Henri says after a moment's hesitation. "It's the garbage from our flat upstairs."

I take the bag between two fingers. "You own the apartments upstairs?" This is news to me. I didn't know they owned the entire brownstone the shop is in. And I thought they lived in New Jersey. They certainly seemed to complain enough about the commute.

Monsieur Henri nods. "Yes. The second floor we use for storage. The top floor is a little flat. I sleep there sometimes when I have to work late on a gown—" Which hasn't happened, as far as I can tell, in a long, long time. Business hasn't been good enough for any of us to pull any all-nighters. "Otherwise, it sits empty. Our sons use it from time to time—"

"Without permission!" Madame Henri cries in English. "I would like to rent it out, help with some of the costs of the business—and to keep my pigs of sons from thinking they can sleep there whenever they miss the train home after a night of debauchery. But this oaf here does not like the idea!"

"I don't know," Monsieur Henri says, not looking as if his sons' alleged debauchery bothers him that much. "I don't want the responsibility of being a landlord. And supposing we get one of those crazy tenants, eh? Like we read about in the papers? The ones with all the cats, who won't move out? I don't want that."

Madame Henri responds by shaking a balled-up fist at her husband. I smile and slip outside to deposit the trash bag in the can by the stoop. With everyone in New York seemingly scrambling to find a better place to live, it's weird to hear about a place sitting empty . . . well, except for when it's used as an occasional flophouse by a couple of party boys.

"Mademoiselle Elizabeth," Madame Henri says when I come back inside. "Do you know, perhaps, of someone looking to rent a small efficiency?"

"No," I say. "But if I hear of someone, I'll let you know."

"It can't be just anyone," Monsieur Henri insists. "They must have references—"

"And be willing to pay two thousand dollars a month," Madame Henri adds.

"Two thousand?" Monsieur Henri cries in French. "That is robbery, woman! Are you mad?"

"Two thousand dollars a month for a beautiful one-bedroom is perfectly reasonable!" she fires back, also in French. "Do you know how much they are charging for studio apartments? Twice that!"

"In buildings that have a swimming pool on the roof!" Monsieur Henri scoffs. "Which ours most decidedly does not have!"

And the two of them are off and running, arguing back and forth. But I'm not alarmed. I've spent enough time with them by now to know that this is how they are. I mean, they argue all day long . . .

. . . but I've seen Madame Henri fuss over her husband's hair in an extremely loving way, while at the same time accusing him of purposely practicing unhealthy dietary habits in order to expire sooner and be rid of her.

And Monsieur Henri regularly ogles his wife's legs, while simultaneously telling her how much her nagging drives him crazy.

Once I caught them kissing in the back room.

Couples. They're all a little nuts, in their own way, I think.

I hope that when Luke and I are as old as Monsieur and Madame Henri, we can be just like them.

Minus the failing business and degenerate sons, I mean.

It's in the bag!

Ever wonder what a bride should carry on her wedding day? Well, I'm here to let you in on the mystery:

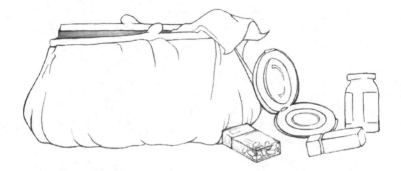

—Lipstick, pressed powder (to control shine), and concealer (in case of blemishes)—
Even if you have your makeup done by a professional, carry these items with you in a small pouch or clutch. You will need them—especially between toasts at the reception (brides, be subtle with makeup fixes at the table . . . excuse yourself for anything more than a quick check in the compact mirror).

—Breath mints—
Trust me, you're going to need them.

—Medications—
If you are prone to migraines, count on getting one on your wedding day. Migraines are often brought on by stress, and what's more stressful than committing yourself for all eternity to your lover in front of hundreds of friends and family members? Make sure you have your prescription migraine medication with you on your special day, or any other medications that might help you through the day, including aspirin, muscle relaxants (go easy on these), beta-blockers, and homeopathics like aromatherapy oils.

—Deodorant—
If you perspire more than average, especially when stressed or overheated, have a minitube of this in your bag for emergencies. You won't regret it.

—Feminine hygiene products—
It happens. Some of us will be having our period on our big day. If you're due for yours, wear protection just in case, and carry some extra for even more security.

And, of course,

—Tissues—
You know you're going to cry—or someone close to you will, anyway. So come prepared.

Lizzie Nichols Designs™

• Chapter 14 •

It is one of my sources of happiness never to desire a knowledge of other people's business.

—Dolley Madison (1768–1849), American First Lady

I completely regret agreeing to let Luke's parents stay with us over the Thanksgiving weekend.

And okay, I know it's his mom's apartment. And I know it's supernice of her to allow us to live in it, rent free (well, in Luke's case).

And I know we all got along great when we were staying at Château Mirac, the de Villiers ancestral home in France, over the summer.

But it is one thing to share a château with your boyfriend's parents.

It is quite another to share a one-bedroom apartment with them . . . while also having promised to prepare a traditional Thanksgiving dinner when, truth be told, you've really never cooked all that much before.

The gravity of the situation didn't really hit me until Carlos, the doorman, buzzed up to say Luke's parents had arrived. An hour before we were expecting them, and while I was in the middle of sorting through several bouquets of freesia and irises, to which I'd treated myself—as well as Mrs. Erickson from 5B—from the flower section at Eli's, and purchased with part of Mrs. Harris's hundred dollars. There's nothing more welcome than having a vase of fresh cut flowers sitting out when people come to visit—and there's no nicer gift for someone who has helped you, as Mrs. Erickson had by recommending Monsieur Henri's to me, either.

But when the flowers are purchased in bunches from a florist, and still have to be arranged, and are lying in messy piles on top of the stove while you look for vases, it's sort of hard to feel the welcoming effect. Especially when you're still in your sweats from doing the grocery shopping—which is still sitting in bags on the kitchen floor—and your boyfriend isn't home from school yet, and the doorman buzzes to inform you that your "guests" are here . . .

"Send them up," I tell Carlos through the intercom. What else could I say?

Then I run around like a crazy person, trying to clean up. The place isn't *that* bad—I'm something of a neat freak—but all of the lovely touches I'd been hoping to have when Luke's parents walked in—a tray of freshly mixed cocktails (kir royales, their favorite), party nuts in bowls, assorted cheeses on a platter—have to be abandoned as I cram the dirty laundry in a hamper, run a quick brush through my hair, slap on a bit of lip gloss, then fling open the door.

"Helloooo!" I cry, noticing that Mr. and Mrs. de Villiers look— well, *older* than when I'd last seen them. But then, who doesn't after a plane ride? "You're early!"

"There was *no* traffic coming into the city from the airport," Mrs. de Villiers drawls in her Texan accent, giving me a kiss on either cheek, as is her custom. "Leaving the city, yes. But coming in? No." Her gaze sweeps the apartment, taking in the grocery bags, the lack of cocktails, and my sweats. "Sorry we're early."

"Oh, it's no problem," I say breezily. "Really. It's just that Luke isn't home from class yet—"

"Well, we will just have to start celebrating without him," Monsieur de Villiers says, as he unveils a bottle of chilled champagne he's managed to procure somewhere along the way from the airport.

"Celebrating?" I blink. "Is there something to celebrate?"

"There is always something to celebrate," Monsieur de Villiers says. "But in this case the fact that the Beaujolais nouveau has been released."

His wife is pulling an Armani wheelie-suitcase. "Where can I park this?" she wants to know.

"Oh, your room, of course," I say as I hurry to produce champagne flutes. "Luke and I will be taking the couch."

Monsieur de Villiers winces as the cork from the bottle of champagne he is opening pops. "I told you we should have stayed in a hotel," he calls to his wife. "Now these poor children will have spinal injuries from sleeping on a pull-out couch."

"Oh no," I say. "The couch is fine! Luke and I are so grateful to you for—"

"It's a fine pull-out couch!" Mrs. de Villiers insists on her way to the bedroom. "I'll admit it's not the most comfortable in the world, but no one is going to suffer a spinal injury!"

I try to imagine how this conversation would go if it were my own parents, and fail. My parents are still in the dark about Luke and me living together, and I have every intention of keeping it that way . . . at least until we announce our engagement. I mean, if we ever get engaged, that is. It's not that they're morally against people living together before they get married. They're just against me living with someone I've only known for a few months.

Which actually says a lot about how much they trust my judgment about people.

Although, looking back on some of my exes, I think maybe they have a point.

"It's fine," I assure Monsieur de Villiers. "Really."

"Well." Mrs. de Villiers has dropped her bag off in the bedroom and returned. "I'm happy to see you've made yourself at home in there."

I realize she's referring to the standing rack from Bed Bath & Beyond—and my vintage-dress collection.

And that she sounds . . . well, *bemused* about it.

And not necessarily in a good way.

"Oh," I say. "Yes. I'm sorry. I know my clothes take up a lot of room. I hope you don't mind—"

"Of course not!" Mrs. de Villiers says—a little too heartily. "I'm glad you're making use of the space. Is that a *sewing machine* I saw on my dressing table?"

Oh. My. God.

"Um, yes . . . well, you see, I needed a table to put it on, and your dressing table is just the right height . . ." She hates me. I can tell. She totally hates me. "I can move it if you need me to. It's no problem . . ."

"Not at all," Mrs. de Villiers says with a smile that's, well, a trifle brittle. "Guillaume, I'll take a little of that champagne. Actually, make that a lot."

"I'll just go move it," I say. "The sewing machine. I'm sorry, I should have thought about it before. Of course you need a place to do your makeup—"

"Don't be silly," Mrs. de Villiers says. "You can do it later. Sit down right now and have some champagne with us. Guillaume and I want to hear all about your new job. Jean-Luc says you're working in a law office! That must be so exciting. I had no idea you were interested in the law."

"Uh," I say, taking the glass Monsieur de Villiers offers me. "I'm not—" Why didn't I move that sewing machine last night, when it occurred to me that Mrs. de Villiers might not appreciate having it sitting there smack in the middle of her dressing table? *Why?*

"Are you doing paralegal work?" Mrs. de Villiers wants to know.

"Um, no," I say. What about all my stuff in the bathroom? I have a ton of beauty products in there. I tried to consolidate it all in my plastic shower caddy from the dorm, but ever since I started working with a model, it's gotten a lot bigger, since Tiffany won't stop giving me samples, and some of them are pretty awesome. Like anything from Kiehl's, which I admit I never heard of until I moved here. But now I'm addicted to their lip balm.

But where would I put all that stuff, if not the bathroom? There's only the one bathroom . . . and that's the place where shower caddies *go* . . .

"Administrative work?" Mrs. de Villiers is asking.

"No," I say. "I'm the receptionist. Do you want me to move my stuff out of the bathroom? Because I totally can. I'm sorry if it seems like my stuff is everywhere, I know there's a lot, but I can really move it—"

"Don't worry about it," Mrs. de Villiers says. She's finished her first glass of champagne and holds out her glass toward her husband for a refill. "When does Jean-Luc get home?"

Oh, God. This is awful. She's already wondering when Luke's going to get here. I'm wondering the same thing. Someone needs to save us from this awkward silence—oh, wait. Monsieur de Villiers is turning on the TV. Thank God. We can watch the news or something—

"Oh, Guillaume, turn that off," his wife says. "We want to visit, not watch CNN."

"I just want to see the weather," Monsieur de Villiers insists.

"You can look outside to see the weather," his wife scoffs. "It's cold. It's November. What do you expect?"

Oh, God. This is excruciating. I'm going to die, I just know it. I saw her disappointed expression when I said I'm just a receptionist at Chaz's dad's firm. Why did she wince like that? Because she can't imagine her son dating a mere receptionist? It's true his last girlfriend was an investment banker. But she was older than me! Well, by a couple of years. But whatever, she had a business degree! I was a liberal arts major. What does anybody expect?

Oh, God. There's an awkward silence. Nooooo . . . Okay, think of something to say. Anything. These are bright, intellectual people. I should be able to chat with them about anything . . . anything at all . . .

Oh! I know . . .

"Mrs. de Villiers, I just love your Renoir," I say. "The one hanging over your bed?"

"Oh." Luke's mother looks pleased. "That little thing? Thank you. Yes, she's adorable, isn't she?"

"I love her," I say truthfully. "Where did you get her?"

"Oh." Mrs. de Villiers looks toward the windows overlooking Fifth Avenue, a faraway gleam in her eyes. "She was a gift from someone. A very long time ago."

I don't have to be a mind reader to know that the "someone" Mrs. de Villiers was referring to had been a lover. It *had* to have been. How else to explain the dewy look that came over her face?

Could it, I couldn't help wondering, have been the same man who keeps calling the apartment, asking for her?

"Um," I say. Because I don't know what else *to* say. Luke's father seems oblivious, switching the channels from New York 1 to CNN. "Nice gift."

The most expensive thing anybody has ever given me is an iPod. And that was from my parents.

"Yes," Mrs. de Villiers says with a catlike smile as she sips her champagne. "Wasn't it?"

"Look." Monsieur de Villiers points at the television. "You see? It's going to snow tomorrow."

"Well, we don't have to worry about it," his wife says. "We don't have to go anywhere. We'll be nice and snug in here."

Oh, God. It's true. We'll all be stuck inside the whole day, me cooking (with Luke's help, hopefully), and his parents . . . God. I don't even know. What are they going to do? Watch the Macy's Thanksgiving Day parade? The football games? Somehow they didn't strike me as parade or football people.

Which meant they were just going to be sitting here. All day. Slowly sucking out my soul with their well-meaning but ultimately barbed comments . . . *You really should consider becoming a paralegal, Lizzie. You'd make a lot more money than a mere receptionist.*

What? Certified wedding-gown specialist? I've never heard of that as a career path. Well, it's true you did do wonders with my wedding gown. But that's hardly a career for a college-educated person. I mean, aren't you a glorified seamstress? Don't you worry that you're wasting all the money your parents paid for your education?

No! Because my education was free! Because my dad works at the college I went to, and free tuition is one of his job benefits!

Oh, God. Why did we all get along so well in France, and yet we have nothing to say to one another here?

I know why. Because they thought I was just Luke's summer fling. Now it's clear I'm more than that, and they aren't happy about it. I know it. I just know it.

"You guys must be starving after your long plane ride," I say as I spring up, determined not to let myself sink into despair. "Let me fix you something to eat."

"No, no," Monsieur de Villiers says. "We are taking you and Jean-Luc out tonight. We have reservations. Don't we, Bibi?"

"Right," Mrs. de Villiers says. "At Nobu. You know how much Jean-Luc loves sushi. We figured it would be just the right pick-me-up for him, considering how hard he's been studying."

"Right," I say, in desperation. Desperation because I'm longing to get out of the same room with them. "I, uh, just got back from the store. I bought some cheese. Let me just put it out for you both. You can snack on it until Luke gets home and we can leave for the restaurant—"

"Don't go to any trouble on our account," Monsieur de Villiers says, waving a hand dismissively. "We can get our own snacks!"

Oh, God. They won't even let me act like a hostess. Which I guess is understandable, since this isn't even my apartment anyway.

Still. They don't have to rub it in so much.

The telephone rings, startling me from my sullen musings. Not my cell phone—the apartment phone, the one listed under Bibi de Villiers's name. The one only a single person has ever called on, since I'd moved in.

The man who leaves the disappointed messages for Bibi! The messages I've never mentioned to Luke.

Or his mother.

"Um, that's probably for you," I say to her. "Luke and I don't use your number. We have our cells."

Mrs. de Villiers looks startled but pleased. "I wonder who that can be," she asks, getting up and heading to the phone. "I didn't tell anyone I was coming to town. I wanted to be free to shop uninterrupted. You know how it is."

Actually, I did. There's nothing more irritating than friends who want to schedule lunch with you when you've blocked out the whole weekend for shopping.

"Hello?" Mrs. de Villiers says, after lifting the receiver and removing the clip-on earring from her right ear.

And I thought my mom was the only woman left without pierced ears.

I know instantly that it's the Guy Who's Been Leaving All Those Messages. I can tell by the surprised but pleased expression on Mrs. de Villiers's lovely face. Also the quick, wary look she darts at the back of her husband's head as she breathes, "Oh, darling, how sweet of you to call. You have? Well, no, I haven't been here. No, I've been in France and then back in Houston. Yes, of *course* with Guillaume, silly."

Hmmm. So Guy Who's Been Leaving All Those Messages knows she's married.

What am I thinking? Of *course* he does. That's why he only calls on her private line.

Wow. I can't believe Luke's mom is cheating on his dad. Or used to be, I guess. Which wasn't necessarily cheating then, either, because they were separated, and in the act of divorcing. They only got back together a few months ago, over the summer . . . because of me.

The question is, now that summer's over, and life's gotten back to normal—if you can call a life where you have three homes, including a château in France, a mansion in Houston, and a Fifth Avenue apartment in Manhattan, normal—will their renewed love be able to survive?

"Friday? Oh, darling, I'd love to, but you know I've blocked that day out for shopping. Yes, the whole day. Well, I suppose I could. Oh, you're so persistent. No, I do admire that in a man. Fine. Friday it is, then. Buh-bye."

Yeah. Maybe not.

Mrs. de Villiers hangs up and puts her earring back on. She's smiling in a pleased kind of way.

"Who was that, *chérie?*" Luke's father asks.

"Oh, no one," Mrs. de Villiers says casually. *Too* casually.

At that moment, I hear Luke's key in the lock. And I nearly crumple with relief.

"You're here!" he cries when he walks in and sees his parents. "You're early!"

"Eh!" Monsieur de Villiers looks pleased. "There he is!"

"Jean-Luc!" His mother throws open her arms. "Come give your mother a kiss!"

Luke crosses the living room to hug his mother, then gives his dad a kiss on both cheeks as well. Then he comes over to me and, giving me a kiss (on the lips, not the cheeks), he whispers, "Sorry I'm so late. I got stuck on the subway. What'd I miss? Anything going on I need to know about?"

"Oh," I say. "Not really."

Because what else am I going to say? *Your parents won't let me make them any snacks, they don't think I'm good enough for you, tomorrow's dinner is going to be a disaster, and by the way, I think your mom's having an affair?*

I may have a big mouth—but I'm learning.

But what about your crowning glory?

Brides have many different options when it comes to head-gear for their special day. While some brides opt to leave their head bare, others opt for a veil, floral wreath, or tiara—or sometimes all three!

There are as many different headdresses as there are brides. Some of my favorites include:

The Wreath: Nothing says "bride" like flowers . . . and a circlet of fresh white rosebuds and baby's breath never goes out of style.

The Tiara: Not just for royalty anymore! Many brides are opting to top their veil with a diamond (or diamante) sparkler.

The Band: Anything from a slim headband to a wider, highly decorated comb to hold both hair and veil in place.

The Bun: This circular band is attached to the bride's updo, from which the veil sweeps.

The Crown: Why cheat yourself? If a tiara works, why not go bigger and better?

The Snood: It worked for your grandmother. A snood is a decorative net fitted over the back of the head, generally holding back the hair in a net.

The Juliet Cap: Like Juliet wore in the famous play—a round skullcaplike hat that sits closely on top of the head, usually decorated in seed-pearls.

And, of course, the ever popular:

Cowgirl Hat: Western brides wouldn't be caught dead without one!

Which one looks best on you? Well, trying them on to find out is half the fun!

• Chapter 15 •

The Puritan's idea of hell is a place where
everybody has to mind his own business.

—Wendell Phillips (1811–1884), American abolitionist

I t's an hour until the turkey will be ready, and I think I
have things under control.

No, really.

For one thing, Mrs. Erickson turned me on to a little New York
secret—precooked turkeys from the local meat market. All you
have to do after it arrives is bang yours in the oven and baste it
every once in a while . . . and it looks (and smells) like you slaved
all day.

And it was completely easy to snow all the de Villiers—even
Luke—that this is what I'd done. All I had to do was make sure I
got up before any of them did—which was no problem, since they
all sleep like the dead—and sneak down to Mrs. Erickson's apartment. I'd had my turkey delivered to her place, where she'd promised to store it until I could pick it up.

Once I had it—and the little bag of giblets that came with it, for
the gravy—I hightailed it back up to Mrs. de Villiers's apartment,
and threw out all the telltale packaging. Perfect.

Luke got up a little while later and started whipping up his con-
tribution to the meal—garlic-roasted onions and Brussels sprouts—

and Mrs. de Villiers insisted on contributing a sweet potato side dish (thankfully minus the marshmallow fluff. Which I love, but Chaz and Shari were already bringing three different kinds of pie, because I like pumpkin, Chaz likes strawberry-rhubarb, and Shari likes pecan, and that's more than enough sweet stuff).

Monsieur de Villiers contributed by puttering around, assembling all his wines in the order in which he wants us to consume them.

So in all, everything is going pretty much according to plan. The guests are arriving. Tiffany—looking resplendent in the suede catsuit Roberta once sent her home for wearing to the office—has shown up with Raoul, who's turned out to be a surprisingly pleasant, fairly normal thirty-year-old, with very good manners—he's brought along a bottle of the Beaujolais that Monsieur de Villiers is so excited about. Apparently, he's something of a wine connoisseur—albeit of the Argentinean variety—himself.

So the two of them immediately start talking grapes and soil, while Mrs. de Villiers sets the table, carefully folding each of her cloth napkins into an upright fan pattern, and using all three forks from her silver set, placing them with extra care beside one another . . . perhaps thanks to the Bloody Marys Luke insisted on preparing for his parents—and has kept filled—since they've woken up. ("How else," he asked me, sotto voce, "are we all going to get along all day in such a small space?")

Not that his parents seem to mind. Once I moved the sewing machine, Luke's mother was all smiles. Although that might have something to do with the fact that Luke's been careful not to leave us alone together again.

Which is fine. I actually have work tomorrow (partners may get the Friday after Thanksgiving as a holiday in busy law firms, but receptionists certainly don't), so it will be up to Luke to keep his parents entertained. His mother, of course, has already made other plans (about which she's informed no one). Luke and his father plan on going to the museums . . .

... where I'll be joining them all day on Saturday, before we head off to the theater together for my first Broadway show—Mrs. de Villiers has four tickets to *Spamalot*. Thankfully they'll be leaving on Sunday, by which time I think my tolerance for sharing a one-bedroom with my boyfriend's parents will have been totally spent.

Tiffany, however, seems completely enthusiastic about the de Villiers . . . fascinated by them, actually. She keeps sidling up to me in the kitchen as I pretend to be sweating over my turkey and whispering, "So . . . that old guy? He's really a prince?"

I rue the day I ever mentioned the whole royalty thing to Tiffany. Seriously, I don't know what I was thinking. Telling something in confidence to Tiffany is like telling it to a parrot. Only a fool would expect it not to be repeated.

"Um, yeah," I say, basting. "But remember, I told you. France doesn't recognize its former monarchs—or whatever—anymore. And, you know. There are like a thousand princes. Or I guess counts is what they really are."

Tiffany, as is her custom, completely ignores my reply.

"So Luke is a prince, too." She is observing Luke across the pass-through, as he arranges a tray of appetizers—shrimp cocktail and crudités—on the coffee table in front of the sofa on which his father and Raoul are having their animated wine discussion. "Man. Did you score in the boyfriend department."

I'm annoyed now. Not just because it's nearly five o'clock and I asked Chaz and Shari to be here at four and there is no sign of them. Which isn't that unusual, especially since it's snowing out, and even the slightest snowfall seems to paralyze New York City . . . but even more so when everyone is off work on a holiday.

Still, it isn't like Shari not to call. Or leave me stranded like this with my future (hopefully) in-laws and no comic relief in the form of my best friend.

Although Tiffany appears to be trying. Unconsciously (the comic part, I mean).

"That's not why I like him," I whisper to Tiffany. "You know that."

"Right," Tiffany says tiredly. "I know, I know. It's because of the doctor thing, he's going to be saving the lives of little children. Yada yada yada."

"Well," I say. "That's not totally why. But yeah, that's part of it. That and the whole part where he's like the best boyfriend who ever lived."

"Yeah," Tiffany says, reaching for a cheese stick from the basket of them I have on the counter, ready to go out to the table as soon as Chaz and Shari get here—whenever that is. "But, you know, doctors, they don't make, like, any money anymore. Because of the HMOs. I mean, unless they go into plastic surgery."

"Yeah," I say, slightly annoyed by this. "But Luke's not doing it to make money. He used to be an investment banker. But he gave it up because he realized saving lives is more important than making money."

Tiffany chews noisily on the cheese stick. "That depends on whose life it is," she says. "I mean, like, some lives are worth more than others. I'm just saying."

"Well." I don't know how to reply to this. "It doesn't matter whether or not he makes money, anyway. Because I plan on making enough money for both of us," I say.

Tiffany actually looks interested when I say this. "Rilly? Doing what?"

"Bridal-gown design," I say. "You know." It would help if she actually paid attention from time to time. "Or, I should say, refurbishment. And restoration."

Tiffany stares at me. "You mean like Vera Wang?"

"Something like that," I say. It doesn't seem worth it to try to explain.

"I didn't know you went to design school," Tiffany says.

"I didn't," I say. "But I majored in fashion history at the University of Michigan."

Tiffany snorts. "Oh, well. That explains a lot."

I glare at her. I only invited her to be nice. I don't need to be insulted in my own home. Or my boyfriend's mother's own home.

Before I can say anything, however, we're interrupted ... and sadly, not by the arrival of Chaz and Shari.

"We are moving on from Bloody Marys," Monsieur de Villiers appears in the pass-through to announce. He is holding one of the bottles of red wine Raoul brought with him. "This is a bottle of the first Beaujolais of the season. You simply have to try a glass. I am sorry your friends are not here yet, but this is an emergency! A wine emergency! Everyone must have some!"

"Oh, that sounds great, Monsieur de Villiers," I say, and accept the glass he's just poured for me. "Thanks."

Tiffany takes a glass as well, then says with a laugh, as Luke's father moves away, "He's sweet."

"Yes," I say, looking after the older man, in his navy-blue sportscoat and spotted ascot. "Isn't he?" How can Bibi de Villiers be cheating on him? It just seems so ... cold.

And completely unlike her in a way. Oh, she's very stylish, and seems to enjoy making people think that the only thing she's got on her mind is the latest Fendi bag and Marc Jacobs couture.

But I saw how her face melted a little when I mentioned the Renoir. She loves that painting—not just the person who gave it to her, but the painting itself. You have to be a little less than shallow to love a painting that much. At least in my opinion.

So what is a woman like that doing, agreeing to meet her lover (if that's what Phone Guy is) behind the back of the husband with whom she's been newly reunited?

Not that I'm about to say anything about it, though. When Luke got home the first night his parents arrived and his mother asked, after she'd kissed him hello, "Darling, did I get any messages here in the apartment? A friend said he'd left several ..."

Luke had just shrugged and said, "I never got any messages for you. Lizzie? Did you ever come home to find any messages for my mom?"

I'd nearly swallowed my tongue, I'd been so embarrassed.

"Messages? You mean on the answering machine?" I'd been stalling for time, but all I ended up doing was making myself look like a bigger idiot than Luke's mother already thinks me.

"That is generally where people leave messages," she'd said, not altogether unkindly.

Great. Now she thinks I'm an even bigger idiot.

"Um," I'd said, still stalling for time. "Uh." Great. Because stammering always helped.

Then, as always, my tendency to babble kicked in . . . for once to my advantage.

"Well, you know," I'd said, "a few times I came home and the light was blinking, but when I pressed play there was never anything on the tape. Maybe the machine is broken or something."

To my everlasting relief, Mrs. de Villiers had nodded and said, "Oh, yes, of course, it might be. It's quite old. I suppose I should stop being such a technophobe and get voice mail, anyway. Well, another thing to put on the shopping list!"

Great. Now Luke's mom was going to enroll in a voice mail plan, because I'd made her think there was something wrong with her perfectly functional answering machine.

But what was I supposed to have said? *Oh yes, Mrs. de Villiers, this man with a sexy foreign accent left multiple messages, but I erased them because I assumed he was your lover and I want you and your husband to stay together?*

Yeah. That'd make me more popular than ever with Luke's parents.

"What do you think of the wine?" Raoul pops his head across the pass-through to ask Tiffany and me. He is darkly handsome—but not objectionably good-looking or what Shari would call a "pretty boy." He has an easy smile and lots of chest hair peeping from the open collar of his shirt . . . and he only has just the one button undone.

"It's great," I say.

"I love it." Tiffany leans across the pass-through to kiss him, practically putting her knee in my bowl of cranberry relish. "Just like I love you . . ."

The two of them are exchanging baby-talk and I'm doing my best not to vomit when the buzzer rings.

"Ah," I hear Luke say. "That must be them at last." He picks up the intercom phone and tells Carlos to send Chaz and Shari up.

Finally. And about time, too. My turkey was in danger of drying out. Just how long can you keep poultry warming, anyway? Especially poultry that's already been cooked once—or however they make precooked turkeys.

I pull it from the oven, relieved to see that the skin is dark golden in color, and not blackened as I'd started to fear it might have become, and let it rest in its own juices, as the little handbook that came with it—and Mrs. Erickson, who, at seventy, knows from good turkey—advised.

The doorbell rings, and Luke goes to answer it. "Hey!" I hear him say cheerfully. "What took you so—hey, where's Shari?"

"I don't want to talk about it." Chaz is trying to keep his voice low, but I can still hear him. "Hey, Mr. and Mrs. de Villiers. Long time no see. You guys are lookin' good."

Tiffany has popped down from the kitchen counter and is now leaning her sinewy body (I'm positive she isn't wearing Spanx beneath all that leather) through the doorway to peer at Chaz.

"Hey," she says, sounding disappointed. "I thought he was bringing your girlfriend. That friend of yours you're always talking about, Shari. Where is she?"

I pop my head out the kitchen doorway and see Chaz handing over two pie boxes to Luke. The door to the hallway is closed. And Shari is nowhere in sight.

"Hey," I say, coming out of the kitchen with a smile. "Where's—"

"Don't ask," Luke mouths, coming toward me with the pie boxes. In a louder voice, he says, "Look, Chaz spent all day baking not one but two pies for dessert. Strawberry-rhubarb and your favorite, Lizzie—pumpkin. Shari's feeling under the weather, so she couldn't make it. But that just means there's more for the rest of us, right?"

Has he lost his mind? He tells me my best friend can't make Thanksgiving dinner because she's under the weather—and he expects me not to ask?

"What's wrong with her?" I demand of Chaz, who has headed directly to the bar Monsieur de Villiers has set up on his wife's antique rolling drink cart, and is helping himself to a whiskey—straight—that he quickly downs before pouring another. "Is it the flu? It's going around. Is it stomach or head? Does she want me to call her?"

"If you're gonna call her," Chaz says, his voice rough from the whiskey—and something else maybe, "you better do it on her cell. Because she's not home."

"Not home? When she's sick? She's—" I widen my eyes . . . then lower my voice, so the de Villierses and Tiffany and Raoul can't hear me. "Oh my God, she didn't go into the office, did she? She went to the office when she's not feeling well—and on a public holiday? Chaz, has she completely lost her mind?"

"It's entirely possible," Chaz replies. "But she's not at the office."

"Where is she, then? I don't understand . . ."

"Neither do I," Chaz says, going for his third whiskey. "Believe me."

"Charles!" Monsieur de Villiers has finally caught on that Chaz is helping himself at the bar—and not to the wine Raoul brought, either. "You must try the wine this young man brought with him. It's the new Beaujolais! I think you will like it better than whiskey, even!"

"I highly doubt that," Chaz says. But the liquor seems already to have improved his mood. "How you doing there, Guillaume? You're lookin' good in that cravat there. Is that what you call it? A cravat? Or is it an ascot?"

"Well, I don't know," Monsieur de Villiers confesses. "But it doesn't matter. You must come and try a glass of this—"

He leads Chaz away before I can ask him any more questions.

"So your friend's sick, huh?" Tiffany slinks over to thrust her concave stomach at me. "That's too bad. I was looking forward to meeting her. Hey, so what's the deal with all these paintings on the walls? Are they real or what?"

"Could you excuse me for a moment please?" I ask Tiffany. "I just have to, um, check the turkey."

She shrugs. "Whatever. Hey, Raoul. You should tell them about that racehorse you owned that one time—"

I hurry into the kitchen, where Luke is trying to find a place to put down the pies—no easy task, considering all the food the granite counters are practically sagging under.

"So what did he say to you?" I stand on tiptoe to hiss in his ear. "Chaz, I mean. About Shari. When he came in?"

Luke just shakes his head. "Not to ask. I think that means—not to ask."

"I have to ask," I sputter. "He can't just come in here without my best friend and say not to ask where she is. Of course I'm going to ask. I mean, what does he think?"

"Well, you asked," Luke says. "What did he say?"

"That she was sick. But that she wasn't at home or at the office. But that doesn't make any sense. Where else could she be? I'm calling her."

"Lizzie." Luke looks helplessly at all the food, some of which is still sizzling on the stove. Then he looks back at me. Something in my expression must have told him not to pursue it, though, since he just says with a shrug, "Go on. I'll start bringing stuff out to the table."

I give him a quick kiss, then hurry over to where my cell phone is charging (my Happy Thanksgiving call to my parents had worn out my battery, since they'd forced me to speak to each of my sisters, their various children, and Grandma, too—who hadn't even wanted to talk to me, as doing so required taking her attention away from the episode of *Nip/Tuck*—"I just adore that Dr. Troy"—she was watching, *Dr. Quinn* apparently not being on yet).

"Uh, I'll be right back," I say to my guests. "I just have to run to the store to get some more, um, cream."

Mrs. de Villiers—the only one, besides Luke, who knows how very, very far it is from her apartment to any store that might be open and selling cream on Thanksgiving Day—looks at me in horror. "Can't we do without?" she wants to know.

"Uh, not if we want whipped cream with our pumpkin pie!" I cry.

And slip out the door. Fortunately, no one even seemed to notice I'm not wearing a coat. Or carrying my purse, for that matter.

As soon as I get to the door to the emergency exit, I start dialing. Inside the stairwell, it's cold . . . but private. And for once I get excellent reception. Shari picks up on the second ring.

"I don't want to talk about it right now," she says. She knew it was me from the caller ID. "Just enjoy your meal. We'll talk about it tomorrow."

"Uh, no, we *won't*," I say. "We'll talk about it right now. Where are you?"

"I'm fine," Shari says. "I'm at Pat's."

"Pat's? Your boss? What are you doing there? You're supposed to be here. Look, Shari, I know you and Chaz had a fight, but you can't leave me alone with all of them like this. Tiffany is wearing a suede BODYSUIT. With a zipper that goes from her throat to her crotch. You can't do this to me."

Shari is laughing. "I'm sorry, Lizzie," she says. "But you're just going to have to fend for yourself. I'm not leaving here."

"Come *on*!" I'm begging, but I don't care. "You guys fight all the time. And you always make up."

"It's not a fight," Shari says. "Listen, Lizzie, we're right in the middle of dinner over here. I'm really sorry. I'll call you tomorrow and explain, okay?"

"Shari, don't be this way. What did he even do this time? I can tell he feels terrible about it. He's already had three scotches, and he only just got here. Just—"

"Lizzie." Shari's voice sounds different. Not sad. Not happy. Just different. "Listen. I'm not coming over. I didn't want to tell you, because I didn't want you to freak out—I want you to enjoy your holiday. But Chaz and I didn't just have a fight, okay? We've broken up. And I moved out."

~ Lizzie Nichols's Wedding Gown Guide ~

Finding the perfect dress for your bridesmaids . . .

I know what you're thinking. You're remembering all the hideous dresses you were forced by your sisters and friends to wear at their weddings, and you want to get revenge by choosing something similarly frightening, and forcing them to wear it.

Well, stop right now.

This is your opportunity to be the bigger person . . . also, to accumulate some good bride karma (and let's face it, all of us can use a little of that).

It is impossible to find a dress that looks good on everyone—unless of course your bridesmaids are all Victoria's Secret models (but even then there are going to be issues over the color of the material. Not even covergirls look good in every shade).

But you can significantly reduce your bridesmaids' angst by:

Picking a dress that flatters the most figure-challenged person in the group. If it looks good on your size-eighteen niece, it will look good on your size-eight roommate. Or—and I know this is radical—give your bridesmaids a color that you know they all look good in (black is flattering to nearly everyone), and ask them to pick their own dresses. True, they won't all match completely. But neither do their personalities. And that's what you love them for anyway, not how they look.

If you really want them to all have the same dress, pick one that they can afford, or pay for all the dresses yourself. Yes, I know—they made you pay for yours when you were *their* bridesmaid, so why should you pay for theirs? But we are RISING above their level, remember? Asking your friends and family to spend three hundred bucks or more on a dress they will never wear again (DO NOT tell yourself that they will. Surrender the fantasy, they WON'T) is unreasonable. Pick one they can all easily afford—or pay for it yourself.

Alterations, alterations, alterations. A good seamstress can fix any number of problems with fit. Employ one. And make sure your bridesmaids get to her in plenty of time for her to make any necessary adjustments.

Your wedding is supposed to be a happy time. One reason some brides have a difficult time with it is because they refuse to be flexible and to think of anyone else's feelings save their own. DO NOT BE THAT BRIDE.

Your bridesmaids will thank you for it.

LIZZIE NICHOLS DESIGNS™

• Chapter 16 •

**What you don't see with your eyes,
don't witness with your mouth.**

—Jewish proverb

I t wasn't any one thing," Shari is telling me over a bubble tea break at a place near where she works called the Village Tea House. I wanted to meet at Honey's. But Shari said she is over dive bars. Which I guess I can understand.

But I sort of prefer red vinyl booths to velvet throw pillows on the floor. And diet Coke to herbal tea with tapioca on the bottom. They don't serve diet Coke at the Village Tea House. I asked. They only serve beverages with "natural" ingredients here.

Like tapioca is natural.

"We just . . . grew apart, I guess," Shari goes on with a shrug.

I am still having trouble processing all of this. About Shari and Chaz breaking up, I mean, and her moving out . . . and missing my Thanksgiving dinner, which, not to brag, turned out pretty darn well.

Well, except for the part where Mrs. de Villiers insisted we all play charades after dinner, and her team of Luke, Tiffany, and herself creamed my team of myself, Chaz (who was so drunk he could barely move), Monsieur de Villiers (who doesn't understand anything about how to play), and Raoul (ditto). Not that I am competitive or anything. I just hate boring party games like that.

Oh, and the part where I had to drag myself to work this morning at Pendergast, Loughlin, and Flynn, even though practically no one called and I was the only one there, except for all the junior partners, of course. And Tiffany, who showed up hungover (of course), claiming she and Raoul went out after leaving my place and "got so wasted" drinking at Butter with a bunch of other models (I don't see how these girls can drink so many high-caloric cocktails, like mojitos and cosmos, and stay so thin).

"I don't understand how you could grow apart," I say to Shari, shaking my head, "when you were *living with* each other. I mean, Chaz's apartment is not all that big."

"I don't know." Shari shrugs again. "I guess I just fell out of love with him."

"It was the curtains, wasn't it?" I can't help asking gloomily.

Shari gapes at me. "What? The curtains you made?"

I nod. "I shouldn't have gone with Chaz's choice of material." Chaz had insisted I make their living room curtains out of a bolt of red satin he'd found in a Chinatown thrift shop. I wouldn't have agreed—I was thinking a muted sage linen—except that the material was embroidered with gold Chinese characters (the clerk at the shop had said they spelled "good luck"), and had such a deliciously kitsch look to it that I agreed with Chaz that it really livened up the place, and that Shari would get a kick out of it.

But when I'd come over to hang the finished curtains, Shari had asked me pointedly if I was trying to make their apartment look like Lung Cheung, the neighborhood Chinese restaurant where we used to eat as kids back in Ann Arbor.

"No, of course it wasn't the curtains," Shari says with a laugh. "Although with the gold couches, they do sort of make the place look like a bordello."

I groan. "We really thought you'd like it."

"Listen, Lizzie. It wouldn't have mattered what anybody did to that place. I was never going to like living there. Because I didn't like who I was when I was living there."

"Well, maybe this is a good thing, then," I say. I'm trying to put a positive slant on things, I know. But Chaz was so devastated by Shari's moving out, it's hard not to want to see him happy again . . . even if Shari doesn't look all that devastated herself. In fact, Shari looks better than I've seen her since we moved to New York. She's even got on some makeup, for a change.

"Maybe some time apart will help you guys to figure out what went wrong," I say. "And make you appreciate what you had more. Like . . . you two could start dating again! Maybe that's what went wrong in the first place. When you're living with someone, you kind of stop dating. And that can take all the romance out of the relationship." You know what else can take all the romance out of a relationship? Sleeping on a pull-out couch with your boyfriend's parents in the next room. But I don't mention this.

"But maybe if you guys are *dating*," I go on, "the fire of your love will be reignited, and you'll get back together."

"I am never getting back together with Chaz, Lizzie," Shari says, calmly removing her tea bag from her mug and laying it on the side of the earthenware plate we've been provided for this purpose.

"You never know," I say. "I mean, a little time apart might actually make you miss him."

"Then I'll just call him," Shari says. "I still want to be friends with him. He's an amazing, funny guy. But I don't want to be his girlfriend anymore."

"Was it all the cookies?" I ask. "You know, that he doesn't have a job, and had nothing to do all day but read and bake and clean and stuff?" Which actually sounds like a dream existence to me. With all the work I'm being saddled with—Monsieur Henri has me practicing ruching . . . like I didn't master the art of ruching in eighth grade, when I realized ruching hides a less-than-flat tummy. I'm getting a little tired of playing Sewing Kid to Monsieur Henri's Mister Miyagi—I barely have time to run the vacuum once in a while, let alone do any baking.

On the other hand, I *am* learning a lot. Mostly about the challenges of parenting teen boys in the new millennium. But also about running a bridal-design business in Manhattan.

"Of course not," Shari says. "Although speaking of jobs, I should be getting back to mine soon."

"Just five more minutes," I beg. "I'm really worried about you, Shari. I mean, I know you can take care of yourself, and all of that, but I still can't help feeling like this is all my fault. If I had just moved in with you and not Luke, like we were supposed to—"

"Oh, please," Shari says with a laugh. "Chaz and I breaking up had nothing to do with you, Lizzie."

"I let you down," I said. "And for that, I am so, so sorry. But I think I can make it up to you."

Shari's straw hits the tapioca at the bottom of her mug. "Oh, this ought to be good," she says, about my offer to make it up to her. Not about the tapioca. Although Shari has always loved stuff like that.

"Seriously," I say. "Did you know that there's an empty apartment just sitting above Monsieur Henri's?"

Shari keeps on slurping. "Go on."

"Now, I know Madame Henri wants two thousand a month for it. But I have seriously been doing so much work for them—they're totally dependent on me at this point. So if I ask them to let you live in the apartment at a reduced rate—say, fifteen hundred a month—they'll have to say yes. They'll just HAVE to."

"Thanks, Lizzie," Shari says, putting down her mug and reaching for her raffia slouch bag. "But I've got a place."

"At Pat's? Living with your *boss*?" I shake my head. "Shari, come on. Talk about taking your work home with you—"

"It's actually pretty cool," Shari says. "She has a ground-floor place in Park Slope, with an actual yard in the back, for her dogs—"

"Brooklyn!" I'm shocked. "Shari, that's so far!"

"It's actually a straight shot on the F," Shari says. "The stop is right outside where I work."

"I mean from me!" I practically yell. "I'll never see you anymore!"

"You're seeing me now," Shari says.

"I mean at night," I say. "Look, won't you let me at least talk to the Henris about you possibly moving into the place above the shop? I've seen it, and it's really cute, Shari. And pretty big. Considering. It's on the top floor, and the place below it is just used for storage. You'd have the whole building to yourself after work hours. And one whole wall is exposed brick. You know how much you love that look."

"Lizzie, don't worry about me," Shari says. "I'm good, really. I know this whole thing with Chaz seems like the end of the world to you. But it's not to me. It's really not. I'm happy, Lizzie."

And just like that, it hits me. Shari really *is* happy. Happier than I've seen her since we moved to New York. Happier, really, than I've seen her since college. Happier than I've seen her since those early days back at McCracken Hall, when she first started going out with (or sleeping with, basically) Chaz.

"Oh my God," I say, as reality finally sinks in. "There's someone else!"

Shari looks up from her bag, which she's digging through to find her wallet. "What?" She looks at me strangely.

"There's someone else," I cry. "That's why you say you and Chaz are never going to get back together. Because you've met someone else!"

Shari stops looking for her wallet and stares at me. "Lizzie, I—"

But even in the winter afternoon light, spilling in through the Village Tea House's less-than-clean windows, I can see the blush slowly suffusing her cheeks.

"And you're in love with him!" I cry. "Oh my God, I can't believe it! You're sleeping with him, too, aren't you? I can't believe you're sleeping with someone I haven't even met. Okay, who is he? Spill. I want all the details."

Shari looks uncomfortable. "Lizzie, look. I have to get back to work."

"That's where you met him, isn't it?" I demand. "At work? Who is he? You've never mentioned a guy at work. I thought it was all women. What is he, like the copier repairman or something?"

"Lizzie." Shari isn't blushing anymore. Instead, she's gone kind of pale. "This really isn't how I wanted to do this."

"Do what?" I stir the tapioca at the bottom of my mug. I am totally not eating it. Talk about empty carbs. Wait—does tapioca even have carbs? What *is* tapioca, anyway? A grain? Or a gelatin? Or what? "Come on. You've only been gone from work for like ten minutes. No one's going to die if you're gone five minutes more."

"Actually," Shari says. "Someone might."

"Come on," I say again. "Just admit I'm right, and that there's someone else. Just say it. I'm not going to believe you're really over Chaz until I hear you say it."

Shari, her lips set in a straight line, stabs at her tapioca with her straw. "All right," she says, her voice so soft I can barely hear her above the pan flute music they're playing over the speakers in every corner of the tea shop. "There's someone else."

"I'm sorry," I say. "I couldn't hear you. Would you mind repeating that a little louder, please?"

"There's someone else," Shari says, glaring at me. "I'm in love with someone else. There. Are you satisfied?"

"No," I say. "Details, please."

"I told you," Shari says, diving back into her bag and pulling a ten-dollar bill from her wallet. "I don't want to do this now."

"Do what?" I demand, grabbing my coat as she shrugs into hers and clambers to her feet. "Tell your best friend about the guy you just dumped your long-term boyfriend for? When would be a good time to do it? I'm just wondering."

"Not now," Shari says. She's picking her way past floor pillows on which our fellow tea-drinkers are sitting. "Not when I have to get back to work."

"Tell me on the way," I say. "I'll walk you back."

We reach the door and step out into the cold winter air. A semitrailer barrels by on Bleecker Street, followed by a stream of cabs. The sidewalk is crowded with busy shoppers taking advantage of the Black Friday sales. Somewhere in this city, Luke is being dragged in and out of museums by his father, and Mrs. de Villiers is having her clandestine meeting with her lover.

Apparently, she isn't the only one who's been up to clandestine meetings.

Shari is uncharacteristically silent on our walk back to her office. Head ducked, she keeps her gaze on her feet . . . which is actually important to do in New York City, what with so many of the sidewalks being in such a sorry state of disrepair.

She's clearly upset. And I'm upset that I've upset her.

"Look, Share," I say, trotting along behind her. She's walking about a million miles an hour. "I'm sorry. I didn't mean to make light of the situation. Honest. I'm happy for you. If you're happy, I'm happy."

Shari stops walking so abruptly, I practically run into her.

"I'm happy," she says, looking down at me. She's standing on the curb and I'm in the gutter. "I'm happier than I've ever been. For the first time in my life, I feel like I'm living with purpose—like what I do has meaning. I'm helping people—people who need me. And I like that feeling. It's the best feeling in the world."

"Well," I say. "That's great. Could you let me up on the sidewalk, though? Because I'm afraid I'm gonna get run over."

Shari reaches down and pulls me by the arm up onto the sidewalk beside her. "And you're right," she says. "I *am* in love. And I want to tell you all about it. Because that's a big part of why I'm so happy right now, too."

"Cool," I say. "So spill."

"I don't even know where to start," Shari says, her eyes shining—and not just because it's cold enough out to make them water.

"Well, how about a name?"

"Pat," she says.

"The guy you're in love with is named Pat?" I laugh. "How weird! That's your boss's name!"

"The girl," Shari corrects me.

"The girl what?"

"The *girl* I'm in love with," Shari says. "*Her* name is Pat."

Know your . . .
Wedding-veil lengths!

Shoulder—This veil just brushes—what else?—your shoulders. Remember, the taller the bride, the longer the veil should be. This length not recommended for petite brides.

Elbow—This veil extends to just past your elbows. The more detailed your dress, the simpler you want to keep your veil.

Fingertip—The ends of this veil hit you just at mid-thigh, or fingertip length. The longer the veil, the more attention is taken away from the bride's midsection. So this length is recommended for fuller-figured brides.

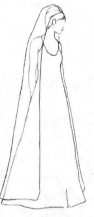

Ballet—The ballet length veil extends to the ankles (presumably this veil got its name for being a longer veil that brides still needn't worry about tripping over).

Chapel—This veil sweeps the floor, and sometimes drags upon it. If you choose this length, please practice walking in it before the ceremony, to avoid any veil-snagging disasters.

Lizzie Nichols Designs™

Chapter 17

There are a terrible lot of lies going about the world, and the worst of it is that half of them are true.

—*Winston Churchill (1874–1965), British statesman*

can't sleep.

And it's not just the metal bar cutting into the middle of my back through the inadequately thin sofa bed mattress beneath me, either.

Or the fact that I can hear my boyfriend's father snoring, even though he's separated from me by several dozen feet and a wall.

It's not even the slight traffic noises I can hear through the double-paned windows overlooking Fifth Avenue.

It doesn't have anything to do with the incredibly rich meal I just had at Jean Georges, one of New York's premier destination restaurants for gourmands, which cost as much as twenty yards of dupioni silk . . . per *person*.

Or even with the fact that my boyfriend's mother came back from her day of Black Friday "shopping" loaded down with plenty of gift bags but looking oddly vital and glowing . . . especially for a woman who'd allegedly just slogged through the pre-Christmas hordes at Bergdorf Goodman. It wasn't just my imagination, either. Her husband kept looking at her and going, "What is different? You have done something different! Is it your hair?"

In response to which Bibi de Villiers merely called him an old goat (in French) and waved him away.

And it isn't even that my boyfriend and I are going to be on two different continents during our first New Year's Eve as a couple, missing that vital Happy New Year stroke-of-midnight kiss.

No. It's not any of those things. I know that. I know what's keeping me up—I know it perfectly well.

It's the fact that earlier today (or yesterday, I guess, considering it's well after midnight by now), my best friend announced that she's in love with her boss.

Her female boss.

And get this: her boss loves her back. Even asked her to move in.

And Shari was happy to oblige.

Not that there's anything wrong with that. I mean, I love Rosie O'Donnell. That documentary about her gay cruise ship line totally made me cry.

And I think Ellen DeGeneres is a goddess, too.

But my best friend, who has always, by the way, liked GUYS? Not just LIKED guys, but has always SLEPT WITH guys—way more guys than me, I might add—and who has never expressed sexual interest in a woman the whole time I've known her?

Well, except for that girl Brianna in the dorm.

But Shari was really drunk that night and said she just woke up with Brianna in her bed and no idea how she got there.

Wait. Was that a sign? Because Brianna (and her boyfriend, actually) was always hitting on me. But I just told her I wasn't interested. Why didn't Shari just say she wasn't interested, like I always did?

Although Lord knows I've never drunk as much as Shari (she can afford the empty calories. I can't).

Still.

But wait. Shari always did like those foreign films at the Michigan Theater in Ann Arbor. You know, the French ones about young girls coming of age sexually, usually with another, older girl as their mentor, or whatever.

God. That was a sign, too.

And now that I think of it, there was that time Kathy Penne-baker—God. It always goes back to Kathy Pennebaker, doesn't it?—invited us over to a slumber party, then wanted to take a group bubble bath. I was like, "Um, aren't we a little old for a group bubble bath—at *sixteen*?"

But Shari, if I recall correctly, actually *joined* Kathy in her parents' bathroom, while I stayed downstairs to watch my then-crush, Tim Daly, on a *Wings* marathon.

God. I'd *wondered* what all that splashing had been about. I even yelled up the stairs for them to keep it down, because I couldn't hear what Tim was saying to Crystal Bernard.

Jeez. How embarrassing.

So, okay. I shouldn't have been so surprised.

And I guess, considering how much Shari has been talking about Pat, it isn't *that* surprising. I mean, we all knew she liked her. We just didn't know she LIKE liked her.

And what's not to like? Because, after Shari dropped her little bomb, and I stood there on the curb with my mouth hanging open like an idiot, Shari grabbed my hand and said, "Come meet her."

I was too stunned to resist. Not that I'd wanted to. I was completely curious to meet this person for whom Shari had dumped Chaz, the previous love of her life.

And, okay, Pat is no Portia de Rossi.

But she's a slender, vibrant woman in her early thirties, with a cascade of bright red ringlets going down her back, and skin the color of milk, with a quick laugh and bright, twinkling blue eyes.

She shook my hand and said she'd heard a lot about me and that she supposed hearing about her and Shari was a shock, but that she loved Shari very much, and, more important, her dogs, Scooter and Jethro, seemed to love Shari very much.

To which I didn't know what to say, except that I'd like to meet Scooter and Jethro someday.

So Shari and her new girlfriend invited me over to watch the Jets game next weekend.

I seriously don't know which is more shocking to me: that my best friend is in love with a girl, or that she's started watching professional football.

In any case, I said I'd be there. And then Shari walked me to the elevator.

"Are you sure you're okay about this?" Shari wanted to know, as we waited for the rickety two-person lift to arrive. "Because you look kinda . . . well, the way you looked that day Andy showed up at Luke's cousin's wedding."

"I'm sorry," I said. "Because I don't feel that way at all. I'm totally happy for you. That's all. I just . . . how long have you known?"

"How long have I known what?"

"You know. That you like girls."

"I don't," Shari said with a smile. "I like *some* girls. Just like I like *some* guys. Just like *you* like *some* guys." Her smile faded, and she added seriously, "It's about the person's soul, Lizzie, not the parts they have on the outside. You know that."

I'd nodded. Because that's true. At least, that's how it's supposed to be.

"I don't love Pat because she's a woman," Shari went on, "any more than I loved Chaz because he's a man. I love them both for who they are on the inside. It's just that I realized the one I'm most romantically interested in is Pat. Possibly because she doesn't leave the toilet seat up."

I stared at her until Shari nudged me. "That was a joke," she said. "It's okay for you to laugh."

"Oh," I said. And laughed. But then my laughter faded as I thought about something else.

"Shari," I said. "What about your mom and dad? Have you told them yet?"

"No," Shari said. "That's a conversation best saved for the next time I see them in person. Christmas vacation, I think."

"Are you going to take Pat to meet them?"

"She wants to go," Shari says. "But I'm trying to spare her. Maybe after they've gotten used to the idea."

"Right," I said. I tried to push down the spurt of jealousy I felt that Shari's girlfriend actually *wants* to meet her parents, whereas my boyfriend has expressed not the slightest iota of interest in meeting mine. There were much more important things to take under consideration, after all. Like, I couldn't even imagine how Dr. and Mrs. Dennis were going to react to the news that their daughter is in a romantic relationship with a woman. Dr. Dennis will probably head straight to his liquor cabinet. Mrs. Dennis will head straight to the phone.

"Oh God!" I'd stared at Shari, wide-eyed. "You know what's going to happen, don't you? Your mom is going to call my mom. And then my mom is going to find out I'm not actually living with you anymore. And then she'll know I'm living with Luke."

"She'll probably just be grateful," Shari said, "that you and I aren't a couple."

"Yeah." My shoulders sagged with relief. "You're probably right about that. Hey—" I glanced at her in some alarm. "We're not, are we? I mean . . . you never felt about *me* the way you feel about Pat, did you?"

Please say no, I was praying. *Please say no, please say no. Because I value Shari's friendship more than anything, and if it turned out she was in love with me, well, how could we be friends anymore? You can't be friends with someone who's in love with you if you don't love that person back the same way . . .*

Shari regarded me with an expression I might almost have called sarcastic.

"Yes, Lizzie," she said. "I have been in love with you since the first grade when you showed me your Batgirl Underoos. The only reason I'm with Pat is because I know I can't have you because you stubbornly refuse to love me and not Luke. Now come over here and kiss me, you little minx."

I blinked at her. And she burst out laughing.

"No, you idiot," she said. "Although I love you dearly as a friend, I have never been romantically interested in you. You're actually not my type."

I don't want to sound pejorative, but her tone seemed to imply that she couldn't understand why *anyone* would be interested in me romantically.

I didn't say so at the time, but I was kind of wondering the same thing. I mean, doesn't Pat realize that Shari is an inveterate blanket hog (as I discovered to my disadvantage when we were forced to share a sleeping bag at camp that time those mean girls threw mine in the lake) and has, to my knowledge, never once returned a book she borrowed? It was a miracle that Chaz, a known bibliophile, even put up with her as long as he did. I purposely never loaned Shari my clothing, because I knew I'd never see it again.

Of course Shari never asked to borrow any of my clothing. My style is just a little too retro for her, I guess.

But, whatever.

"You have a type?" I asked her with a raised eyebrow. "Because you seem to cover a pretty wide range—"

"Primarily," Shari interrupted, "I like people who can keep their mouths shut once in a while."

"Well, then, it's no wonder you and Chaz broke up," I said, just as the elevator, groaning with the strain, finally arrived.

"Ha ha," Shari said. Then, giving me a hug, she said, "Take care of him for me, will you? Don't let him slide into one of his funks where he stays inside all day reading Heidegger and never ventures out except to buy booze. Promise?"

"Like you have to ask," I said. "I love Chaz like the brother I never had. I'll make sure to get Tiffany to invite him out with her and some of her model friends. That should cheer him up."

"That ought to do it, all right," Shari agreed.

And the elevator doors closed and she was gone.

And that was that.

Well, except for the part where now I can't sleep a wink, because I keep replaying it all over and over in my head.

"Hey." The word, spoken so softly beside me, causes me to jump. I turn my head. Luke is awake, and blinking at me sleepily.

"Sorry," I whisper. "Did I wake you?" I hadn't been making any noise. Had I managed to wake him with my noisy thoughts? I've read that couples can become so close that they can read each other's minds. *Ask me to marry you, Luke. Luke, ask me to marry you. Luke. I am your father . . .* Oh no, wait—

"No," he says. "It's this damn metal bar—"

"Oh yeah. It's killing me, too."

"Sorry about this," Luke says with a sigh. "We just have to put up with them for one more night and then they'll be gone."

"It's all right," I say. I can't believe he's worrying about me when he has something so much bigger to worry about—his mother's secret affair, I mean.

Except of course he doesn't know about that. Because I haven't told him. How can I? He's so happy his parents are back together.

And something like that could totally sour him against marriage forever. I mean, what if he concludes, from his mother's catting about—not to mention Shari's recent abandonment of Chaz, and his own ex-girlfriend's leaving him for his own *cousin*—that women are incapable of fidelity?

And things between us have been going so well—familial visitations aside. Even having Tiffany and Raoul to Thanksgiving dinner didn't prove the disaster I thought it would, as they provided a welcome distraction for Chaz, who seemed to take great pleasure in watching Tiffany gad about in her thigh-highs and catsuit—I really think Luke might have forgotten all about that whole "people our age don't even know what love is" thing.

Maybe I'll even be getting an extraspecial present for Christmas. The kind that comes in a very small box.

Hey. You never know.

"Well," Luke says, his lips suddenly in my hair, "I think you're a trouper. You've gone above and beyond the call of duty. And hey—did I mention that turkey you made was delicious?"

"Oh," I say modestly. "Thanks."

Well? He doesn't need to know it came already cooked.

"I think you're a keeper, Lizzie Nichols," he says, his lips now moving lower than my hair, and toward some other parts of my body that can appreciate lips more than hair.

"Oh," I say in a different voice. "Thanks!" A keeper! Why, that's *practically* a marriage proposal. Calling someone a keeper is like saying you never want to throw them back into the dating pool for someone else to snatch instead. Right?

"And you're sure," he says, from down there, "that you and Shari never—"

I sit up and glare at him in the darkened room. "Luke! I told you! No!"

"Whatever!" he says with a laugh. "I'm just asking. You know Chaz is going to ask, too."

"I told you." I can't believe this. "You can't say anything to Chaz. Not until Shari's told him. I wasn't even supposed to say anything to you—"

Luke laughs—not very nicely, I might add. "*Shari* told you something and asked you to keep it a secret?"

"I *am* capable of keeping some things to myself, you know," I say indignantly. Because, seriously . . . if he only knew what I've been keeping to myself since I moved in.

"I know," he says with a laugh. "I'm just teasing you. Don't worry, I won't say anything to him. But you know what Chaz is going to say."

"What?" I ask, relenting—but only because he looks so handsome in the moonlight spilling in from the windows.

"That if Shari was going to decide to become a lesbian, why did she have to do it *after* they'd broken up?"

I yank the sheet up over the parts of my body he seems to be finding so interesting.

"For your information," I say, "Shari is not a lesbian."

"Bi, lesbian. Whatever. What's with this?" He tugs at the sheet.

"What's with the labels?" I demand, tugging back. "Why do people have to be defined by their sexual preference? Can't Shari just be Shari?"

"Sure," Luke says, looking taken aback. "Why are you being so defensive about this?"

"Because," I say. "I don't want people to call Shari my 'lesbian friend.' And I'm sure she doesn't, either. Well, actually, I'm sure Shari doesn't care. But that's not the point. She's just Shari. I don't call Chaz your 'heterosexual friend.'"

"Fine," Luke says. "I'm sorry. I've never had my best friend's girl-friend ditch him for another girl before. I'm a little confused at the moment."

"Welcome to the club," I say.

Luke rolls over to stare at the ceiling.

"Obviously," he says after a moment's silence, "there's only one thing we can do."

"What?" I ask suspiciously.

He shows me.

And, in the end, I have to admit—he has a point.

Which he makes—nice and emphatically, I might add.

Feeling the glove . . .

Some brides opt for a more formal look by donning gloves on the big day. Gloves come in many lengths, and can be the perfect accessory for the fashion conscious or merely traditional bride. They have a practical use, as well—brides who wear gloves certainly needn't worry about their manicure . . . or smearing their own messy fingerprints on their pure white gown.

The most common types of bridal gloves are:

Opera Length—These long white gloves stretch from the fingertips to the upper arm.

Elbow length—Like the opera length, only these end just above the elbow.

Gauntlet—These kinds of gloves are hand-and-fingerless, covering only the forearm.

Fingerless—Just like the lace ones Madonna used to wear. Or the woolly ones Bob Cratchitt is often pictured wearing.

Wrist—These gloves cover the hand only, like ski gloves.

Gloves should be removed for the ring part of the ceremony (it is considered ill-bred to wear rings OVER glove fingers. If your glove does not open at the wrist, cut a small hole beneath the wedding finger of your left-hand glove so you can easily wiggle your finger through to receive the ring) and of course while dining.

Brides with very muscular arms or those wearing long sleeves should avoid gloves altogether.

• Chapter 18 •

No one gossips about other people's secret virtues.

—Bertrand Russell (1872–1970), British philosopher

The Monday after Thanksgiving, we got slammed at the Pendergast, Loughlin, and Flynn reception desk. I don't know if there have ever been any official studies on this, but I would say, just judging from my own observations, divorce requests definitely go up after a long holiday weekend.

A sentiment with which I could actually sympathize, having spent mine with the de Villierses . . . who are all very charming people, but not without their annoying quirks. Like Mrs. de Villiers's annoying quirk of talking about Dominique, Luke's ex, and how happy she and Blaine, Luke's cousin, are. Apparently Dominique is doing a great job managing Blaine's financial affairs . . . and he needs the help, because his band, Satan's Shadow, is superhot on the indie metal circuit.

Another hot topic of conversation for Mrs. de Villiers is Blaine's sister's pregnancy. Vickie isn't even due until the spring and doesn't even know the baby's sex yet, but Luke's mother is already buying tiny onesies and booties and cooing over how much she can't wait to have a grandchild of her own, making Luke look extremely uncomfortable and putting back my woodland-creaturing of him weeks, possibly even months.

And Mr. de Villiers's annoying quirk wasn't much better. His was not looking where he's going and consequently putting his foot through my Singer 5050—which I purposely moved from the dressing table to the floor beneath my hanging rack, thinking no one would trip over it there, since there was a metal bar in the way.

And yet somehow Luke's father managed to destroy it . . . or at least the bobbin.

He apologized profusely and offered to pay for a new one. But I told him it was all right, that the machine was old and I'd been intending to get a new one anyway.

I swear I don't know where some of the things that come out of my mouth even come from.

Anyway, they're gone. They left Sunday afternoon, after much kissing and talk of all the fun they're going to have at Château Mirac over Christmas and New Year's. Of course, they pressured me to come along, but I could tell they didn't really mean it. Well, Luke did, of course. And maybe his dad did.

But his mom? Not so much? The smile she gave me as she said, "Oh, do come, Lizzie, it will be such fun," didn't go all the way up to her eyes. They didn't crinkle at the sides like they normally did when she smiles.

No. I know where I'm not wanted. And that's at the de Villierses' familial holiday celebration in France.

Which is fine. It is. It's totally cool. I explained I only had the long weekend off anyway, which I'd be spending flying home to see my parents, before returning to work on Monday.

I don't think it's my imagination that Mrs. de Villiers looked kind of relieved about that. I mean, that she was getting her son all to herself.

Which you would think she'd realize makes the grandchild production thing kind of difficult. But maybe she has other candidates in mind . . . ones who aren't working two jobs, one of them nonpaying, and the other hardly worth bragging to her girlfriends about. I mean, a receptionist? So not as glamorous, say, as an investment banker or market analyst . . .

Especially not the Monday after Thanksgiving, when everybody and their mother seems to want a divorce lawyer. Tiffany says the only busier time in the office is right after New Year's, which is when a lot of proposals take place, so people want to come in for their prenups.

I've said, "Pendergast, Loughlin, and Flynn, how may I direct your call?" so many times, my throat is getting sore, and I'm starting to rasp a little. Fortunately, Tiffany has come in early (as usual) to shoot the breeze, and is willing to spell me for a few minutes while I run to the ladies' room to spray a little Chloraseptic down my throat.

"So Raoul says he can get your friend Shari in to see his internist," Tiffany says, as she takes my chair. "You know, if she's still sick. Is she still sick?"

"She's not sick," I say, opening my drawer and pulling out my Meyers handbag—which barely fits in there, thanks to the back issues of *Vogue* which Tiffany insists on saving. "She and Chaz broke up."

"They did?" Tiffany swings her wide, blue-eyed gaze up at me. "Right before your party? God, no wonder he said she was sick. How totally embarrassing. So is one of them moving out? Which one? Oh my God, why didn't you *tell* me?"

Because I've been trying really hard not to mention anything about it to anyone—especially people like Tiffany who could conceivably say something to Chaz's father. Obviously Luke knows, but he's the only person I've told. I'm really trying not to be such a gossip these days. Shari asked me not to say anything to anyone until she'd had a chance to speak to Chaz about it—which I hope to God she has, because I don't know how much longer I can keep from saying anything to him when he calls the office to return his father's phone calls. Between that and the thing about Luke's mom, I am BURSTING with secrets.

And it's driving me mental.

"I don't know," I say. "Look, let me just go spray my throat and I'll be right back—"

Tiffany doesn't get a chance to reply, though, because the phone chirps and she has to grab it. "Pendergast, Loughlin, and Flynn, how may I direct your call?"

The ladies' room of the law offices is actually situated outside the lobby, by the elevator doors. To get in, you have to punch in a code. This is not to keep random tourists from wandering in off the street to use the Pendergast, Loughlin, and Flynn bathrooms, since for one thing random tourists can't even get into the building without an appointment and passing a security screening. I don't actually know why all the offices in this building keep the doors to their ladies' (and men's. The management of this building is not sexist) rooms locked, and require a code to enter.

In any case, one of the duties of the receptionist at Pendergast, Loughlin, and Flynn is to give the code to any clients or visiting lawyers who ask for it. The code is very easy to remember: 1-2-3.

And yet some clients (and lawyers) have to be given the code two, even three times before they retain it. This can be annoying to the receptionist, though of course we never show it. Still, it makes me wonder why we need the lock at all, since in all the time I've been using the ladies' room at Pendergast, Loughlin, and Flynn, no one has ever been in it at the same time I have. It's the most underused bathroom in all of New York.

The day I go in to spray my throat (and put on a little lipstick and fluff up my hair) is no exception. I'm alone in the very clean, very beige bathroom. I'm gazing at my reflection in the huge mirror hanging above the sinks, grateful that last night I finally got to sleep in my own (well, Luke's mother's own) bed, instead of on the pull-out couch, because the bags under my eyes from tossing and turning around so much are finally starting to fade. I swear, when I am a certified wedding-gown specialist with my own shop, and I finally have some money to spare, I am going to buy one of those Pottery Barn pull-out couches that don't have the metal bar across the middle, that are actually comfortable.

Well, first I'm going to buy my own apartment so I actually have a place to keep my stuff where it won't get tripped over and broken.

Then I'm buying the couch.

And I probably won't even have to worry about ever sleeping on it again, because the next time Luke's parents come to visit, they can just stay at Luke's mother's apartment, and not mine—

It's as I'm enjoying this lovely fantasy that I hear something. At first I think it's just the heel of my shoe on the tiles beneath me. But then I realize I'm not alone in the Pendergast, Loughlin, and Flynn ladies' room. The door to the last stall is closed.

I'm about to sneak away to give the person some privacy when I hear the noise again. It's kind of a whimpering noise. Like a little kitten.

Or someone crying.

I duck down to see if I recognize the person's shoes beneath the stall door. Instantly I realize I'm looking at the feet of Jill Higgins, New York's current most famous bride-to-be. Because on those feet are a pair of Timberlands.

And nobody wears Timberlands to Pendergast, Loughlin, and Flynn but Jill.

Who is apparently taking a break in the bathroom to cry for a while before her next appointment with Chaz's dad.

I know, as an employee of the firm, I should quietly leave the ladies' room, and pretend like I never heard what I'm hearing.

But as a not-yet-certified wedding-gown specialist—and more important, a girl who knows what it's like to be constantly ragged upon (as my sisters have ragged upon me for my entire existence)—I can't just turn and walk away. Especially since I know—I just know—I can help her. I really can.

Which would explain why I walk over to the door of her stall and quietly tap on it—although I'll admit, my heart was thumping. I really need this job, after all.

"Um ... Miss Higgins?" I call through the stall door. "It's me, Lizzie. The receptionist?"

"Oh ..."

I've never heard so much emotion piled into a single word. That "oh" is laden with fear—I guess about what I'm going to say or do, having caught John MacDowell's fiancée weeping in the bathroom. Am I going to call the press? Pass her a box of Kleenex? Run and get Esther? What?—regret, self-loathing, embarrassment, and even what sounds like a healthy dose of mortification.

"It's okay," I say through the door. "I mean, I sometimes feel like crying in here myself. In fact, most days."

This elicits a burble of laughter from the woman in the stall. But it's a tearful burble.

"Do you want me to get you something?" I ask. "Like tissues? Or a diet Coke?" I don't know why I thought she might want the latter. It's just that a nice cold diet Coke always makes me feel better. Except hardly anyone ever offers me one.

"No-oo-oo," Jill says in a tremulous voice. "I'm okay. I think. It's just—"

And before I know it, she's off—*really* crying this time, in big huge gasping baby sobs.

"Whoa," I say. Because I know what it's like to cry like that. I've been there. I've done that.

And I know there's only one thing that ever makes me feel better when I've got that big a crying jag going on.

"Hang on," I say to Jill through the stall door. "I'll be right back."

I run out of the bathroom. Then, so as to avoid Tiffany (who, after all, is probably wondering what happened to me. Especially since she doesn't technically start work for half an hour, and I've left her sitting in my chair, answering all the calls that I should be picking up), I zip through the locked back door to the office (code to get in: 1-2-3), and hurry into the Pendergast, Loughlin, and Flynn kitchen.

There, I seize an armful of items—under the watchful gaze of an intern on a coffee break—and hurry back to the ladies' room, where I find Jill still lustily weeping.

"Hang on," I say, setting my armful of pilfered treats down on the counter by the sinks. "I'm coming." I survey the assortment before me. I really don't have time to make a careful selection. I can see that urgent help is needed, and right away. I grab the first plastic-wrapped confection I see, and kneel down beside the stall to hand it through the gap beneath the door.

"Here," I say. "Drake's Yodels. Dig in."

There is stunned silence for a moment. I wonder if maybe I have just committed a huge faux pas. But hey, when I cry, Shari always gives me chocolate. And it makes me feel better *immediately*.

Well, maybe not immediately, but eventually.

But maybe Jill's problems are so huge that it's going to take more than just a Yodel to make her feel better.

"Th-thank you," she says. And the snack cake (although, really, if you ask me Yodels are more of a dessert than a snack) disappears from my hand. A second later I hear plastic crinkling.

"Do you want some milk with that?" I ask. "I have both whole and two percent. There was skim, too, but, well, you know. Also, I have a diet Coke. And a regular Coke, if you need the sugar."

More crinkling. Then I hear a tearful, "Regular Coke would be good."

I crack the can open for her, then pass it beneath the stall door.

"Th-thanks," Jill says.

For a moment there's no sound except soft slurping. Then Jill says, "Do you have any more Yodels?"

"Of course I do," I say soothingly. "And Devil Dogs, too."

"Yodels, please," she says.

I pass another one under the stall door.

"You know," I say conversationally. "If it's any consolation, I know what you're going through. Well, I mean, not *exactly*, but, you know, I work with a lot of brides. Most of them aren't under the kind of pressure you are, of course. But, you know. Getting married is *always* a little stressful."

"Oh, yeah?" Jill asks with a bitter laugh. "Do all their future mother-in-laws hate them the way mine hates me?"

"Not all of them," I say. I've helped myself to a Devil Dog. Just the creamy filling inside, though. It's less carbs than the cake part. I think. "What's up with yours?"

"Oh, you mean besides the part where she thinks I'm a gold digger out to rob her son of his rightful inheritance?" I hear more crinkling plastic. "Where do I start?"

"You know," I say. *Don't do it*, a voice inside my head is saying. *Do not do it. It's not worth it.*

But a different voice is telling me that it is my duty, as a woman, to help, and that I cannot let a girl who has suffered as much as this one has to continue to wallow in misery . . . especially when she doesn't *have* to.

"When I said I work with a lot of brides, I didn't mean here," I go on. "I mean, not *just* here. I'm actually a certified wedding-gown specialist. Well, *I'm* not. I mean, I'm not certified. Yet. But I work with someone who is. Anyway, my specialty is restoring vintage or antique gowns, and refurbishing them to fit modern brides. Just in case that information is at all helpful to you."

For a second, there is no sound from the stall. Then I hear some more crinkling. Then the toilet flushes. A second later, the stall door opens and Jill, looking red-eyed and pink-faced, her hair a blowsy mess, with Yodel crumbs all over the front of her woolly sweater, comes out, staring at me warily.

"Are you kidding me with this?" she demands, not in what you would call a teasing or even friendly manner.

Oops.

"Look," I say, straightening up from where I've been leaning against the bathroom wall. "I'm sorry. I just heard, you know, through the grapevine, that your future mother-in-law was trying to make you wear some dress that's been handed down in their family for generations or something. And I just wanted to let you know that—you know. I can help."

Jill is blinking at me, her expression devoid of any emotion whatsoever. She's not wearing any makeup, I notice. But then she's one of those healthy, outdoorsy girls who can get away with it.

"Not just me, I mean," I add hastily. "Lots of people can help, this whole town is filled with people who can help. Just don't go to this one guy, Maurice? Because he'll just charge you a lot and he won't actually fix it. The gown, I mean. Monsieur Henri—that's where I work—is the place to go. Because, you know, we don't use chemicals or anything like that. And we care."

Jill blinks at me some more. "You *care*?" she repeats, sounding incredulous.

"Well, yeah," I say, realizing—a little belatedly—how I must sound to her. Because it isn't as if she isn't hounded all day by people who want something from her—the press, for a quote or a photo; the public, for what it's like to be engaged to one of the richest bachelors in New York; even her beloved seals, the ones she's willing to throw out her back for, are probably always after her for fish. Or whatever it is the seals in the Central Park Zoo eat.

"Look," I say. "I know you're going through a rotten time right now, and it must seem like everybody and his brother wants a piece of you or whatever. But I swear that's not why I'm telling you this. Vintage clothing—it's my life. I mean, you can see what I have on, right?" I point at the dress I'm wearing. "This is a rare long-sleeved, kimono-style dress from the 1960s by the designer Alfred Shaheen, who was better known for his authentic South Seas designs—basically Hawaiian shirts—but who also made some hand-screened Asian prints as well. This dress is a fantastic example of his work—see the wide, obi-style belt? Which is actually a good look for me, because I have more of a pear shape, you know, so I want to emphasize my waistline and not my hips so much? Anyway, this dress was in pretty bad shape when I found it in the bottom of the dollar bin at the place where I used to work back in Ann Arbor, Vintage to Vavoom. It had this really gross stain on it—grape jelly, I think—and it was actually floor length because I think it was meant to be a hostess dress. And it was way too big for me in the boobs. But I just threw it in a pot of boiling water and gave it a good soak, then I dried it out, cut it off to mid-knee, hemmed it, redid the darts, and, boom."

I do a little pivot for her, the way Tiffany had taught me to.

"And now I've got what you see here. What I'm trying to say"—I pivot over to where she's standing, gaping at me—"is that I know how to take someone else's trash and turn it into treasure. And that if you want me to, I can do it for you. Because what would stick it to your future mother-in-law more than you walking down the aisle in the dress she's forced onto you, looking way, way better in it than she ever did?"

Jill shakes her head. "You don't understand," she says.

"Try me."

"That—that thing she wants me to wear. It's . . . hideous."

"So was this," I say, indicating the Alfred Shaheen. "Grape jelly. Floor length. Bullet boobs."

"No. This is worse. Way worse. It's got like—" Words seem to defy Jill. So she uses her arms to make a circle. "This hoop skirt thing. And there's . . . *stuff*. Hanging. It's got this plaid thing—"

"The MacDowell clan tartan," I say gravely. "Yes. Yes, of course it would have that."

"And it's like a million years old," Jill says. "And it smells. And it doesn't fit."

"Too big or too small?" I ask.

"Too small. Way too small. There's no way anybody could make it fit. I already decided." She tosses her head, her blue eyes glittering. "I'm not wearing it. I mean, she already hates me. What's the worst that can happen?"

"True," I say. "Do you have something else in mind?"

She looks at me blankly. "What do you mean?"

"I mean, do you have another dress in mind? Have you shopped for another gown?"

She shakes her head. "Oh, right. When would I have time to do that? In between manicures? What do you think? No, of course not. What do I know about any of this stuff? I mean, John, he keeps telling me just to go to Vera Wang or whatever, but it's like every time I even think about going into one of those places—you know, those designers—I get all short of breath, and . . . well, it's not like I've got girlfriends, or whatever, who are into that stuff. Everyone I know, they've got like monkey shit all over their shoes. *Literally.* What do they know from bridal gowns? Really, I was just thinking maybe I'd fly home and pick something up back at the mall in Des Moines. Because at least there I know what I'm getting myself into—"

Something cold and hard grips my heart. I recognize immediately what it is, of course. Fear.

"Jill." I reach for another Devil Dog. I need it. For sustenance. "Can I call you Jill?"

She nods. "Yeah, whatever."

"I'm Lizzie," I say. "And please, don't ever say that word around me again."

She looks at me blankly. "What word?"

"Mall." I shove a fingerful of delicious filling into my mouth and let it melt. Ahhhh. Better. "No. Just no, okay?"

"I know," she says, her eyes suddenly bright with tears again. "But seriously. What else am I gonna do?"

"Well, for starters," I say, "you're going to bring the MacDowell clan bridal gown, tartan and all, to me, here." I pass her one of my business cards from my purse. "Can you come this afternoon?"

Jill squints down at the card. "Are you serious?"

"Dead serious," I say. "Before we make any drastic decisions involving the mall, let's just see what we have to work with, okay? Because you never know. You may have something salvageable. And then you won't have to deal with the mall *or* the high-fashion boutiques. And it would be a really nice in-your-face to your mother-in-law if we could make it work."

Jill narrows her eyes at me. "Wait. Did you just say 'in-your-face'?"

I look at her guiltily over the second fingerful of Devil Dog filling I've just stuffed into my mouth. "Um," I say around my finger. "Yeah. Why?"

"I haven't heard anybody say that since eighth grade."

I pop my finger out of my mouth. "I was always kind of a late bloomer."

For the first time since coming out of the toilet stall, Jill smiles. "Me, too," she says.

And the two of us stand there grinning idiotically at each other . . .

At least until the door to the ladies' room swings open and Roberta comes in, freezing mid-step when she sees us.

"Oh, Lizzie," she says, smiling at Jill. "There you are. Tiffany just asked me to check on you because you'd been gone from the desk for so long—"

"Oh, sorry," I say, sweeping the remains of the junk food I'd looted from the kitchen into my arms. "We were just—"

"I was having a blood sugar issue," Jill says, reaching out to grab another Coke and a Yodels from the pile in my arms, "and Lizzie was just helping me through it."

"Oh," Roberta says, smiling even harder. Well, what's she going to do? Yell at me for sneaking the entire contents of the Pendergast, Loughlin, and Flynn snack closet into the ladies' room for one of their most high-profile clients? "Great. So long as you're both all right."

"We are," I say cheerfully. "In fact, I was just heading back to the desk—"

"And I have a two o'clock with Mr. Pendergast," Jill says.

"Okay, then," Roberta says. Her smile is practically frozen onto her face. "Good!"

I hurry out to the lobby, where Tiffany's eyes widen perceptibly when she sees who's following me. Esther, Mr. Pendergast's assistant, is waiting by the reception desk. She looks even more surprised than Tiffany to see Jill Higgins following behind me and Roberta.

"Oh, Miss Higgins," she cries, her gaze going straight to the Yodel crumbs on Jill's chest. "There you are. I was getting worried. The security desk called and said they'd sent you up some time ago—"

"Sorry," Jill says smoothly. "I stopped for a snack."

"I see," Esther says, darting a quick look at me.

"She was hungry," I say, indicating the snack cakes and sodas— and minicartons of milk—in my arms. "Want some?"

"Er, no, thank you," Esther says. "Won't you come with me, Miss Higgins?"

"Sure," Jill says, and starts following Esther out—only to fling me an enigmatic look over her shoulder as she rounds the corner . . . a look I am in no shape to interpret, since I'm getting ready to be yelled at by my boss.

But Roberta doesn't say anything except, "Well. That was, er, nice of you, to, er, help Miss Higgins."

"Thanks," I say. "She said she was feeling light-headed, so—"

"Quick thinking," Roberta says. "Well. It's past two, so—"

"Right." I dump the stuff from the kitchen onto the reception desk—causing Tiffany to make a small noise of protest and give me a dirty look. "Sorry, Tiff," I say. "But I gotta run. My shift's up for the day—"

And then I bolt out of there like a bike messenger with a clear shot up Sixth Avenue . . .

~ Lizzie Nichols's Wedding Gown Guide ~

A word on . . .

Shoes!

Of course you want to look your best on your wedding day, and higher heels can help emphasize a nice figure, and improve a less-than-perfect one. Keep in mind, however, that you will be spending a LOT of time on your feet on your wedding day. If you insist on heels, wear a pair at a height you are somewhat used to.

If your wedding heels are still less than comfortable by the time the big day rolls around, it's always a good idea to bring a second pair of shoes to wear during your "downtime," such as while you're waiting for the photographer to set up, et cetera.

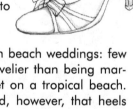

One word on beach weddings: few things are lovelier than being married at sunset on a tropical beach. Keep in mind, however, that heels and sand do not mix. If you are being married on a beach, skip the shoes altogether. Just be sure to put some bug repellent on your ankles to ward off sand fleas or you'll be scratching throughout the ceremony.

LIZZIE NICHOLS DESIGNS™

• Chapter 19 •

If you reveal your secrets to the wind, you should
not blame the wind for revealing them to the trees.

—*Kahlil Gibran (1883–1931), poet and writer*

*a*t five of six that day, I give up hope that Jill Higgins is
going to walk up and ring the bell to Monsieur Henri's.
I've been, I know, too presumptuous. Why would Jill
Higgins, who is marrying one of the richest men in Manhattan,
choose me—a woman she knows only as the receptionist at the law
firm where she is getting her prenup negotiated—as her certified
wedding-gown specialist?

Especially since I'm not even certified! Yet.

I haven't mentioned to Monsieur and Madame Henri that I've
given their name and address to one of the most famous brides-to-
be in the city. I don't want to get their hopes up. Business has not
been good, and there've been conversations (in French, of course,
so I won't understand what they're saying) about packing it up for
good when Maurice finally opens his shop down the street and
steals away the last of their customers. The Henris have mentioned
decamping for the cottage in Provence.

There would be a significant loss of income if this were to take
place, since they've taken out a second mortgage on the building in
order to pay for the boys' college tuition, and the home in which

they live in New Jersey has depreciated considerably with the current housing sales slump. Plus there's the small fact that the two boys, Jean-Paul and Jean-Pierre, adamantly refuse to move to France, or even transfer to colleges less expensive than New York University, to which they commute daily from home (when they aren't sneaking overnight stays in the apartment upstairs).

Of course, I have no doubt that if the decision to give up the shop is ever made, the boys will end up doing precisely as their mother insists. Money, not discipline, is what is lacking in the Henri family—at least if the way Monsieur Henri piles the work on me at the shop is any indication. For someone who claims his business is going under, Monsieur Henri certainly seems to have enough sewing for me to do, day in and day out. He's had me make so many lace ruffles—the same ones I'd admired in his shop window, months ear-lier, and swore to myself I'd learn to create on my own—that I can practically do them in my sleep. And I've completely mastered the art of the sewn-on diamond drop, for that all-over shimmer effect. And don't even get me started on ruching.

Madame Henri is fussing at her husband for him to hurry and pack up so they can leave, because the Rockefeller Center Christmas tree lighting—scheduled to take place tonight—makes the traffic so impossible that it takes an hour, practically, just to navigate out of the city, when the bell to the front door of the shop rings, and I look up to see a pale face, framed by a curtain of blond hair, peering at me urgently.

"What is this?" Madame Henri wants to know. "We have no appointments today."

"Oh," I say quickly, getting up and going to the door. "This is a friend of mine." I open the door to let Jill in . . .

. . . and only then notice that there is a chauffeured black Town Car with smoked windows parked with its motor running in front of the fire hydrant, and that behind Jill stands a tall, athletic man I immediately recognize as—

"Oh!" Madame Henri drops her purse and flings both her hands to her cheeks. She's recognized Jill's companion as well. Which, considering how often his face appears on the front page of the *Post*, isn't any wonder.

"Um, hi," Jill says. Her cheeks are very red from the cold outside. She's carrying a garment bag. "You said to stop by. Is this a bad time?"

"This is a perfect time," I say. "Come on in."

The couple step in from the slight snow flurry that has started up, lightly coating their hair and shoulders with drops that sparkle more than any crystal I've ever sewn onto anything. They bring with them the smell of cold and good health and . . . something else.

"Sorry," Jill says, wrinkling her nose. "That's me. I came straight from work and I didn't have time to change. We wanted to beat the tree traffic."

"That intoxicating odor," John MacDowell says, "that you're smelling right now is seal excrement. Don't worry, you get used to it."

"This is my fiancé, John," Jill says. "John, this is Lizzie—"

John sticks out a large hand, and I shake it.

"Nice to meet you," he says, seeming to mean it. "When Jill told me about you—well, I really hope you can help us. My mother—I mean, I love her and everything, but—"

"Say no more," I say. "We completely get it. And, believe me, we've probably seen worse. May I introduce you to my boss, Monsieur Henri? He owns this shop. And this is his wife, Madame Henri. Monsieur and Madame, this is Jill Higgins and her fiancé, John MacDowell."

Monsieur Henri has been standing nearby staring at the three of us with a stunned expression on his face. When I say his name, he takes a quick step forward, his hand extended. "*Enchanté*," he says. "I am very pleased to make your acquaintance."

"Nice to meet you, too," John MacDowell says politely. Madame Henri practically faints when he says the same thing to her. She hasn't been able to utter a sound since the couple entered the shop.

"Shall we see what you have here?" I ask, taking the garment bag from Jill.

"I'm warning you," John says. "It's bad."

"*Really* bad," Jill adds.

"We are used to bad," Monsieur Henri assures them. "That is how we came by our endorsement from the Association of Bridal Consultants."

"It's true," I say gravely. "The National Bridal Service has given Monsieur Henri their highest recommendation."

Monsieur Henri inclines his head modestly while at the same time moving behind Jill to help her out of her down parka. "Perhaps we can get you some tea? Or coffee?"

"I'm fine," John says, handing over his own parka. "We're . . ."

His voice trails off. That's because I've opened the garment bag. And now all five of us are staring at what I've revealed.

Monsieur Henri nearly drops the coats, but at the last second his wife darts forward to scoop them up.

"It's . . . it's hideous," Monsieur Henri breathes—thankfully in French.

"Yes," I say. "But it can be saved."

"No." Monsieur Henri shakes his head, like someone in a daze. "It cannot."

I can see why he might feel that way. The gown isn't promising, to say the least. Made of yards and yards of clearly valuable antique lace over cream-colored satin, it's a princess cut, with an enormous full skirt, made even bigger by a hoop sewn into the hem. The neckline is a typical Queen Anne style, with enormous poufed sleeves that end in tartan bows at the wrists. Draped along the skirt is more tartan, held in place with gold toggles.

It looks, in other words, like something out of a high school drama club's production of *Brigadoon*.

"It's been in my family for generations," John says apologetically. "All the MacDowell brides have worn it—with various degrees of alteration. My mother is the one who put in the hoop when she wore it. She's from Georgia."

"That explains a lot," I say. "What size is it?"

"A six," Jill says. "I'm a twelve."

Monsieur Henri says in French, "Impossible. It is too small. There is nothing we can do."

"Let's not be hasty," I say. "Obviously the bodice will have to go. But there's enough material here—"

"You are going to chop up the ancestral gown of the richest family in the city?" Monsieur Henri demands, again in French. "You've lost your mind!"

"He said other brides have altered it," I remind him. "I mean, come on. We can at least try."

"You cannot fit a size-twelve woman into a size-six gown," Monsieur Henri snaps. "You know it cannot be done!"

"We can't fit her into *this* gown the way it is now," I say. "But fortunately it's too long on her." I take the gown from the hanger it's on and hold it up to Jill, who stands with her arms at her side, looking alarmed. "See? If it were too short, I'd say you were right. But like I was saying, if we unstitch the bodice—"

"My God, are you mad?" Monsieur Henri looks shocked. "Do you know what the mother-in-law will do to us? She could even take legal action—"

"Jean," Madame Henri says, speaking for the first time.

Her husband glances at her. "What?"

"Do it," she says in French.

Monsieur Henri shakes his head. "I am telling you, it cannot be done! Do you want me to lose my certification?"

"Do you want Maurice to steal away what little business we have left when he opens his shop down the street?" his wife demands.

"He won't," I assure them both. "Not if you let me do it. I can. I *know* I can."

Madame Henri nods at me. "Listen to her, Jean," she says.

The issue is no longer up for debate. Monsieur Henri may wield the needle, but his wife wears the pants in the family. Once she has ruled, there is no more argument. Madame Henri's word is always final.

Monsieur Henri's shoulders sag. Then he looks at Jill. Both she and her husband-to-be are staring at us, wide-eyed.

"When is the wedding?" Monsieur Henri asks weakly.

"New Year's Eve," Jill says.

Monsieur Henri groans. And even I have to swallow hard against the soreness that has suddenly crept back into my throat. New Year's Eve!

Jill notices our reaction, and looks worried. "Does that . . . I mean, will you have enough time?"

"A month." Monsieur Henri stares down at me. "We have a *month*. Not that it matters, since what you are saying cannot be done in any amount of time."

"It can if we do it the way I'm thinking we should do it," I say. "*Trust me.*"

Monsieur Henri takes a final look at the monstrosity on the hanger.

"*Maurice,*" his wife hisses. "Remember Maurice!"

Monsieur Henri sighs. "Fine. We will try."

And I turn, beaming, toward Jill.

"What was that all about?" she asks nervously. "I couldn't tell what you were saying. It was all in French."

"Well," I start to say . . .

Then realize what she's just said.

I turn guiltily toward Monsieur and Madame Henri, who are both staring at me in horror. It's hit them at the same time as it's hit me: we've just had an entire conversation in their native language—which I'm not supposed to understand.

But hey. It's not like they ever asked.

I give the Henris a shrug. Then, to Jill, I say, "We'll do it."

She stares at me. "Okay . . . but how?"

"I haven't completely figured that out yet," I admit. "But I have an idea. And you're going to look great. I promise."

She lifts her eyebrows. "No hoop skirt?"

"No hoop skirt," I say. "But I'm going to need to take your measurements. So if you could just come with me back to the dressing room—"

"Okay," she says. And follows me past Monsieur and Madame Henri, who continue to stand there, looking stunned. I can see that they are going over in their heads every conversation they have ever had within earshot of me.

And that's a *lot* of conversations.

Behind the curtains that make up the walls of the dressing room, the smell of seal is stronger than ever.

"I'm really sorry," Jill says. "I'll totally change before I come the next time."

"That's okay," I say, trying to take only shallow breaths. "At least you know that guy must *really* love you, if he's willing to put up with *that*."

"Yes," Jill says, with a smile that makes her normally merely attractive face stunningly beautiful for a moment. "He does."

And I feel a twinge. Not of jealousy, really, although there's a little of that in it, I guess. But mostly it's caused by the fact that I want what she has—not an engagement to the richest bachelor in Manhattan; not a future mother-in-law who is making it her single goal in life to ruin any chance at joy I might have on what is supposed to be the happiest day of my life.

But a guy who would go on loving me even if I smelled like seal poo. Not just go on loving me, but want to spend the rest of his life with me—although I'd settle at this point for coming to Ann Arbor for Christmas with me—and be willing to verbalize that desire in front of a room full of friends, family members, and sneaky members of the press who happened to worm their way into the church.

Because right now, that's something I'm pretty sure I don't have.

But hey. At least I'm working on it.

∼ Lizzie Nichols's Wedding Gown Guide ∼

Time to ask the age-old question: White, ivory, or cream?

Believe it or not, there are many different shades of white. Don't believe me? Check out the paint section of your local hardware store. You've never seen so many different names for what many people consider a single color—everything from Eggshell to Navajo to Blush.

The days of the traditional snow-white wedding gown are long gone, and many brides are opting to take advantage of this trend by picking out gowns in off-white, beige, pink, and even blues. To find the color that flatters your skin tone best, follow this easy guide:

Snow White—Dark of hair? Then traditional white really will look best on you. Whites with a blue or lavender tint will complement you as well.

Cream—Blond? Your light locks will best be set off by a cream-colored gown. The hint of gold will echo the tawny highlights in your crowning glory (your hair, not your tiara). Remember Princess Diana, on *her* special day . . .

Ivory—In between? Ivory looks good on nearly everyone. That's why it's used on so many walls.

LIZZIE NICHOLS DESIGNS™

● *Chapter 20* ●

To a philosopher all news, as it is called, is gossip,
and they who edit it and read it are old women over
their tea.

—*Henry David Thoreau (1817–1862),*
American philosopher, author, and naturalist

Where have you been?" Luke wants to know, when I finally
stagger home later that evening, my arms loaded down
with books.

"The library," I say. "Sorry, did you call? You're not allowed to
have your ringer on there."

Luke is laughing as he comes over to take the books from my
arms. "*Scottish Traditions*," he reads aloud from the covers. "*Your
Scottish Wedding. Tartans and Toasts.* Lizzie, what's going on? Are
you planning a visit to the Emerald Isle soon?"

"That's Ireland," I say, unwinding my scarf. "I'm doing a Scottish
bridal gown for a client. And you're never going to believe who the
client is."

"You're probably right," he says. "Have you eaten? I've got some
leftover turkey reheating in the oven—"

"I'm too excited to eat," I say. "Come on. Guess. Guess who the
client is."

Luke shrugs. "I don't know. Shari? She's having some kind of lesbian wedding?"

I glare at him. "No. And I told you, don't—"

"Label her, yes, yes, I know," Luke says. "All right, I give up. Who's your client?"

I flop down onto the couch—my sore throat really *is* bothering me a little. It feels great to sit down—and say triumphantly, "Jill Higgins."

Luke has gone into the kitchen to pour some wine. "Am I supposed to know who that is?" he asks across the pass-through.

I can't believe it. "Luke! Do you even read the paper? Or watch the news?"

But even as I ask it, I know the answer. The only paper he reads is the *New York Times,* and all he ever watches are documentaries.

Still, I try.

"You know," I say as he comes forward with a glass of cabernet sauvignon in each hand. "That girl who works in the seal enclosure at the Central Park Zoo? And she threw her back out returning one of the seals to the enclosure? Because they jump out when the water level gets too high, you know, from excessive snow or rain." I am able to add this last bit because Jill just told me about it, in the dressing room while I was taking her measurements, when I asked her to tell me how she and John met.

"And while she was in the emergency room she met John Mac-Dowell—you know, of the Manhattan MacDowells? Well, they're getting married at like the biggest wedding of the century practically, and Jill asked *me* to fix her wedding dress for her." I am still so stoked, I'm bouncing up and down on the couch. "Me! Of all the people in New York! I'm doing Jill Higgins's wedding gown!"

"Wow," Luke says, smiling his beautiful, even-toothed smile. "That's great, Lizzie!"

It's clear he has no idea what I'm talking about. None.

"You don't understand," I say. "This is huge. See, the press has been savage to her, calling her 'Blubber' and stuff, just because she's not some skinny model, and works with seals, and she cries in front of them sometimes, because they won't stop hounding her, and her mother-in-law is making her sign this prenup and wear this hideous—you can't even imagine how hideous—wedding gown, and I'm going to fix it, and everything will be perfect, and Monsieur Henri will finally start getting some business, and then he'll be able to pay me, and then I can quit working for Chaz's dad, and do what I love full-time! Isn't that *great*?"

Luke is still smiling—just not as much as before. "That *is* great," he says. "But—"

"I'm not saying it's going to be easy," I interrupt, thinking I know what he's about to say. "I mean, we only have a month—less than a month now—to get the dress done, and it's going to take a *lot* of work. Especially if I'm going to do to it what I think I'm going to have to do to it, just so it will fit. So you're probably not going to see very much of me for a while. Which is just as well, since you have finals anyway, right? I'm seriously going to have to work late if we're going to pull this off. But if we do, Luke—just think! Maybe Monsieur Henri will let me run the shop! I mean, he's been wanting to retire and move to France . . . this way he could do it and not have to sell the place at a loss. Then I can start saving my money, and maybe—please, God—get some small-business loans or something, and eventually be able to *buy* the business—building and all—from him someday—"

Luke is looking distinctly nonplussed by all this. I know it's a lot of information all at once. But I can't help thinking he could be a *little* more excited for me.

"I *am*," he insists when I mention this (a little churlishly, I admit, but hey, my throat hurts). "It's just . . . I didn't know you were serious about this bridal-gown thing."

I blink at him. "Luke," I say. "Were you not there this summer, when all those friends of your parents were coming up to me, telling me I should open my own bridal-gown design business?"

"Well, yes," Luke says. "But I just thought—you know. That that would be something you'd do down the line. Maybe after getting a business degree."

"A business degree?" I screech. "Go back to school? Are you kidding me? I just graduated. Wait, I haven't *even* graduated yet! Why would I want to go *back*?"

"Lizzie, you need more to open your own business than just a talent for refurbishing vintage clothing," Luke says a little dryly.

"I know that." I shake my head. "But that's what I'm doing at Monsieur Henri's. Learning the ropes of running your own business. And, Luke, I really think I'm ready. To take it to the next level, I mean. Or I will be, depending on how this thing with Jill Higgins goes."

Luke looks dubious. "I don't see how one wedding dress can make such a huge difference."

I gape at him. "Are you kidding me? Have you *heard* of David and Elizabeth Emanuel?"

"Uh." Luke hesitates. "No?"

"They designed Princess Diana's wedding gown," I say, feeling a little sorry for him. I mean, really. He knows a lot about the principles of biology, which he's studying this semester. But not so much about popular culture.

But that's just as well, because really, which would you *rather* your doctor know about?

"And because of that one dress, they got superfamous," I go on. "Now, I am in no way putting Jill Higgins in the same category of fame as Princess Diana. But, you know, *locally* she's pretty well known. And when it gets out we're doing her dress, well, it's going to be very good for business. That's all I'm saying. And since she's getting married on New Year's Eve, there's a bit of a time crunch, so—"

"So you're not going to be around much," Luke says. "Don't worry, I understand. And you're right, what with my finals, you won't be seeing much of me anyway. Not to mention the fact that I leave for France in just three weeks. For a couple of people who live together, we sure don't seem to see each other much."

"Except when we're sleeping," I agree. "But, you know. Then we're unconscious."

"Well," Luke says. "I guess I'll just have to be happy with what I can get. Although I was kind of hoping you could spare a little of your precious time to go tree-shopping with me."

"Tree-shopping?" I stare at him for a few seconds before I realize what he's talking about. "Oh, you mean you want to put up a Christmas tree?"

"Well, yeah," Luke says. "Even though we won't be able to spend the real holiday with each other, I was still hoping we could have our own private celebration before we both take off to be with our families. And to do that, we need a tree . . . especially since I got you a little something special, and I need a place to put it."

My heart melts. "You got me a Christmas present? Ahhh, Luke! How sweet!"

"Well," he says, looking pleased by my reaction, but a little embarrassed as well, for some reason. "It's not really so much of a Christmas present, I realize now, as an investment in the future—"

Wait . . . did he just say what I *think* he did?

An investment in the *future*?

"Come on," Luke says, getting up abruptly, and going into the kitchen. "You've got to eat something. Your voice is sounding a little scratchy. We don't want you coming down with something. You have a wedding dress to design!"

The big send-off

Traditionally, wedding guests have been provided with tiny sachets of raw rice to open and then toss at the happily wedded couple as they leave the venue at which the wedding ceremony has taken place (usually a church). The rice represents fertility. Tossing it at the couple is supposed to represent your wish for them to have good luck and abundance in their future lives together.

In recent years, however, many churches and other buildings in which weddings are performed have banned the throwing of rice. The stated reason for this ban is that the uncooked rice is harmful to birds if swallowed. This is, in fact, an urban myth. Many species of birds and ducks depend on raw rice as a main staple of their diet.

The problem with the rice is that it actually poses a danger to humans . . . the hard granules are slippery beneath the feet, and many wedding sites choose to avoid a lawsuit by the banning of rice.

A popular substitute for rice these days is birdseed. However, this can pose just as big a risk to the health of your guests as rice, when it comes to creating a slippery surface.

Furthermore, rice, birdseed, and even confetti are extremely difficult to clean up, and for venues that perform multiple weddings per day, cleaning up after each bridal couple's departure (since no bride wants to step in the rice or confetti of a previous bride) is time-consuming and expensive.

That's why I always recommend bubbles as a wedding favor. Guests can create a pretty "canopy" of bubbles under which the newly wedded couple can duck on their way to their carriage or limo. And no one has ever filed a lawsuit from slipping on a bubble.

Just maybe from getting one in the eye.

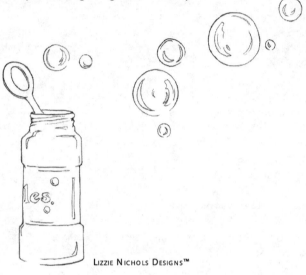

• Chapter 21 •

I lay it down as a fact that if all men knew what others say of them, there would not be four friends in the world.

—Blaise Pascal (1623–1662), French mathematician

*a*n investment in the future?" Shari sounds dubious on the other end of the phone. "But that could be anything. Stock certificates. One of those World Trade Center coins from the Franklin Mint."

"Shari." I can't believe she's being so dense. "Come on. Luke is not going to get me something from the Franklin Mint. It's an engagement ring. It *has* to be. He's trying to make up for not going home with me to meet my parents."

"By buying you an *engagement ring*?"

"Yes. Because what better thing to give me right before I leave to go back home?" I'm a little giddy just thinking about it. "It's like, even though *he* can't be there, the *ring* will be, so everyone will know how serious it is between us. Oh, hold on." I press the hold button, then line 2. "Pendergast, Loughlin, and Flynn, how may I direct your call?"

I send the call to one of the junior partners, then hit the button to line 1 again.

"It makes sense," I say to Shari. "I mean, we've been going out for six months. We've been living together for four. It's not as if it would be completely out of left field if he proposed."

"I don't know, Lizzie." Shari sounds like she's shaking her head. "According to Chaz, Luke is the kind of person who, um . . . lacks follow-through."

"Well, maybe because of my careful tutelage," I say, recalling Chaz's not very charitable warning of several months earlier—which was just Chaz, being jealous of the fact that Luke has a girlfriend who actually likes him, and not her female boss, "he's changed."

"Lizzie." Shari sounds tired. "People don't change. You know that."

"They can change in small ways," I say. "Look how when you first started going out with Chaz, he had that thing, remember, where he ate pork chops and Rice-A-Roni every night? You totally weaned him off that."

"By telling him if we didn't have something else once in a while, I was going to stop sleeping with him," Shari says. "But when I'm not around, that's still all he ever eats."

"Ooooh," Tiffany chimes in, beside me, from over the top of the bridal magazine she's reading. Because I brought a bunch of them in to work, for inspiration. "When you and Luke do get married, you could totally have your company's PR person send out a press release, you know, to like *Vogue* and *Town & Country*, and they'll send reporters out to cover your wedding, and that will just get you *more* clients. And free publicity."

I stare at her. For someone who is so ditzy that she has, upon occasion, forgotten to lock the office door after closing for the day, Tiffany can be pretty savvy.

"That's good," I say to her. "That's *very* good."

"Hello," Shari says. "Are you talking to me? Or to Miss Hairspray for Brains over there?"

"Hey, now," I say. "Come on."

"Well, I'm trying," Shari says. "But seriously, Lizzie. I know you love Luke and all. But do you really see yourself with him fifty years from now? Even *five* years from now?"

"Yes," I say, taken aback by the question. "Of course. Why? What's wrong with him?" The other line chirps. "Crud. Hold on." I press line 2. "Pendergast, Loughlin, and Flynn, how may I direct your call? Mr. Flynn? One moment please."

A second later, I'm back with Shari. "Seriously. Why do you sound like you think Luke and I don't have a future?"

"Well, honestly, Lizzie," Shari says. "What do the two of you have in common? Except sex?"

"Lots of things," I insist. "I mean, we both like New York. We both like Château Mirac. We both like . . . wine. And Renoir!"

"Lizzie," Shari says. "Everybody likes that stuff."

"And he wants to be a doctor," I go on. "And help save people's lives. And I want to be a certified wedding-gown specialist. And help make brides look good. *We're practically the same person.*"

"You're making a joke out of it," Shari says. "But I'm serious. One of the reasons I realized Chaz and I were wrong for each other, and Pat and I so right, is that intellectually Pat and I are compatible. And I don't think the same could be said about you and Luke."

I feel tears sting my eyes. "You think he's intellectually superior to me, is that it? Just because he likes documentaries and I like *Project Runway*!"

"No," Shari says, sounding exasperated. "What I mean is, he likes documentaries and you like *Project Runway* . . . and yet you guys only ever watch documentaries. Because you're so busy trying to get him to like you, that you just do whatever he wants, instead of telling him what *you* really want to do. Or watch."

"That is not true," I cry. "We watch shows I like all the time!"

"Oh, yeah?" Shari lets out a bitter laugh. "I had no idea you were such a *Nightline* fan. I always thought you were more of a David Letterman type of girl. But hey, if *Nightline* is what floats your boat—"

"*Nightline* is a totally good show," I say defensively. "Luke watches it so he can stay abreast of world issues, since he often misses the evening news, being busy at the library, studying—"

"Face it, Lizzie," Shari says. "I know you think you've found your handsome prince—literally. But do you really think of yourself as the princess type? Because I sure don't think of you that way. And I'm pretty sure Luke doesn't, either."

"What is *that* supposed to mean?" I demand. "I'm totally the princess type! Just because I make my own clothes instead of waiting for a fairy godmother to come along and sprinkle me with fairy dust—"

"Elizabeth?" It's only then that I notice that Roberta has approached the reception desk. And that she does not look happy.

"Uh," I say to Shari. "Ihavetogobye."

I hang up. "Hi, Roberta," I say. Beside me, Tiffany has pulled her feet from the desk and is making herself look busy by pulling open a drawer and arranging bottles of her fingernail polish in rainbow order.

Expecting to receive a warning about making personal calls on the firm's time, I'm surprised when Roberta says, "Tiffany, it's nearly two. Would you mind taking over for Lizzie a few minutes early so I can have a word with her in private?"

"Sure," Tiffany says with a furtive glance at me that screams, *You are so busted!* And causes my stomach to twist into an immediate knot.

I follow Roberta back to her office, conscious of Daryl's—the fax and copier supervisor—pitying glance. He apparently thinks I'm busted, too.

Well, whatever! If Pendergast, Loughlin, and Flynn wants to fire me over one personal call, then they better fire everyone else at the firm, too! I've overheard Roberta on the phone with her husband plenty of times!

Oh, God. Please don't let me get fired . . . please . . .

I think I'm going to throw up.

It's only when I walk into Roberta's office and see that the *New York Post* is open on her desk to a large picture in the center of the second page that I realize this might not be about my using the firm's phone for personal calls. Because even though they're upside down, I can make out the words, "Blubber's New Mystery Pal." And I can see that the photo is of me walking Jill to her Town Car after her fitting the night before.

The knot in my stomach turns into something that feels more like a fist.

"Correct me if I'm wrong," Roberta says, holding the paper up. "But isn't this you?"

I swallow. My sore throat, which had been miraculously cured by Luke's "investment for your future" remark, comes back with a vengeance.

"Um," I say. "No."

Honestly, I don't know where the lie comes from. But once it's out, there's nothing I can do to stuff it back in.

"Lizzie," Roberta says. "It's obviously you. That's the same dress you wore to work yesterday. You can't tell me there's another one like that anywhere in Manhattan."

"I'm sure there are loads," I say. And I'm not lying this time, either. "Alfred Shaheen was a very prolific designer."

"Lizzie." Roberta sits down behind her desk. "This is very serious. I saw you talking to Jill Higgins in the ladies' room yesterday. And then, apparently, you met her somewhere after work. You know the firm takes the confidentiality of its clients extremely seriously. So I'm going to ask you again. What were you doing yesterday with Jill Higgins—and, if this photo is to believed, her fiancé, John Mac-Dowell?"

I swallow again. I wish I had a Sucrets. Also, that I didn't need this job so badly.

"I can't tell you," I say.

Roberta raises a single eyebrow. "I beg your pardon?"

"I can't tell you," I say. "But I can tell you that it has nothing whatsoever to do with the firm. Honestly. It has to do with a completely different business. But it's a business that also has confidentiality clauses. That I really can't violate."

Roberta's other eyebrow rises to join the first. "Lizzie. Are you telling me that this is you in the picture?"

"I can neither confirm nor deny it," I say, parroting the phrase Roberta herself told me to say whenever reporters call the firm, requesting information about people on whom they are writing stories.

"Lizzie." Roberta does not look amused. "This is very serious. If you are harassing or otherwise bothering Miss Higgins—"

"I'm not!" I cry, genuinely startled. "*She* came to me!"

"For what?" Roberta demands. "What other line of work are you in, Lizzie?"

"If I told you that," I say, "you'll know why she came to see me. And she hasn't given me permission to tell anyone that. So I can't say. I'm sorry, Roberta."

I can't believe that I'm doing this. I mean, actually NOT spilling a secret for a change. This is a real sign of my inner growth. I should totally be celebrating.

Too bad I feel so much like vomiting.

"You can fire me if you want to," I go on. "But I promise you, I am not bothering Jill. If you don't believe me, call and ask her. She'll tell you."

"She's *Jill* to you now?" Roberta says with more than a little sarcasm in her tone.

"She told me I could call her that," I say, wounded. "Yes."

Roberta looks down at the picture. She seems to be at a loss. "This is highly irregular," she says at last. "I honestly don't know what to say about it."

"It's nothing illegal," I say.

"Well, I should hope not!" Roberta cries. "Are you going to be meeting her again?"

"Yes," I say firmly.

"Well." Roberta shakes her head. "All I can say in that case is, try to be more careful not to get your picture in the *Post*. If one of the partners had seen this and recognized you—"

"I had no idea there was a photographer there," I say. "But I'll definitely be more careful in the future. Is that it? Can I go now?"

Roberta looks startled. "Well, you're in an awfully big hurry to get out of here. Christmas shopping?"

"No," I say. "I have to get to that business that I'm doing for Jill."

Roberta's shoulders slump. "Fine," she says. "But fair warning, Lizzie. This firm prides itself on its sterling reputation. Any whiff of impropriety on your part and you're gone. Understand?"

"Totally," I say.

Roberta looks down, dismissing me . . .

. . . and I bolt from her office. Heading back to the reception desk to get my coat and purse, I ignore Daryl's whispered *"Yo! What'd you do this time?"* and Tiffany's *"Oh my God, are you all right? You look like someone just told you that your Prada handbag is a fake."*

"I'm fine," I mutter. "I'll see you tomorrow."

"Seriously," Tiffany hisses, "call me and tell me what she said. I'm collecting Roberta stories to submit to the Smoking Gun."

I wave at her and hurry out, my heart hammering so hard in my chest, I'm afraid it's going to fly out and hit the wall. When the elevator doors open, I rush inside without even looking to see who else is in there before pounding the button for the lobby. It isn't until a voice beside me says, "Well, hello there, stranger," that I look up and see that Chaz is in the car with me.

"Oh my God," I cry. "Were you going up to see your dad? Why didn't you say anything? I'd have held the door for you—oh no, and now you're going down. I'm sorry!"

"Relax," Chaz says. "I wasn't going up to see my dad. I was coming to see you."

"Me?" I'm shocked.

"I was hoping I could take you for a drink," Chaz says. "And pump you for the information I need about my ex in order for me to start rebuilding my male ego so I can learn to love again."

I chew my lower lip. "Chaz," I say. "I am trying really hard not to talk about people behind their backs. It's this whole new thing with me. I have gotten in so much trouble in the past for being a big mouth, and I'm really trying to change. Because despite what *some* people think, people *can* change."

"Sure they can," Chaz says. The elevator has reached the lobby. "Come on. Let me take you for a beer at Honey's."

I'm about to say *I can't.* I know Chaz is hurting, but I have a dress to design. I'm about to say, *I have to get to the shop. We have this huge project—which is another thing I can't talk about—and I'm in a time crunch, so I'll see you later, okay?*

But then I look into his face and see that it's been a while since he shaved—and, as far as I can tell, changed baseball caps.

Which is how I find myself sitting across from him in one of the red vinyl booths at Honey's, a sweating diet Coke in front of me, listening to the dwarf sing "Dancing Queen," a not entirely unpleasant experience.

"I just need to know," Chaz is saying into his bottle of beer. "I know it sounds stupid, but . . . I mean . . . do you think I did something to . . . turn her?"

"What? Of course not," I cry. "Chaz! Come on. No."

"Well, what happened then?" he demands. "I mean, a person isn't straight one day and then gay the next. Unless maybe I did something to make her—"

"You didn't," I say. "Chaz. Trust me. You didn't. It's exactly like Shari explained to you. She just fell in love with someone else. And that person just happens to be another woman. It's no different than if she'd met some other guy she ended up falling for instead of you."

"Uh," Chaz says. "It's different."

"It's not," I say. "It's still love. Love does crazy things to people. You can't blame yourself. I know Shari doesn't blame you. She still loves you. She told you that, right?"

Chaz grimaces. "She mentioned it."

"Well, it's true. She does still love you. Just, you know. Not romantically anymore. It happens, Chaz."

"So you're saying," Chaz says slowly, "that I could, conceivably, fall in love with a guy sometime?"

"Conceivably," I say. Although to tell the truth I really can't picture Chaz in a homosexual relationship. Or, rather, I can't picture any of the homosexual guys I've known (and dated) actually wanting to be in a relationship with Chaz, seeing as how his fashion sense is less than minimal and he does have an alarming enthusiasm for college basketball and not much interest in home furnishings. I have a much easier time picturing Luke comfortably nesting with another man.

"Have *you*?" Chaz wants to know.

"Have I what?" I glance at the clock above the bar. I really need to get to the shop. I have about a million ideas for Jill's dress and my fingers are itching to get started on them.

"Ever been in love with a woman."

"Well," I say slowly. "There are a lot of women in my life I've really admired, and wanted to be like, and wanted to get to know better. But not, you know, *sexually*."

Chaz is scraping the label off his beer bottle with a thumbnail. "And you and Shari never . . . er . . . experimented?"

"Chaz!" I throw my coaster at him. "No! Ew! You and Luke are exactly alike. That's it, I'm leaving—"

"What?" he cries, looking truly alarmed as he catches my arm before I've made my way completely off the end of the bench. "I was just asking! I thought maybe, you know, all girls do that kind of stuff—"

"Well, they don't," I inform him. "Not that there's anything wrong with it. Now let go of my arm, I have to get to work."

"You just came from work," he points out.

"My other job," I say. "At the bridal shop. We have a really big new job, and I want to get started on it."

"You really like this wedding stuff, don't you?" he says as, over on the karaoke stage, the dwarf switches from Abba to a little Ashlee

Simpson, declaring that, despite what everybody thinks, he didn't steal my boyfriend. "You really believe in it . . . the happy ending, the rice . . . the whole thing."

"Yeah," I say. "Of course I do. And I know you're sad right now, Chaz—and you have every right to be. But someday it will happen for you—I promise. Just like it's going to happen for me, too." Maybe sooner than anyone thinks.

"Well, I hope you're not still counting on making it happen with Mr. Woodland Creature," Chaz says.

I stare at him. "Why shouldn't I be?" Then, when I see him rolling his eyes, I say, "Oh, come on, Chaz. Not your horse thing again. For your information, Luke is doing very well in his classes, and, furthermore, he seems ready to take our relationship to a new level."

Chaz raises his eyebrows. "Threesome?"

I smack him in the center of his baseball cap. "He's gotten me a Christmas present," I say, "that he says is an investment toward my future."

Chaz's eyebrows furrow in a rush. "What's *that* supposed to mean?"

"What else *could* it mean?" I ask. "It has to be an engagement ring."

Chaz frowns. "He hasn't told me about buying any ring."

"Well, he's hardly likely to," I say, "considering what he knows you've recently been through. Do you really think he's going to brag about getting engaged to me when he knows your girlfriend just left you for a woman?"

"Thanks," Chaz says. "You really know how to make a guy feel great."

"Well, you aren't exactly Mr. Charm yourself," I say, "with the whole Luke-not-being-a-horse-you-would-bet-on thing. But you're probably feeling differently about all that now, aren't you?"

"Truthfully?" Chaz shakes his head. "No. An investment toward your future could be anything. Not necessarily a ring. I wouldn't get your hopes up, kid. I mean—no offense—the two of you aren't even spending the holidays together. What does that say about your big happily ever after?"

"Chaz." I regard him steadily from across the booth before I slide out and leave. "I know Shari hurt you. I frankly can't believe she did that, although I know it really wasn't easy for her and she does feel super badly about it. But seriously. Just because your romance didn't work out doesn't mean all romances are doomed. You just need to get back out there, find some pretty philosophy Ph.D. candidate you can talk to about Kant or whatever, and you'll feel better about things. I promise."

Chaz just stares at me. "Someday you're really going to have to describe to me in more detail what life is like on the planet you live on. Because it sounds really great, and I'd like to visit there one day."

I give him a sour smile, and leave the booth, just as the dwarf breaks into his signature piece, "Don't Cry Out Loud."

I hope Chaz takes a cue from him.

Makeup

Many brides opt to have their makeup professionally done on their wedding day. This is often a good idea—if there is a professional doing it, then that's one less thing the bride has to worry about going wrong.

However, too many brides who opt for professional makeup on the big day end up looking as unlike their normal selves as relatives lying in a casket whose faces have been done over by a mortician. Make sure you and your cosmetic specialist are on the same page about color, amount, and shade . . . and make sure he or she uses a light hand. Yes, you want to look good for your photos—but you also want to look natural and pretty up close to your guests as well. A talented professional makeup artist can easily achieve both.

Some makeup tips to remember:

—Have your first meeting with your makeup professional four weeks before your event. That will give the two of you plenty of time to come up with a look with which you are both happy.

—Your makeup should not be so heavy that your neck and face are two visibly different shades. BLEND!

—You will be shiny on your wedding day from nerves and possibly the heat. Make sure you and your bridesmaids have plenty of blotting tissues on hand, as well as powder.

—Curling your eyelashes with a heated curler can create lasting oomph for the eyes.

—Be sure to use waterproof mascara—you *will* be crying. Or at least sweating.

—Under-eye concealer will hide any dark circles from a restless night's sleep.

—And lastly, opt for lipstick that stays on permanently—you will be using your mouth to kiss, eat, and drink throughout the day/evening, and you don't want to have to stop for constant reapplications of your favorite shade.

• Chapter 22 •

Foul whisp'rings are abroad.

—William Shakespeare (1564–1616), English poet and playwright

t didn't take long for the press to figure out where Jill Higgins was meeting her new mystery pal—though I managed to keep my own picture out of the tabloids by not walking her to her car anymore.

In no time word was out all over town that Jill Higgins, the bride of the wedding of the century, was using Monsieur Henri as her personal certified wedding-gown specialist. The next thing anybody knew, we were beating off the hordes of brides descending on the little shop demanding that we work on their gowns, as well. Jean-Paul and Jean-Pierre had to be employed as doormen/bouncers to keep the paparazzi out, and the brides coming in.

Any residual resentment the Henris might have felt toward me for not letting on that I knew French fell by the wayside when they realized they were booking so many appointments with desperate brides, they had to buy a two-year calendar.

Not that either Henri had laid so much as a finger on Jill's dress since she'd brought it in. Monsieur Henri had tried after I told him my plan, telling me that it could never be done and that I was going to get sued by John MacDowell's mother.

His wife, however, calmly lifted the gown from his fingers and handed it back to me, with a gentle, "Jean. Let her get to work."

Which I appreciated. Especially considering the "stupid" remark. She had evidently changed her mind, and now the dress—Jill's dress—hung on a special hook in the back of the workroom, where every day I flung back the sheet that covered it, took in what I'd done the day before, and what I needed to get done in the next few hours, freaked out, then got to work.

They say it's always darkest until right before the dawn. I've worked on enough projects to know how true this saying really is. A week before Christmas—I'd promised to have Jill's dress done by the day before Christmas Eve, so there'd be time for any last-minute alterations before the ceremony on New Year's Eve—I was sure the dress would never get done on time . . . or worse, that it would get done but look awful. It's no joke making a size twelve out of a size six. Monsieur Henri had been right to say such an undertaking was impossible.

Except it wasn't. Impossible, I mean. It was just really, really hard. It required hours of backbreaking seam snipping, even more of sewing, and the consumption of many, many, many diet Cokes. I was in the shop from two-thirty in the afternoon—as soon as I could make it there after my shift at Pendergast, Loughlin, and Flynn, still my only paying gig—until midnight, sometimes even one in the morning, at which point I would stagger home, fall into bed, and wake at six-thirty the next day to shower and dress and go back to the law firm. I rarely if ever saw my boyfriend, let alone anyone else. But that was all right, because Luke was just as busy studying for his finals. If he hoped to finish his postbac program in a year, he had to cram as many classes as he could into each semester, which meant he had four finals to worry about—basically the academic equivalent of making a size-six dress into a size twelve.

But even though I haven't seen much of my boyfriend in the past few weeks, I've seen plenty of the box he placed under the tiny Christmas tree he bought on the street—complete with a miniature stand—and put in front of the windows, so the twinkling lights he wrapped around it could shine down on Fifth Avenue. I saw it (the box, I mean) the minute I stepped through the door one night after a long, painful battle with the tartan on Jill's dress. It was kind of hard to miss—again, I'm talking about the box.

Because it's huge.

Seriously, the box is the size of a miniature pony. Or at least a cocker spaniel. It's almost bigger than the tree itself. It is definitely NOT a ring box.

But, as Tiffany said, when I mentioned this to her, "Oh, maybe he's one of those."

"One of what?" I asked.

"You know, one of those guys who don't like it when their girl-friend guesses what they're giving to her, so they put it in like a million different boxes inside of boxes, so she won't be able to shake it and guess."

This makes brilliant sense, of course. Luke knows perfectly well I can't keep a secret (though I've been doing pretty well since moving to New York. Really, I think I'm maturing). It's a short step from not being able to keep a secret to not being able to keep from snooping in one's Christmas presents. It's true I already accidentally snagged the silver foil wrapping paper on the box just a little by vacuuming too close to it the other night. But I stopped myself from peeling the foil back.

I know Tiffany's right, and that Luke is doing the box-within-the-box thing. That's just so like him.

Which is why I did the same for the sleek leather wallet I got him from Coach. The box I used to disguise the much smaller box the wallet actually comes in is a box Mrs. Erickson gave me that used to contain multiple bottles of dishwashing liquid that she bought two years ago during a trip to Sam's Club in New Jersey. It's taken her this long to get through enough bottles to throw out the box.

I just hope Luke doesn't take a big sniff of his gift. Because if he does he'll get a snootful of liquid Dawn.

And then, before I know it, it's the day before Christmas Eve, and I'm as nervous as a kid about to visit the Santa in the mall. Not about Luke's gift to me—although that has me plenty jittery—or about the fact that the two of us are about to spend over a week apart in totally different parts of the world, but about what Jill's going to think of her dress. Because—as these things do—it had finally come together a few days before, and now . . . well, even Madame Henri had looked at it, then at me, and said gravely, "Good. Very good."

Which, from her, is high praise indeed. But even more meaningful was her husband's critique, which included several scratchings of the chin . . . much pacing . . . two or three pointed questions about tartan ribbon . . . and finally a nod and a *"Parfait."*

Not the ice cream, but "perfect."

But he isn't the critic of whose opinion I'm most afraid. We still need to make sure Jill likes it.

She finally shows an hour after we've shut down the shop—shooed out the last appointment for the day, pulled down the blinds, and finally, switched off the lights in the front room, to make it look as if everyone had gone home. This is, of course, to throw off the paparazzi.

Then, when the doorbell rings at precisely seven o'clock, Madame Henri hurries to unlock the door, still not flicking on any lights. Two shadowy forms slip inside. At first I think Jill has brought her fiancé and I feel a burst of irritation with her—everyone knows it's bad luck for the groom to see the bridal gown before the wedding.

But then I remember how Jill had come to each fitting alone, looking so hounded, not just by the press, but by her own social isolation, seeing as how her family lives so far away, and her friends know no more about wedding gowns than she does.

And I'm glad she's brought John with her, because he's really done everything he could to make things easier for her—even recently intervening in the prenup negotiations, and demanding that Jill be given a fair agreement or his parents will be stricken from the guest list for the reception, a bold move that succeeded perfectly, and made Mr. Pendergast so giddy that he ordered an extra round of champagne for everyone at the firm's Christmas party at Montrachet (from which I'd had to duck out early to get back to work on Jill's dress, thus missing the highlight of the evening: Roberta getting so drunk, she was found making out with Daryl, the fax and copy supervisor, in the cloakroom—unfortunately by Tiffany, who took snaps of the event with her camera phone, and e-mailed them to all of us).

So that's why, when Madame Henri finally judges it safe to switch on the lights, I'm shocked to see that the person Jill has brought with her is not loyal, lovable John at all, but an older woman—almost an exact replica of her, as a matter of fact—whom she introduces as her mother.

My surprise is followed quickly by a rush of relief. *Yes.* Jill has an ally at last—one besides me and her husband-to-be, I mean.

"Lizzie, hello," Mrs. Higgins says, pumping my hand with the same heartiness her daughter habitually employs in her handshakes, as if she's unaware of her own strength, which in Jill's case is considerable, given the fact that she routinely lifts hundred-pound seals. "I'm so glad to meet you. Jill's told me so much about you. She says you practically saved her life . . . and that you're very generous with—what were they again, honey? Yoodles?"

"Yodels," Jill says, looking embarrassed. "Sorry, I had to tell her about that time we met, in the bathroom—"

"Oh, sure," I say with a laugh. "We have more in the back if you want some—" Given all the work I've been doing, the low-carb diet has completely fallen by the wayside. I have no idea how much weight I've gained recently, but it's not inconsiderable. And yet I find it really hard to care, I'm so excited about Jill's dress.

"No, that's okay," Jill says, laughing. "I'm good. So. Are you ready?"

"I'm ready if you are," I say. "Let's go."

And I take her into the back, while Monsieur and Madame Henri offer Mrs. Higgins a chair and some champagne.

My fingers are shaking as I lower the rich ivory folds over Jill's head, but I try to hide my nervousness by explaining, "All right, Jill, this cut is what we call an empire waist. It means the waistline falls just beneath the breasts, which on you is the narrowest part of your body. What this will do is allow the skirt to fall straight down your body, kind of flowing around it, which is what some- one with your body type wants. The empire waist was made popular by Josephine, the wife of Napoleon Bonaparte, who adapted it from Roman togas she saw depicted on ancient art. Now, as you can see, we've gone off the shoulder, because you have such nice shoulders, we wanted you to show them off. And then this right here—this is the original tartan that was hanging off the old dress—and we're using it as a sash beneath the breastline, see? It emphasizes your tiny waist. And finally, here are some gloves—I was thinking above the elbow, so that they almost reach the dangling straps there . . . Well." I've steered her in front of a full-length mirror. "What do you think? I was thinking hair up, with maybe some curly tendrils hanging down, to sort of complete the Grecian urn look . . ."

Jill is staring at her reflection. It takes me a minute to realize that her silence isn't disapproval. Her eyes are as wide as quarters and just as shiny. She's holding back tears.

"Oh, Lizzie" is all she seems able to say.

"Is it terrible?" I ask nervously. "It's all the original dress. I just took out the seams . . . well, pretty much *all* the seams. It was hard, but I really think this style suits you. You have sort of classic propor- tions, and there's nothing more classic than Grecian urns—"

"I want to show Mom," Jill says in a choked voice.

"Okay," I say, hurrying behind her to lift the four-foot train I've attached to the back of the gown. "This hooks up, you know, into a sort of drapy bustle off the back for when you're dancing. I didn't want it to get in your way. But I wanted you to have some presence, you know, because St. Patrick's Cathedral is so huge—"

But she's already tearing out of the back room and into the front of the shop, where her mother and the Henris are waiting.

"Mom!" Jill cries when she bursts through the curtain separating the shop from the back room. "Look!"

Mrs. Higgins chokes on the champagne she is in the act of swallowing. Madame Henri wallops her on the back a few times and the woman is finally able to recover enough to say, her eyes glistening as much as her daughter's, "Oh, honey. You look gorgeous."

"I do," Jill says, sounding shocked. "I do, don't I?"

"You really do," Mrs. Higgins says, hurrying over to get a closer look. "That's the dress she gave you? The old battle-axe—I mean, John's mother?"

"This is the dress," I say. I feel funny inside. I can't really explain it. But it's like a combination of excitement and joy at the same time. Really, the only appropriate way to describe it would be to say it feels like someone's opened up a bottle of champagne—*inside* me. Or, as Tiffany would say, up my cootchy. "Obviously, I modified it a bit."

"A bit!" Jill echoes with a giggle. Yes! A giggle! From Blubber! This is big. *Really* big.

"It's just so lovely," Mrs. Higgins coos. "She looks like . . . well, like a princess!"

"Speaking of which, we need to talk headpieces," I say. "I was telling her she should wear her hair up, with just a few curly tendrils hanging down in back. So maybe a tiara isn't a bad idea. I think it would look really pretty against her hair—"

But it's clear no one is listening to me. The two Higgins ladies are staring at Jill's reflection in the shop mirror, murmuring softly to each other, and giggling. To look at them, it would be hard to imagine that just weeks ago the bride had been weeping in a ladies' room and often showed up for her fittings smelling of seal poo.

"Well," Madame Henri says to me, when I walk over to join the couple, since it's clear neither client nor her mother is listening to me. "You did it."

"I did," I say, still feeling a little bit dazed.

Then Madame Henri does something that surprises me. She reaches down and clasps my hand in hers. "For you," she says with a smile.

Then Madame Henri slips something into my hand. I look down and see a check. With a lot of zeroes on it.

A thousand dollars!

When I look up again, I see that Monsieur Henri is looking embarrassed but pleased.

"Consider it your Christmas bonus," he says in French.

Touched, I rush over to hug him—and his wife—spontaneously. "Thank you!" I cry. "You're both just—*fantastique!*"

"So, you're coming, right?" Jill asks me later as I'm carefully helping her out of the dress. "To the wedding, right? And the reception? You know you're invited. You and a guest. You can bring that boyfriend of yours I've heard so much about."

"Oh, Jill," I say, smiling. "That is so sweet of you. I'd love to come. Only Luke won't be able to make it. He's going to France for the holidays."

Jill looks confused. "Without you?"

I make sure my smile stays in place. "Sure. To visit his parents. But don't worry. I wouldn't miss your wedding for the world."

"Great," Jill says. "So I know I'll have at least one friend. Besides my family and the guys from the zoo, I mean."

"I think you'll be finding out soon that you have a lot more friends than you know," I say, meaning it.

Walking home that night, I feel as if I'm floating on a cloud. The thousand-dollar check and wedding invitation are the least of it. The fact that she'd liked it—*really* liked it!—is all I can think about.

And she'd looked so good! Just like I'd known she would. Mrs. MacDowell was going to DIE when she saw Jill coming down the aisle. Just die. She had given her future daughter-in-law that dress to humiliate her, because she didn't approve of her son's choice.

Well, who was going to be humiliated now, when "Blubber" turned out to be the most beautiful bride of the season?

And I was going to be there to watch it all take place! Honestly, I have the best job in the entire world. Even, you know, if it doesn't pay what you'd call a regular salary.

I'm still floating as I head into our building and up the elevator to our apartment. I'm still floating when I unlock the door and find Luke inside, with the Christmas tree's lights lit, holding a bottle of wine and going, "There you are! Finally!"

"Oh, Luke!" I cry. "You won't believe it. But she loved it. Absolutely loved it. And Monsieur and Madame Henri gave me a Christmas bonus, and Jill invited me to her wedding—too bad you're going to miss it. But the important thing is, she really, really loved the dress. And she looked great in it, too. No one will be calling her 'Blubber' ever again."

"That's great, Lizzie!" Luke has poured us each a glass of wine. It's only then that I realize the lights are off—all except the Christmas-tree lights and a few candles. He's set up a cheeseboard and some bowls of snacks he knows I like—spicy nuts and candied orange peel. It's so festive—and romantic.

Then he says, as he hands me one of the glasses of wine he's poured, "I couldn't have picked a more perfect gift for you then. Do you want to open it now?"

Couldn't have picked a more perfect gift for me? Because everything else is going so perfectly and proposing to me will just make my evening that much better? That's the only thing I can think of that he could mean.

"Of course I want to open it now," I cry. "You know I've been dying to ever since you put it there!"

"Well, have at it," Luke says. Which is a strange thing to say to someone you're about to propose to under a Christmas tree. But whatever.

Taking my wineglass with me, I go to sit on the parquet beside my gift and wait until he's seated by his.

"Do you want to go first?" I ask, thinking that my gift to him is really going to be a letdown after the tears of joy that are going to follow his to me. But he says, "No, you first. I'm so excited to see what you think," so I shrug and dig in.

When I peel off the wrapping paper to find beneath it a giant box that says "Quantum-Futura CE-200" on it, I begin to lose my happy, floaty feeling. But when I see that the picture on the box is of a sewing machine, the floating feeling goes away entirely.

And when I look up questioningly and see Luke beaming at me from across his wineglass, not looking at all like he's about to propose, I actually start feeling . . . well. Pretty bad.

"It's a sewing machine!" he cries. "To replace the one my dad broke. But this one is way better than the one he kicked. The lady at the store said it's the top of the line. You can do all sorts of embroidery and stuff with it. It comes with a minicomputer inside!"

I blink down at the gigantic box. An investment for my future. That's what he'd said.

And that's what he'd given me, all right.

And before I know what's happening, I'm crying.

Weddings are supposed to be a happy time. That's why no one, least of all the bride, ever wants to admit that some-times—well, weddings just don't happen. Maybe the groom gets cold feet. Maybe the bride does. Maybe the couple decides the timing isn't right after all. Maybe a beloved family member passes away, making everyone uncomfortable with the idea of holding a celebration during a time of mourning. In any event, things happen.

That's why the savvy bride purchases wedding insurance. Like travel insurance, wedding insurance will guarantee that you don't lose the entirety of your deposits on things like venues, cakes, photographers, food suppliers, wedding limos, flowers, honeymoon, even your gown . . .

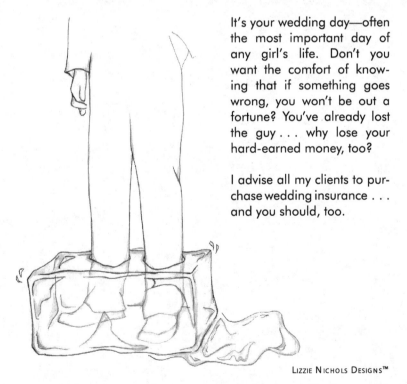

It's your wedding day—often the most important day of any girl's life. Don't you want the comfort of knowing that if something goes wrong, you won't be out a fortune? You've already lost the guy . . . why lose your hard-earned money, too?

I advise all my clients to purchase wedding insurance . . . and you should, too.

LIZZIE NICHOLS DESIGNS™

• *Chapter 23* •

Love and scandal are the best sweeteners of tea.

—Henry Fielding (1707–1754), English writer

W hat's the matter?" Luke cries, watching me break down. "What . . . did I get the wrong one? Why are you crying?"

"No—" I can't believe this. I can't believe I'm crying in front of him. I can't believe I don't have better control of myself. This is ridiculous. It's not his fault. It's my fault. I'm the one who got the ridiculous idea that when he said my gift was an investment for my future, that he meant . . . that he meant . . .

"That I meant what?" he asks bewilderedly.

And then, to my horror, I realize I've been speaking out loud. No! I've been so good! I've been so careful! I've laid out so many tiny bread crumbs for him to follow! I can't bash him over the head with a mallet now. Not when he's come so close—

"That you were giving me an engagement ring," I hear myself sob, "and that you were going to ask me to marry you!"

There. I've done it. It's out. It's floating out in the universe now, for anyone to hear—even Luke.

And, just as I'd known, deep down—just as I'd always known, somehow, even before Shari and Chaz tried to warn me—he's horrified.

"*Marry* you?" he bursts out. "Lizzie . . . I mean, you know I love you. But . . . we've only been going out for six months!"

Six months. Six years. It doesn't make any difference. I realize that now. There are some woodland creatures that, no matter how many bread crumbs you leave out for them . . . no matter how patiently you wait . . . are never going to be yours. They'll never let themselves be tamed. Because they prefer to run wild and free in the forest.

And that's what Luke is. Everyone else could see it. Just not me. I'm the only idiot who refused to acknowledge the truth. That he's happy to live with me now. But not forever. Six months. Six years. He's never going to let himself get tied down.

At least not by me.

"I thought we were having fun," Luke is saying. He appears to be genuinely upset. "I love living with you, it's been great—but marriage. I mean, Lizzie, I can't even see where I'm going to be next year, let alone four years from now, when I'm finished with medical school—if I even get into medical school! Which I don't even know if I will! How can I ask you to marry me? How can I ask *anyone* to marry me? I'm not even sure—I mean, I can't say for sure if I'll *ever* get married. I don't know if marriage is something that will *ever* even be on my radar."

"Oh," I say quietly.

Because what else can I say to this? Obviously, this is a conversation we ought to have had some time ago. I mean, if he isn't even sure marriage is something he wants down the line . . . not just with me, but with *anyone* . . .

Except that maybe he might have realized it was something he wanted if I'd played it cooler. But of course now I've ruined everything by opening my big mouth. If I had just hung on for a bit longer . . .

But no. A year from now . . . two . . . he'll still be saying the same thing. I can see that by the panic in his eyes. It's completely different than what I see in John MacDowell's eyes when he looks at Jill. Or even what I used to see in Chaz's eyes when he looked at Shari.

How could I have been so blind? How could I not have seen that that look was never in Luke's eyes?

"It's okay," I say gently. I'm so tired. So, so tired. I've been working so hard. And tomorrow I have to get on a plane and fly home.

Thank God. All I want, at that moment, is to be home and in my mother's arms . . . the way Jill flew to her mother's arms, only for a different reason. Jill's was joyful.

Mine? Not so joyful.

"God, Lizzie," Luke is saying. "I feel so terrible. If there was ever anything, anything I did to make you think—but I mean, you told me that thing, about how you want to open your own shop. So I just assumed you felt the same way. That marriage wasn't even in the equation. Because supposing we get married and I get into medical school out in California? You'd have to give up the shop! You wouldn't want to do that. Give up your business, for me? Of course not. Or supposing after I graduate, I get some job in like Vermont or something . . . Would you want to go to *Vermont* with me?"

The answer, of course, is yes. Yes, actually, I would. I would go anywhere, Luke. Anywhere. And give up anything. As long as we could be together.

But clearly he doesn't feel this way about me.

"I just . . ." Luke is going around, turning on the lights. I blink in the sudden brightness. "Lizzie, I'm so sorry. Oh God. I've really fucked everything up, haven't I?"

"No," I say, shaking my head, and using the back of my wrist to dry the tears from my cheeks. "No, you haven't. I'm sorry. I'm the silly one. I just have weddings on the brain, or something. A hazard of the profession. It's just—"

"It's just what?" he asks, coming up to me and putting his arms around my waist. "Lizzie—what can I do to make this right between us? Because I want to. I want to keep having fun, like we were—"

"Yeah," I say. I'm about to shrug it off. Because what's the point, really?

But somehow this time . . . I can't. I just can't. Maybe because of the joy I'd just seen on Jill's face. Maybe because I'm realizing I'm not actually going to get to casually reply, when one of my sisters asks if that's an engagement ring on my finger, "Why, yes. Yes, it is," when I go home tomorrow. I don't know.

But it's time, I realize, to be honest. With Luke. And with myself.

"Fun's great," I say. "But, you know, Luke . . . I *want* to get married someday. I really do. And if you don't . . . well, what's the point of even being together? I mean, don't you think it'd be better for us to break up, so we can get back out there and try to find the person we *can* picture a future with?"

"Hey," Luke says, pressing his lips to my hair. "Hey, don't talk like that. I didn't say I can't picture a future with you. I'm just saying that right now I can't picture a future for myself—let alone with anyone else! So how can I presume to put you in it, as well . . . much as I might like to see you there?"

I rest my cheek against his chest. I can feel the crisp starch of his white button-down, and smell the light scent of the eau de cologne he wears as aftershave. It's a smell I've come to associate with sex and laughter.

Until now.

"I know," I say, gently pushing him away. "And I'm really sorry. But I have to go."

And I turn and head into the bedroom, where my suitcase for tomorrow's trip sits. The only thing I haven't packed yet is my toiletries. I go into the bathroom to do that now.

"You're kidding me with this, right?" Luke's followed me. "This is a joke."

"It's not a joke," I say, slipping my toothbrush and facial soap into my Luscious Lana toiletries bag. I can barely see what I'm doing, because my eyes are so filled with tears. Stupid eyes.

I brush past him to stuff my toiletry bag and cosmetics bag into my suitcase. Then I wrench up the little pull handle and begin dragging my bag to the door.

"Lizzie." Luke darts in front of me. His expression is anxious. "What is the matter with you? I've never seen you like this—"

"What?" I demand, a little more sharply than I mean to. "You've never seen me angry before? You're right. That's because I've been trying to be on my best behavior with you, Luke. Because I've been trying to prove to you that I'm worthy of you. Worthy of being with a guy as great as you. It's like . . . it's like this apartment. This beautiful apartment. I've been trying to act like the kind of person who would live in a place like this . . . a place with a little Renoir girl on the wall. But you know what I figured out? I don't *want* to be the kind of person who would live in a place like this. Because I don't *like* the kind of people who live in places like this—people who cheat on their husbands and lead girls to believe they've got a future together when they don't because they're not interested in marriage, only in having fun. Because I think I'm worth more than that."

Luke blinks at me. "Who's cheating on their husband?" he asks, puzzled.

"Ask your mother who she met for lunch the day after Thanksgiving!" I say before I can stop myself. Inwardly, I groan. Okay, that's it. I have to get out. Now. "Good-bye, Luke."

But Luke doesn't take the hint and get out of my way. Instead, he sets his jaw.

"Lizzie," he says in a different tone from before. "You're being ridiculous. It's ten o'clock at night. Where do you even think you're going?"

"What do you even care?" I demand.

"Lizzie. I *care*. You *know* I care. How can you just walk out like this?"

"Because," I say. "I can't do for now. I need forever. I *deserve* forever."

I shove past him, unlock the door, and pull my suitcase out into the hallway, stopping only to grab my coat and purse along the way.

It's sort of hard to make a superdramatic exit like that, though, when you have to stand there and wait for the elevator to come. Luke leans in the doorway, staring at me.

"You know I'm not going to run after you," he says.

I don't say anything.

"And I'm leaving for France tomorrow," he goes on.

I stare at the numbers above the door of the elevator as they light up, one by one. They're a bit blurry, because of my unshed tears.

"Lizzie," he says in his infuriatingly reasonable tone. "Where are you going to go, huh? You're going to find a new place over Christmas vacation? This city shuts down the week between Christmas and New Year's. Look, let's just use this time apart to cool off a little, okay? Just . . . just be here when I get back. So we can talk. Okay?"

Thankfully, the elevator finally comes. I get on it. And, not caring that the uniformed elevator attendant is listening, say, "Good-bye, Luke."

The elevator doors close.

Lizzie Nichols's Wedding Gown Guide

The party's over . . .

What to do with your gown now that your wedding is through?

Well, many women choose to save their wedding gown for their future daughters or granddaughters to wear at their own weddings. Others may choose simply to store their wedding gowns for the sake of posterity.

Whichever you choose, it's important to have your wedding gown cleaned after its final wearing, as even hidden stains, such as those from champagne or perspiration, can discolor the delicate material over time.

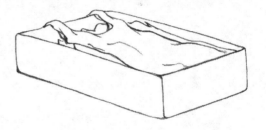

But some women, once their dress has been cleaned and placed in a preservation box, may find that it no longer holds the sentimental value for them that it once did. Perhaps their marriage ended in divorce, or even the death of their spouse.

While it may hold painful memories for you, don't throw your wedding gown away—donate it to Lizzie Nichols Designs™ or any one of numerous 501(c)(3) charities that exist to help impoverished brides have the wedding of their dreams—501(c)(3) charities are fully tax deductible, so you'll be making your accountant happy, too.

You'll be helping a fellow bride in need, and you'll be replacing possibly unhappy memories with new, joyful ones. Try it . . . you won't be sorry!

LIZZIE NICHOLS DESIGNS™

Chapter 24

There is only one thing in the world worse than being talked about, and that is not being talked about.

—Oscar Wilde (1854–1900), Anglo-Irish playwright, novelist, and poet

It's my fault," I say.

"It's not your fault," Shari says.

"No," I say. "It is. It *is*. I should have asked him. Back in France, I should have just asked him how he feels about marriage. You know? I could have avoided all of this if I hadn't played that stupid woodland creature game. For once, if I actually *had* opened my mouth, I might have spared myself a lot of pain and hardship."

"Yes," Shari says. "But you wouldn't have gotten laid as much."

"True," I say with a tearful sigh. "So true."

"Better?" Shari wants to know as she presses the cool washcloth against my forehead.

I nod. I am stretched out on her girlfriend Pat's futon couch, in their nice big living room in their Park Slope apartment. On either side of me is a large Labrador retriever. Scooter, on the left, is a black Lab. Jethro, on the right, is a golden.

Even though we've only just met, I love them both very, very much.

"Who's a good boy?" I ask Jethro. "Who?"

I see Pat look uneasily at Shari. Shari says, "Don't worry. She'll be all right. She's just had a bit of a shock."

"I'll be fine," I say. "I'm just going back home tomorrow to visit my family. But I'll be back. I'm not staying in Ann Arbor. New York didn't chew me up and spit me out. Not like it did Kathy Pennebaker."

"Of course you're coming back," Shari says. "We're coming back on the same flight on Sunday. Remember?"

"Right," I say. "I'll be back, and I'll be fine. I'll land on my feet. Because I always do."

"Of course you do," Shari says. "We're going to go to bed now, all right, Lizzie? You stay out here with Scooter and Jethro. And if you need anything—anything at all—don't be shy about coming to wake us up. I'll leave the hall light on, just in case. Okay?"

"Okay," I murmur as Jethro licks my hand in long, steady strokes. "Good night."

"Good night," Shari and Pat call. And turn out the light and leave the room.

I hear Pat whisper to Shari, "Wait . . . did he really give her a *sewing machine*?"

"Yes," I hear Shari whisper back. "She'd convinced herself he was getting her a ring."

"Poor thing," Pat murmurs.

Then I can't hear them anymore, because they go into their bedroom and close the door.

I lie there, blinking in the semidarkness. I'd come out of Luke's mother's building, hailed a cab, and instructed the driver to take me to Park Slope. I'd had to call Shari to get the exact address. She'd been able to tell by my tone that it was an emergency and had instructed me to come right over without even asking for details. That's what best friends do for each other, after all.

Pat's place is very pretty and pleasant, a basement apartment with a lot of wainscoting and sage-colored walls and spider plants hanging in baskets from the ceiling. There are pictures of ducks on the walls. The blanket Pat put over my shoulders when I came, weeping, through the door, had a mallard duck on it.

There is something very comforting about ducks used as an item of decor. I personally wouldn't want a duck motif in my house, but I am heartened by the fact that someone does.

Maybe, I think, as I lie there between Jethro and Scooter, whose hot, stinky breath I find almost as comforting as the ducks, *Shari and Pat will let me move in here with them.* Just until I can find a place of my own. That would be nice, three girls against the world. The world of men. Men who aren't sure they see marriage in their future . . . or at least, not marriage with a girl like me.

"It's my fault" was what I'd kept telling Shari, when I first came through the door. "I mean, how can I expect him to know he wants to marry me when he only met me six months ago?"

"Well, even if marriage isn't important to him," Pat had said crisply, "he might have realized it'd be important to a girl who earns her living making wedding dresses."

"I don't actually earn my living that way," I'd informed her.

"The guy is a rat fink," Shari had replied. "Here, drink this."

The whiskey helped. Hearing Shari call Luke a rat fink didn't. Because deep down inside, I know he's not a rat fink. He's just a guy who, up until a few months ago, didn't know what he wanted to do with his life. Or rather, he knew . . . he was just afraid to take the risk and try it. Until I came along and encouraged him.

Maybe that's his problem with marriage. Maybe he's just afraid to take the risk and admit that there might be a girl out there with whom he could picture spending the rest of his life. Obviously that girl isn't me. But maybe that's just because, despite everything I've been telling myself for the past six months, Luke and I aren't right for each other after all. Maybe I haven't even met my soul mate yet. Or maybe I have, and I missed him.

Or maybe, like Chaz is always saying, you make your own soul mate.

Maybe the truth is that getting married isn't the be-all and end-all of the universe. Lots of perfectly happy people aren't married. They don't sit around crying about it. In fact, they'd probably laugh at the idea of ever getting married. There's nothing wrong with being single . . .

. . . which is what I keep telling my mother and sisters when I get back to Ann Arbor the next day. Because of course they can all tell by my reddened, weepy eyes that something is wrong.

"Luke and I broke up," I tell them. "He wasn't ready for a commitment, and I was."

And Rose and Sarah have a few snarky things to say about it. Rose: "I knew it wouldn't last. I mean, you met him while you were on vacation. Vacation flings never last." Sarah: "Guys never want a commitment. That's why you should have just let yourself get pregnant. Once he knows there's a bun in the oven, he commits fast enough. I mean, when his mom finds out she's about to be a grandma, anyway."

But I don't want to get my husband the way Rose and Sarah got theirs. Because that's as dishonest as my whole woodland creature strategy.

And look how that turned out.

Fortunately Shari's Christmas Eve announcement to her parents about her new girlfriend takes all the attention off me, and is soon the talk of the neighborhood, thanks to Mrs. Dennis's speed dial. Dr. Dennis, I later learn, responds to the news with a mere tightening of the lips and a trip to his liquor cabinet.

But Mrs. Dennis has soon appointed herself the community spokeswoman for PFLAG. "It stands for Parents, Families, and Friends of Lesbians and Gays," Shari's mother proudly tells mine over Christmas Day dinner. "It's the national organization for promoting the health and well-being of gay, lesbian, and bisexual persons, as well as their families and friends."

"Well," Mom says. "How nice."

"Would you like to join?" Mrs. Dennis asks. "I have a pamphlet right here."

"Oh," Mom says, putting down her forkful of Yorkshire pudding. "I'd love to."

Shari winks at me from across the table. *Did he call?* she mouths. Because Shari is convinced that, despite what I think, it's not over between me and Luke, and that he's going to call me, and we'll talk things out, and everything will be fine.

Shari lives in a fantasy world. Possibly due to all the ducks.

Christmas Day is always a zoo at the Nichols household, because Mom hosts all of her children and grandchildren, in addition to Grandma and the Dennises and the occasional graduate assistant of my dad's who can't afford plane fare home for the holidays, and so comes over with a dish from their native country to share (which is how our holiday meals often consist of beef Wellington with a side dish of malai koftas and a basket of fresh-baked poori).

There is no escape from the shrieking of the under-six set, and the relentless cheer of Mom's caroling with the Muppets record, and Dad's grad student's patient explanation to everyone at the dinner table that the defocusing effect of the radial field gradient is compensated by ridges on the magnet faces which vary the field azimuthally, and Rose's breakdown because her latest EPT showed two blue lines instead of the one she expected, and Sarah's fury because she asked for white gold diamond stud earrings, and her husband, Chuck, got her yellow gold instead ("I mean, is he *color blind?*").

And through it all I clutch my cell phone in my hand, occasionally thinking I feel it jump—but it's only my own heartbeat I feel, I guess, because he doesn't call, not even to wish me a merry Christmas.

And I don't call him because—well, how can I?

It's when I'm seeking some kind of relief from the stream of tears and chatter of the rest of the house that I stumble across Grandma in the basement rec room, perched in front of the television in the La-Z-Boy she demanded my parents buy her, watching *It's a Wonderful Life*—the original, not colorized, version.

"Hey, Gran," I say, sinking down onto the couch. "Jimmy Stewart, huh?"

Grandma grunts. I don't miss the bottle of Bud in her hand. It's one of the special ones Angelo, Rose's bohunk husband, prepared for her, filled with nonalcoholic beer instead of the real thing. Not that it makes any difference. Grandma will act drunk later anyway.

"That's when they knew how to make *real* movies," Grandma says, gesturing toward the screen with her beer bottle. "This one. What's that other one, with that Rick? Oh, right. *Casablanca*. Those were real movies. Nothing blowing up. No talking monkeys. Just smart talk. Nobody knows how to do that in movies anymore. It's like everyone in Hollywood got retarded."

I think I feel my phone vibrate. But it's nothing. A second later, I have to bow my head to hide my tears.

"This guy's good," Grandma goes on, indicating Jimmy Stewart with her beer bottle. "But I like that Rick, who owned the café in *Casablanca*. Now, he was the real deal. You remember when he helps the girl's husband win the money, so she doesn't have to sleep with that Frenchie to get it? That's a real man, for you. What does Rick get for going to all the trouble? Not a thing. Except peace of mind. I don't want that Brad Pitt phony baloney. What'd he ever do, except take his shirt off, and adopt a lot of orphans? Rick never takes his shirt off. He doesn't need to! We don't need to see him naked to know he's a real man! That's why I'd take Rick over that Brad Pitt any day. Because he's such a real man, he doesn't need to take his shirt off to prove it. Hey. What're you crying for?"

"Oh, Gran," I choke. "Everything—everything is so awful!"

"What're you, pregnant?" Grandma wants to know.

"No, Gran, of course not," I say.

"Don't of course not me," she says. "That's all any of your sisters ever do. Get knocked up right and left. You'd think they'd never heard there's a population crisis. So what's the matter with you, if you're not pregnant?"

"Ev-everything was going so well," I sob. "In N-New York, I mean.

I think I might really be able to make something out of this wedding dress rehab thing. I can figure out which way is First Avenue and which way is First Street. I finally found a place I can afford that does good highlights . . . and then I had to go and cry when Luke gave me my Christmas present, because I thought I was g-getting an engagement ring, and he g-got me a . . . sewing machine!"

Grandma takes a meditative sip of her beer. Then she says evenly, "If your grandfather had ever given me a sewing machine for Christmas, I'd have hit him over the head with it."

"Oh, Gran!" I can barely see, I'm weeping so hard. "Don't you see? It's not the gift. It's that he doesn't want to get married—ever! He says he can't look that far into the future. But don't you think if you love someone, Gran, even if you can't see where you'll be or what you'll be doing twenty years from now, you'd still know you want that person to be there?"

"Well, of course," Grandma says. "And if he said he didn't know, well, you were right to give him the old heave-ho."

"It's more complicated than that, Gran. I mean, don't tell Mom, but Luke and I—we've been l-living together."

Grandma snorts at this information. "Even worse. He's had a taste, and he's still not sure he likes you well enough to make a permanent go of it someday? Tell him toodleloo. Who does he think he is, anyway—Brad Pitt?"

"But, Gran, maybe some guys really do need longer than six months to know whether or not a girl they like is the one for them."

"If he's a Pitt, maybe," Grandma says with a snort. "But not if he's a Rick."

It takes a few seconds for me to digest this. Then I say, "If I move out, I'm going to have to find a whole new place to live. I'll probably have to pay even more in rent than I am now. Because I got the girl-friend deal on my current place."

"Which would you rather have," Grandma asks, "money? Or your dignity?"

"Both," I say.

"So? Find a way to have both, then. You're up to the challenge. You're the one who was always going around, claiming you could fix anything with a glue gun and a needle and thread. Now go open your grandma another beer. And make it a real one this time. I'm tired of this nonalcoholic crap. It's just empty calories for *nothing*."

I get up and take Grandma's empty beer bottle from her. Her gaze is glued back to the screen. Jimmy Stewart is running down the street, wishing Mr. Potter a merry Christmas.

"Gran," I say. "How come you like Sully on *Dr. Quinn* so much, but you hate Brad Pitt? Isn't Sully always taking his shirt off, too?"

Grandma looks up at me as if I've lost my mind. "That's *television*," she says. "That isn't *movies*. That's completely different."

You did it! You're married at last! All that hard work, all those grueling hours . . . now it's time to head to the reception and PARTAY!

But wait . . . do you have your wedding toast ready?

Not just best men and fathers of the bride are standing up to say a few words at wedding receptions anymore. These days, more often than not, the bride herself is paying a hefty portion of the cost of the wedding. So why shouldn't she take a moment to say a few words?

The best bridal speeches include a little bit of everything—humor, warmth, and yes, even some tears. But here are some absolute musts:

Thank guests who've traveled a long way to get to the ceremony/reception, or otherwise have gone out of their way to be with you.

Thank everyone for their gifts and generosity (this does not preclude your having to write thank-you notes later).

Thank any of your friends who have put up with you during the wedding preparations. This includes any members of the bridal party who have gone above and beyond for you (of course, anyone who agrees to stand up with you at your wedding is going above and beyond for you, so you should probably include them all).

Thank your mom and dad. Especially if they're paying. Even if they're not, acknowledge any special role they might have had in your courtship/ceremony.

Thank your future husband for putting up with you. A funny story about how you met or fell in love would also work.

Finally, toast your guests, and thank them again for coming to help you celebrate your special day.

Then get wasted. Only not so much that you mess up your dress.

LIZZIE NICHOLS DESIGNS™

Chapter 25

Gossip is the art of saying nothing in a way
that leaves practically nothing unsaid.

—Walter Winchell (1897–1972), American news commentator

a *sewing machine?*" Tiffany looks shocked. "No. No way."

"It's not the sewing machine," I say to her. "I mean, that was the catalyst for the conversation in which I later realized he doesn't feel about me the same way I feel about him."

"But a *sewing machine?*"

It's the Monday after Christmas, the first day back at work, and my second day back in New York. I'd spent what was left of Sunday scouring the want ads, trying to find an apartment that—unlike the empty one sitting over the shop, which Madame Henri wanted two thousand bucks a month for—I could afford.

But it was hopeless. The only places I saw for a thousand dollars or less a month were roommate shares. In Jersey City. And urged potential sharers to keep an open mind.

It was especially depressing to be sitting in Luke's mother's Fifth Avenue apartment, with the Mirós on the wall and the steps to the Metropolitan Museum of Art right outside the double-paned windows, looking at ad after ad that stated *hombres de preferencia*.

Hombres? I don't want to live with a bunch of hombres. I just wanted *one* hombre . . .

And he still hasn't called, much less left me a note. I came back to find the apartment exactly as I'd left it . . . clean, my sewing machine still in its box, sitting next to the now completely dried-out little Christmas tree. The box I put Luke's present in is beside it, still wrapped. He hadn't even bothered to see what I'd gotten him.

I wonder if I can take both gifts back and exchange them for cash. It's not like I don't need the money.

"So it's not even like a *present*," Tiffany points out. "Because his dad BROKE your sewing machine. So he got you something he actually OWED you. Not even something, like . . . *new*. Something you already have that he *broke*."

"Right," I mutter. "I know. Okay?"

"But I mean . . . what kind of present is THAT? If Raoul broke something of mine—or God forbid his DAD came to visit and broke something of mine—I would expect him to replace it, and not try to pass the replacement off as a CHRISTMAS PRESENT. Because he still owes you a PRESENT."

"I know," I say, and am relieved when the phone rings. "Pendergast, Loughlin, and Flynn, how may I direct your call?"

"Lizzie." I'm surprised to hear Roberta's voice on the other end of the line. "Is Tiffany there yet?"

"Yes," I say. Tiffany had come into work early, as usual, to ask how my Christmas had gone, and tell me all about hers, which had been spent at Raoul's godmother's estate in the Hamptons, where they'd made drunken love on a polar bear skin rug, and Raoul had gifted her with a canary diamond cocktail ring and a fox stole, which she is wearing inside because, as she says, "It's part of my OUTFIT," of snakeskin pants and a silk blouse.

"Good," Roberta says. "Could you ask her to take over the desk while you come back here and see me please? And kindly bring your coat and purse with you."

"Oh. Okay." I hang up slowly, feeling all the blood in my body dropping to freezing temperature.

Tiffany must read from my expression that something is wrong, because she tears her attention away from her ring for a moment and goes, "What?"

"Roberta wants me to come back to her office," I say. "Right now. And she wants me to bring my purse and coat."

"Oh, shit," Tiffany says. "Shit, shit, shit. That fucking bitch. The day after Christmas, too. Talk about a fucking Grinch."

What did I do? I'm wondering, as I stand up and reach for my coat. I was so careful. *No one saw Jill and me together after that one time. I'm sure of it.*

"Listen," Tiffany says, sliding into the chair I've just vacated. "Just because we won't be working together anymore doesn't mean we can't be friends. I really like you. You invited me to Thanksgiving dinner. No one else in this fucking place ever invited me anywhere. So I'm going to be calling you. Do you hear me? We'll hang. If you want to go to the shows during Fashion Week, whatever . . . I'm here. Got it?"

I nod dumbly and start for Roberta's office. I can see that someone is in there with her already. As I get closer, I can see that the someone is Raphael, from the security desk downstairs. What is Raphael doing up here? I wonder.

"You wanted to see me, Roberta?" I say, stepping into her office.

"Yes," Roberta says coldly. "Come inside and close the door, will you, Lizzie?"

I do as she asks, glancing nervously at Raphael, who is looking nervously back at me.

"Lizzie," Roberta begins, not even bothering to invite me to sit down. "You recall a conversation we had a few weeks ago about your having been photographed by the press in the company of one of our clients, Jill Higgins, don't you?"

I nod, not trusting myself to speak, because my throat has gone dry with terror. Why is Raphael here? Have I broken the law? Is he going to arrest me? But he isn't even a real cop . . .

"You assured me at that time that your relationship with Miss Higgins had nothing whatsoever to do with this office," Roberta goes on. "So kindly explain to me why I opened the *Journal* this morning to find this."

Roberta hands me a copy of the *New York Journal,* open to the second page . . .

. . . on which there is splashed a huge black-and-white photo of Monsieur Henri and his wife, standing in front of the shop and grinning ear-to-ear beneath the headline "Meet the Designers of Blubber's Wedding Gown!"

The first thing I feel is a bubble of outrage burst inside my chest. Designers! They aren't the designers of Jill's dress! That's me! I am! How dare they try to pass themselves off—

But then as my gaze skims the article, I see that the Henris haven't tried anything of the sort. They are extremely upfront about the fact that Elizabeth Nichols—"an exceptionally talented young woman," according to Monsieur Henri—is the one who refurbished Miss Higgins's wedding gown, after having met Miss Higgins "at the law offices of Pendergast, Loughlin, and Flynn, where Miss Nichols works as a receptionist, and where Miss Higgins sought representation for the handling of her prenuptial agreement with husband-to-be John MacDowell."

And then—grainy but still recognizable—is a picture of me, hurrying through the doors to the lobby of the very building in which I'm standing now.

And all I can think is, *Gray Cords! It was Gray Cords! I knew he was trouble the first minute I saw him!*

Also, *Why, oh, why, did the Henris have to open their mouths about me and how Jill and I met? True, I never told them it was a secret—but why did I tell them anything about it at all? I should have just said she was a friend. Oh God. I'm such an idiot!*

"You know how much we here at Pendergast, Loughlin, and Flynn pride ourselves on keeping our association with our clients private," Roberta is saying. I can hear her voice only dimly through the roaring in my ears. "You were warned once before. You know I have no choice now but to let you go."

I look up from the newspaper article, blinking rapidly. The reason I'm blinking so much is that my eyes have filled with tears.

"You're *firing* me?" I cry.

"I'm sorry, Lizzie," Roberta says. And she actually looks as if she means it. Which helps. Kind of. "But we talked about this. I'll make sure your last check gets mailed out to you promptly. I'll just need your office key. Then Raphael will escort you out."

My cheeks burning, I dig around in my bag until I find my key chain. Then I remove the key to the office doors from it and hand it over. The whole time, my brain searches feverishly for some kind of response to the charges laid against me. But there's really nothing I can say. She *had* warned me. And I didn't listen.

And now I had to pay the price.

"Good-bye, Lizzie," Roberta says, not unkindly.

"Bye," I say. But a bubble of spit, brought on by the fact that I am weeping openly now, prevents me from saying more. I let Raphael guide me with a hand on my arm through the office—conscious of everyone staring, although of course my vision is so blurred I can't actually see whether or not they really are looking at me—and to the elevators. We ride down to the lobby in silence, because there are other passengers on board with us.

When we reach the main floor, Raphael continues to guide me through the lobby, because I still can't see. At the doors to the outside he stops and says a single word to me: "Bummer."

Then he turns around and heads back to the security desk.

I push open the lobby doors and head outside into the bitter Manhattan cold. I have no idea where I'm going, really. Where *can* I go? I have no job, and soon, I'll have no place to live. I have no boyfriend, either, which is really, you know, freeing, on top of the just-getting-fired-and-having-no-place-to-live thing. I feel, in fact, just like Kathy Pennebaker probably did, when she finally admitted that New York City—that big, gutsy, glittering town—had beat her to a pulp and sent her packing.

I'd actually seen Kathy while I'd been home for Christmas. She'd been at the Kroger, pushing a cart in the produce section, looking so washed out and wan, I hardly recognized her.

Is that going to be me someday? I'd wondered, as I'd stared at her from my hiding place behind the nut and dried fruit bins. Will I cease to care what people think of me and go to the grocery store in an overlarge ALLSTATE 400 AT THE BRICKYARD SUMMER RUMBLE NASCAR T-shirt and cropped cargo pants (in the winter)? Will I start dating a guy whose mustache is yellow from nicotine, and who is stocking up on cold medicine—so much so that he can only be planning on mixing up a batch of crystal meth for the weekend? Will I ever actually buy radishes? I mean, for a salad or even just to use as garnish?

And then, hurtling down the street with tears streaming down my face, trying not to slip in the slush beneath my feet, I realize something.

And not just because I've suddenly found myself standing in front of Rockefeller Center, its ice-skating rink and gold statue of a man lying down iconic to New York City's image—the more so with the glittering, towering Christmas tree behind.

No. No, I realize. That will *not* be me. That will *never* be me. I would *never* wear cargo pants in public. I don't think I could bring myself to date someone who has a yellow mustache. And radishes are only good on tacos.

I'm not Kathy Pennebaker. And I will never be Kathy Pennebaker. EVER.

My resolve thus strengthened, I turned around and found a cab—on my first try! At Rock Center! I know! It was a miracle—and gave the driver the address of Monsieur Henri's.

When he pulled up in front of the building, I opened my purse to find I had no cash—except the ten-dollar bill Grandma had given me.

But what choice did I have? I handed over the bill, told the driver to keep the change, and barged into the shop, where I found Monsieur and Madame Henri chuckling over the copy of the *Jour-*

nal with steaming mugs of café au lait in their hands and a plate of madeleines in front of them.

"Lizzie!" Monsieur Henri cried delightedly. "You are back! Did you see? Did you see the story and photo? We are famous! Because of you! The phone won't stop ringing! And the best news of all— Maurice! Maurice is closing his shop down the street and moving it to Queens, instead! All because of you! All because of that story!"

"Yeah?" I unwind my scarf, staring at both of them with fury. "Well, I got fired because of that story."

This wipes the smiles off their faces.

"Oh, Lizzie," Madame Henri begins.

But I hold up a single finger.

"No," I say. "Not a word. You're going to listen to me. First off, I want thirty thousand a year *plus* commissions. I want two weeks' paid vacation, full medical *and* dental. I want at least one sick day per month plus two personal days per year. And I want the upstairs apartment, rent free, all utilities paid for by the shop."

The couple continue to stare at me, openmouthed in surprise. Monsieur Henri is the first one to recover.

"Lizzie," he says, sounding wounded. "What you ask, of course, you deserve. No one is suggesting otherwise. But I don't see how you can ask us to—"

But Madame Henri silences him with a *"Tais-toi!"*

While her husband looks at her with surprise, she says to me, clearly and concisely, *"No dental."*

I practically feel my knees give beneath me, I'm so relieved.

But I don't let on. Instead, I say, with all the dignity I can muster, "Done."

And then I accept their invitation to join them for café au lait and madeleines. Because when your heart is broken, carbs don't count.

Aaahhhh! You're home from the honeymoon! Time to start enjoying wedded bliss, right?

WRONG. You have work to do. Get out your stationery—maybe you've sprung for the thank-you cards that match your invitations; maybe you're merely using your new mono-grammed note cards—and your favorite pen, and *start writing.*

If you were smart, you didn't wait until after the honey-moon to begin the thank-you process, but started writing and sending out thank-you cards *as you received each gift.* If, however, for some horrible rea-son you chose to wait, you have your work cut out for you now. At the very least, you ought to have been saving each gift tag, with a note scribbled on the back as to what the gift actually was. If this is the case, you have it easy: just jot a thoughtful note—MENTIONING THE GIFT RECEIVED BY NAME—to each giver, signing it cordially with both spouses' names.

If you have not kept track of who gave you what, start doing some investigating. Because you can bet that even if you haven't been paying attention, someone has. And that someone—usually a mother or mother-in-law—can tell you exactly what you received from whom.

The reason you must mention the name of the gift received in your thank-you note is so that the giver knows for certain that you received their gift, and that it was acknowledged in some thoughtful way. Writing "Thank you so much for the gift" is neither polite nor satisfying to the giver . . . and in general will guarantee that when the baby shower comes around, you will not be receiving anything from that person.*

Yes, you must handwrite each card. No, you may not send a photocopied or even printed letter of thanks to your guests.

LIZZIE NICHOLS DESIGNS™

*Exception: If a guest gave you a gift of money, it is not necessary or polite to mention the amount in your thank-you note. Call any amount "a generous gift."

Chapter 26

I cannot tell how the truth may be; I
say the tale as 'twas said to me.

—*Sir Walter Scott (1771–1832), Scottish novelist and poet*

Wait," Chaz says. "So he said he couldn't picture a future with you in it?"

I'm carting the second-to-last armload of clothes up the narrow staircase to my new apartment. Chaz, behind me, has the last one.

"No," I say. "He said he couldn't picture the future, period. Because it's too far away. Or something. You know what? The truth is, I don't even remember anymore. Which is fine, because it doesn't matter."

I reach the top of the stairs, turn left, and I'm in my new apartment. MY apartment. And no one else's. Clean, furnished in shabby chic, and featuring faded pink wall-to-wall carpeting and cream-colored wallpaper with pink roses in every room save the bathroom, which is tiled in plain beige, it features floors that slope even worse than the ones in Chaz's place; only four windows—two that look out onto East Seventy-eighth Street from the living room and two that look out into a dark courtyard from the bedroom; a kitchen so tiny only one person can enter it at a time.

But it also boasts a full-size tub in the bathroom, with a scorchingly hot shower, and two tiny, but highly decorative, fireplaces—one of which by some miracle actually works.

And I love every inch of it. Including the queen-size, lumpy bed, in which I've no doubt many unspeakable acts have been committed by the younger two Henris, but which a proper airing and a fresh set of sheets from Kmart ought to cure, and the tiny black-and-white television with rabbit ears, that I intend to replace with a color set as soon as I have enough money saved.

"That sounds like Luke, though," Chaz says, coming into the bedroom where we've assembled the hanging rack along one wall. "You know. That whole follow-through thing we were talking about."

"Yeah," I say. It's been a little over a week since Luke and I broke up—if, indeed, that is what happened that night in the hallway of his mother's apartment building. I haven't heard a word from him.

And the pain is still too raw for me to talk about it very much.

But Chaz seems to be unable to speak of anything else. It's a small price to pay, I suppose, for his helping me to move—he borrowed a car from his parents and everything. He seems to feel it's the least he can do, considering his best friend is responsible for my broken heart and his father's company for my current state of pennilessness.

But I've pointed out that the latter, at least, has turned out to work to my advantage, since it galvanized me into finally demanding the compensation I deserved from my "real" employers. Even Shari was stunned by what she called my "sudden development of *cojones.*"

"Free rent *and* a salary? Good job, Nichols," was what she said over the phone, when I called to tell her the news.

Although, if you think about it, all of this really is Shari's fault. She's the one who went out with Chaz, who was the one who invited us all to Luke's château last summer. In fact, the whole thing could be construed as Chaz's fault. Chaz is the one—as he pointed out on the stairs a little while ago—who told Luke how much I love diet Coke, thus prompting Luke to buy me diet Coke that day in the village, and making me fall in love with him, because of his thoughtfulness.

And Chaz is the one who got me the job at Pendergast, Loughlin, and Flynn that I later lost.

Of course, if he hadn't invited us to France, I'd never have met Luke. And if he hadn't told Luke about my loving diet Coke, I'd have never fallen in love with Luke. And if I hadn't fallen in love with Luke, I probably wouldn't have moved to New York. And if I hadn't moved to New York, I wouldn't have gotten the job at Chaz's dad's firm, and then I never would have met Jill, and thus made my dream of being a certified wedding-gown refurbisher a reality.

So. Everything really is all Chaz's fault.

Which is why it's only fitting he help me move.

"Well," Chaz says, as I take the last dress from him, and slip it onto the hanging rack. "That's it. You sure that's everything?"

Even if it's not, I can't go back now. I left the key to Luke's mother's apartment with the doorman, along with a note—brief but cordial—thanking Luke for the use of the place, and asking that he get in touch with me about any outstanding bills or issues concerning the place.

There is no way I can ever go to the Met again. I'll be too nervous about running into him. Though I'm going to miss poor Mrs. Erickson, for whom I'd also left a good-bye note, since she's spending the holidays in Cancún, and doesn't even know I've moved out. I even stood in front of the Renoir girl, and wished her a fond farewell. I hope Luke's next girlfriend—whoever she is—appreciates her.

"I'm sure," I say to Chaz.

"Well, then I guess I better run the car back," he says. "I don't want to deal with holiday parking and all that."

"Oh, right," I say. I'd almost forgotten that it's New Year's Eve. I've got Jill's wedding to go to in a few hours. Which reminds me. "What are you doing tonight, anyway? I mean, with Luke still out of town, and Shari—well, with Pat. Do you have any plans?"

"They're having a party at Honey's," Chaz says with a shrug. "I figured I'd hang out there."

"You're going to spend New Year's Eve in a karaoke bar with strangers?" I can't keep the incredulity from my voice.

"They aren't strangers," Chaz says, sounding wounded. "The dwarf with the bow staff? That bartender who's always yelling at her boyfriend? Those people are like family to me. Whatever their names are."

And suddenly I'm taking his arm.

"Chaz," I say. "Do you own a tux?"

Which is how, nine hours later, I find myself standing beside Chaz in the Grand Ballroom at the Plaza Hotel (now the Plaza Luxury Condominiums), a glass of champagne in one hand, and the clutch that matches my 1950s pink silk Jacques Fath evening gown in the other, as Jill Higgins, now MacDowell, standing on top of the ballroom's grand piano, prepares to throw her bouquet.

"Here," Chaz says. "Give me that stuff. You better get up there."

"Oh," I say. Despite my reservations—once I'd made sure that Jill's dress looked perfect (which it did) and that her mother-in-law's eyes bulged out when she saw her in it (they did), I'd been reluctant to stay long at the reception. It's weird to be at a wedding where the only people you know are the bride and groom, who certainly don't have much time to spend with anyone but family on the big day—I was having a pretty good time. Chaz declared that there was no way he was going home before twelve ("I'm not getting into a monkey suit just to change into jeans before the ball drops"), and the truth was, he was right. Jill's friends from the zoo were hysterically funny, and as out of their element as I was. And John's friends weren't anywhere near as snooty as I'd expected—the opposite, in fact. Just about the only person, in fact, who didn't seem to be having that good a time was John's mother, and that, apparently, had to do with the fact that someone overheard Anna Wintour say that Jill's gown was "cunning."

Cunning. The head of *Vogue* called something I made—well, rehabbed—*cunning*.

Which actually is no surprise to me, because I think it's pretty cunning, too.

In any case, it's clear Jill will be Blubber to the press no more, and that seems to have depressed John's mother . . . so much so that she's currently sitting with her head in one hand at the head table, shooing away solicitous waiters who keep coming by with ice water and aspirin.

"Everybody," Jill is yelling from on top of the piano. "Get ready! The person who catches it is the next one to tie the knot!"

"Go on," Chaz encourages me. "I've got your bag."

"Don't lose that," I say. "It's got all my needles and emergency sewing kit and everything in it."

"You sound like a nurse," he assures me with a laugh. "I won't lose it. Just go!"

I hurry to the front of the room where the bridesmaids and assorted female zoo employees are gathered before the grand piano, thinking to myself bemusedly that for someone who habitually wears nothing but jeans and a baseball cap, Chaz cleans up *very* nicely. My heart actually skipped a beat when I opened up the door and saw him standing there in his "monkey suit," ready to escort me.

Then again, I suppose *all* men look handsome in tuxedos.

"Okay," Jill calls. "I'm going to turn around and do it so it's fair. Okay?"

I reach the front of the room, and jostle in with all the other girls. I see Jill notice me. She smiles and winks before she turns around. What does *that* mean?

"One," Jill calls.

"ME!" shrieks the woman beside me, whom I recognize as one of the other seal keepers at the zoo. "THROW IT TO ME!"

"Two," Jill calls.

"No, ME!" another woman screams, leaping up and down in her festive though aggressively bright charmeuse satin pantsuit.

"Three!" Jill says.

And her bouquet of white irises and lilies soars through the air. For a moment, it's silhouetted against the warm gold lights from the ceiling. I lift up my arms, not expecting much—I've never caught a ball on the fly before in my life—and so am shocked when the bouquet falls neatly into my outstretched hands.

"Whoa," Chaz says, when I run up to him triumphantly a little while later, to show off my bounty. "If Luke saw you with that, he'd probably pass out."

"Look out, bachelors of Manhattan!" I yell, brandishing my bouquet. "I'm next! I'm next!"

"You're drunk," Chaz says, looking pleased.

"I'm not drunk," I say, blowing some of my hair from my face. "I'm high on life."

"Ten," the people around us suddenly start chanting. "Nine. Eight."

"Oh!" I cry. "New Year's! I forgot it's New Year's!"

"Seven!" Chaz joins the chanting. "Six!"

"Five," I yell. Chaz is right, of course. I *am* drunk. Also, cunning. "Four! Three! Two! One! HAPPY NEW YEAR!"

The people who managed to remember to hold on to their wedding favors—New Year's horns—blow on them, hard. The band launches into "Auld Lang Syne." And above our heads, a net is released, and hundreds of white balloons tumble softly down, like snowflakes, to land in piles around us.

And Chaz reaches for me, and I reach for him, and we kiss happily as the clock strikes midnight.

Here is a bona fide cure for any postwedding-reception hangover:

Pour 5 ounces of tomato juice into a tall glass. Add a dash of lemon (or lime) juice and a splash of Worcestershire sauce. Sprinkle in 2 or 3 drops Tabasco sauce, then add pepper, salt, and celery salt to taste. If you're feeling adventurous, add some ground horseradish. Add ice, then garnish with celery stick and lime wedge.

Finish off with 1.5 ounces of vodka.

Enjoy.

LIZZIE NICHOLS DESIGNS™

Chapter 27

Rumor travels faster, but it don't stay put as long as truth.

—Will Rogers (1879–1935), American actor and humorist

wake to pounding.

At first I think the pounding is just coming from inside my head.

I open my eyes, not recognizing where I am for a few moments. Then my vision clears, and I see what I had originally taken for big pink blurry blobs floating before my eyes are actually roses. And they're on the walls.

I'm in the bed in my new apartment above the bridal shop.

And, I realize when I turn my head, I'm not alone.

And someone is knocking on the door.

These are far too many realizations to have at once. Any one of them would be confusing enough all on its own. But considering the fact that they all occur to me simultaneously, it takes me a minute to process what's actually going on.

The first thing I notice is that I'm still in my Jacques Fath evening gown—rumpled now and stained with chocolate cake. But it is very firmly *on* . . . as are my Spanx beneath it.

Which is good. *Very* good.

I notice furthermore that Chaz is fully dressed as well. That is, his tuxedo pants and jacket are still on, but he appears to have lost his tie, and his shirt is more than halfway unbuttoned, the studs—his grandfather's onyx and gold studs, I remember him telling me—gone, as are his shoes.

I rack my poor, addled brain, trying to remember what happened. How did Chaz—my best friend's ex-boyfriend; my ex-boyfriend's best friend—end up sleeping, even if fully clothed, in my new bed?

And then, as I take in other facts—such as that Jill's bouquet is sitting on my bedside table, looking wilted but really not worse for wear, and that my shoes appear to have vanished—I begin to recall the chain of events that led to this startling early-morning discovery: Chaz and I sharing a New Year's kiss that started out as merely a friendly peck . . . at least, that's how I'd intended it to be.

But then Chaz was throwing his arms around me and turning it into something more.

I'd pushed him away—laughingly—only to realize he wasn't laughing. Or at least, not as much as I was.

"Come on, Lizzie," he said. "You *know*—"

But I'd laid a hand over his mouth before he could finish whatever it was he'd been about to say.

"No," I'd said. "We *can't*."

"Oh, why the hell not?" Chaz had demanded against my fingers. "Just because I met Shari first? Because you know if I'd met you first—"

"*NO*," I'd said, pressing my hand down even more firmly. "That's not why, and you know it. We're both feeling very vulnerable and alone right now. We've both been hurt—"

"Which is all the more reason we should seek solace in each other," Chaz said, taking my hand in his and moving it away from his mouth—so he could kiss it! "I really think you should take all your frustrations over Luke out with me. Physically. I promise to lie very still while you do it. Unless you want me to move."

"Stop it," I'd said, wrenching my hand away. How could he make me laugh so much during what was supposed to be such a serious moment? "You know I love you—as a *friend*. I don't want to do anything that might jeopardize our relationship . . . as *friends*."

"I do," Chaz said. "I want to do things that might jeopardize our relationship as friends a *lot*. Because we're *always* going to be friends, Lizzie. No matter what. I really think it's the whole physical part of our relationship that needs a lot more work."

"Well," I'd said, still laughing. "You're just going to have to be patient then. Because I think we both need time to grieve for what we've lost . . . and to heal."

Chaz, not unsurprisingly, made a disgusted face at this—both the idea of it as well as the way I'd put it seemed to displease him. But I'd continued, undaunted, "If, after a suitable amount of time, we're both still interested in taking our friendship to another level, we can reevaluate."

"How much time are we talking about?" Chaz had wanted to know. "I mean, to grieve and heal? Two hours? Three?"

"I don't know," I'd said. It had kind of been hard to concentrate, considering the fact that he still had his arms around me, and I could feel those studs of his grandfather's pressing through the silk of my dress. That wasn't all I felt pressing through it, either. "At least a month."

He had kissed me again after that, as we swayed back and forth to the music.

And I don't think it was just the champagne that made me feel as if it were raining gold stars all around us, instead of white balloons.

"Well, at least a week," I'd said, when he'd finally let me up to breathe.

"Deal," he'd said. Then he'd sighed. "But it's going to be a long week. What have you got on under there, anyway?" His hands were at the waistband of my panties, which he could feel beneath my dress.

"Oh, those are my control-top Spanx," I'd said, deciding in that moment that in this and all future relationships, I was going to be ruthlessly, even brutally honest—even to my own disadvantage—such as by admitting to a guy that I wear control-top panties. Not just panties, either, but basically bicycle pants.

"Spanx," Chaz had murmured against my lips. "Sounds kinky. I can't wait to see you in them."

"Well," I'd said, welcoming yet another opportunity to be brutally honest. "I can tell you right now it's not going to be as exciting as you might expect."

"That's what you think," Chaz had said. "I just want to let you know that when I look into my future, I see *nothing* but you." Then he'd whispered, *"And you're not even wearing Spanx."*

And then he'd dipped me, so that suddenly I was giggling up at the ceiling, from which the last of the balloons were still falling, in fat, lazy arcs.

The rest of the night was a blur of more kissing, and more champagne, and more dancing, then more kissing, until finally, staggering out of the Plaza just as fingers of pink light were beginning to stretch across the sky above the East River, we tumbled into a waiting cab, and then somehow, into my bed.

Only nothing had happened. Obviously nothing had happened because (a) we're both fully clothed, and (b) I wouldn't have *let* anything happen, no matter how much champagne I might have had.

Because this time, I'm going to do everything the *right* way, instead of the Lizzie way.

And it's going to work, too. Because I'm *cunning.*

I'm lying there thinking about how cunning I am—also about how untidy a sleeper Chaz is, considering the fact that his face is all smushed against one of my pillows, and that, even though he isn't a drooler, like I am, he's definitely a snorer—when I realize that the pounding sound I'd thought was actually my hangover is coming from the door.

Someone is knocking on the outer door to the building—which actually has an intercom, but it's broken (Madame Henri swore to me it would be fixed by the end of next week).

Who could be pounding on the door at—oh God—ten in the morning on New Year's Day?

I roll out of bed, then climb unsteadily to my feet. The room sways . . . but then I realize it's only the slanting floors that make me feel as if I'm about to fall. Well, the floors and my severe hangover.

Clinging to the wall, I make my way to the door of my apartment and unlock it. In the narrow—and chilly—stairway to the ground floor, the pounding is louder than ever.

"Coming," I call, wondering if it could be a UPS delivery for the shop. Madame Henri had warned me that by taking occupancy of the apartment on the top floor of the brownstone, I'd be responsible for signing for all after-hours deliveries.

But does UPS even deliver on New Year's Day? It can't possibly. Even Brown must give its workers the day off.

At the bottom of the stairs, I struggle with all of the various locks, until finally I can pull the door open—though I've kept the security chain on, just in case the person outside is a serial killer and/or religious fanatic.

Through the three-inch crack between the door and frame, I see the last person in the world I ever expected.

Luke.

"Lizzie," he says. He looks tired. Also annoyed. "Finally. I've been knocking for hours practically. Look. Let me in. I need to talk to you."

Panicked, I slam the door shut.

Oh my God. Oh my God, it's Luke. He's back from France. He's back from France, and he came to see me. Why did he come to see me? Didn't he get my brief but cordial note in which I gave him my new address so he'd know where to forward my mail, but instructed him not to contact me there?

"Lizzie." He's pounding on the door again. "Come on. Don't do this. I flew all night to get here to say this to you. Don't shut me out."

Oh God. Luke's at my door. Luke's at my door . . .

. . . and his best friend is asleep in my bed upstairs!

"Lizzie? Are you going to open the door? Are you still there?"

Oh God. What am I going to do? I can't let him in. I can't let him see Chaz. Not that Chaz and I did anything wrong. But who would even believe that? Not Luke. Oh, God. What do I do?

"I'm . . . I'm still here," I open the door to say. I've thrown back the chain, but I don't move to let Luke step inside—even though it's freezing, standing there on the stoop in my evening gown, with the bitter cold seeping in around. "But you can't come in."

Luke looks at me with those sad dark eyes. "Lizzie," he says, apparently not even registering the fact that I've obviously slept in my clothes. And not just any clothes, either, but my Jacques Fath evening gown that I've been saving for years for an event fancy enough to wear it to. Not that he would know that. Because I never told him.

"I've been a total ass," Luke goes on, his gaze never straying from mine. "I'll admit, when you brought up . . . well, the marriage thing last week, you really threw me for a loop. I wasn't expecting it. I really did think we were just hanging out, you know. Having fun. But you made me think. I couldn't *stop* thinking about you, as a matter of fact, though I tried. I really tried."

I stand there blinking at him, shivering. This is what he flew all the way back to America—apparently spending his New Year's Eve on a plane—to say? That I ruined his holiday, even though he tried not to think about me?

"I even talked to my mother about it," he says, the winter sunlight bringing out the bluish highlights in his ink-dark hair. "She's not having an affair, by the way. That guy she met the day after Thanksgiving? That's her plastic surgeon. He does her Botox. But that's beside the point."

I swallow. "Oh," I say. And realize, belatedly, that that's why Bibi's eyes hadn't crinkled when she'd smiled at me while issuing her invitation to join them in France for the holidays: she'd just had Botox injected into them.

Still, this doesn't change anything. It doesn't, in fact, change the part about how Luke chose to spend the holidays with his parents instead of going with me to the Midwest to meet mine.

I remind myself of this because I'm trying very hard to keep my heart steeled against him. Because, of course, the hurt is still fresh. Like I'd said to Chaz, we're both still grieving.

But seeing Luke, looking so tired and vulnerable, on my doorstep isn't helping.

"Mom is the one who told me what an idiot I was being," Luke goes on. "I mean, even though she was kind of pissed about the whole thing where you thought she was having an affair. She was trying to keep the Botox from my dad."

I'm finally able to pry my tongue from the roof of my mouth long enough to say, "Dishonesty in a relationship is never a good thing." As I know, only too well.

"Right," Luke says. "That's why I realize how lucky I am, Lizzie, to have you." He reaches out and takes my hand in his icy cold, leather-gloved fingers. "Because even if maybe you do have a reputation for talking too much, there is one thing about you: you do always tell the truth."

Nice. Also, true. Well, mostly.

"Did you come all this way to insult me?" I ask, trying to sound haughty—though of course the truth is that I just feel like crying. "Or is there a purpose to all of this? Because I'm standing here freezing—"

"Oh!" he cries, dropping my hand, and hastily whipping off his coat, which he then drapes gently around my shoulders. "I'm sorry. This would be a lot easier if we could just go in—"

"No," I say firmly, grateful for the coat. Although now my stocking feet are like ice.

"Fine," Luke says with a little smile. "If that's the way you want it. I'll just say what I came here to say and then let you go."

Yes. Because of course that's the kind of thing princes do. Fly thousands of miles just to say good-bye.

Because whatever else they might be, princes are unfailingly polite.
Good-bye, Luke.

"Lizzie," Luke says. "I've never met a girl like you before. You always
seem to know what you want and exactly how to go after it. You aren't
afraid to do or say anything. You take risks. I can't tell you how much
I admire that."

Wow, this is a very nice good-bye speech.

"You came into my life like a . . . well, a tsunami or something. A
good one, I mean. Totally unexpected, and totally irresistible. I honestly don't know where I'd be now if it weren't for you."

Back in Houston with your ex, I want to say.

Only I don't. Because I'm sort of curious to hear what he's going
to say next. Although mostly I just want to run back upstairs to bed.

Except I can't, I remember belatedly. Because there's a snoring
man in my bed.

"I'm not the kind of person who's good at going after what I
want," he goes on. "I guess I'm more cautious. I have to weigh all the
possibilities, calculate each and every risk involved—"

Yes. I know.

Good-bye, Luke. Good-bye forever. You'll never know how much
I loved—

"That's why it took me so long to realize that what I really want
to say to you—" He's fumbling in the front pocket of his charcoal
wool trousers now. And I can't help thinking, Why is he doing
this . . . what's he doing? Is he just trying to torture me? Does he
have no idea how hard I'm trying not to throw myself at him? Why
can't he *just go away*? "What I think I've *always* wanted to say to you,
since the day I met you, on that crazy train, is—"

—*get out of my life, and never contact me again.*

Only that's not what he says. That isn't what he says at all.

Instead, for some reason, he's sunk down onto one knee, in front
of the closed bridal shop, and the lady across the street walking her
dog, and the guy in the minivan looking for a parking space, and the
entire population of East Seventy-eighth Street.

And though I can't believe what I'm seeing, and I'm positive my tired, hungover eyes are playing tricks on me, he's pulled from his pocket a black velvet box, which he opens to reveal a diamond solitaire that glistens in the morning light.

No. No, that's really what he's doing. And there are words coming out of his mouth. And those words are:

"Lizzie Nichols, will you marry me?"

extracts reading groups
competitions books new
discounts extracts extracts events reading groups
competitions new discounts
books new extracts
events books
new extracts reading groups
interviews events books
events extracts extracts
discounts new books events events
new books events events new interviews new books extracts

www.panmacmillan.com

extracts events reading groups
competitions books extracts new books